Have yourself a very
improper Regency Christmas

A SCANDALOUS
Regency
CHRISTMAS

Five Regency-themed Christmas reads from
favourite authors Christine Merrill,
Marguerite Kaye, Annie Burrows,
Barbara Monajem and Linda Skye

A SCANDALOUS
Regency
CHRISTMAS

CHRISTINE MERRILL

MARGUERITE KAYE

ANNIE BURROWS

BARBARA MONAJEM

LINDA SKYE

MILLS &
BOON

Mills & Boon, an imprint of Harlequin (UK) Limited,
Eton House, 18-24 Paradise Road, Richmond, Surrey TW9 1SR

A SCANDALOUS REGENCY CHRISTMAS
© Harlequin Enterprises II B.V./S.à.r.l 2013

To Undo A Lady © Christine Merrill 2012
An Invitation to Pleasure © Marguerite Kaye 2012
His Wicked Christmas Wager © Annie Burrows 2012
A Lady's Lesson in Seduction © Barbara Monajem 2012
The Pirate's Reckless Touch © Linda Skye 2012

ISBN: 978 0 263 91043 8

012-1113

Harlequin (UK) policy is to use papers that are natural, renewable and recyclable products and made from wood grown in sustainable forests. The logging and manufacturing processes conform to the legal environmental regulations of the country of origin.

Printed and bound
by CPI Group (UK) Ltd, Croydon, CR0 4YY

CONTENTS

To Undo A Lady

CHRISTINE MERRILL

To my readers: Merry Christmas!

Christine Merrill lives on a farm in Wisconsin, USA, with her husband, two sons, and too many pets—all of whom would like her to get off the computer so they can check their e-mail. She has worked by turns in theatre costuming, where she was paid to play with period ballgowns, and as a librarian, where she spent the day surrounded by books. Writing historical romance combines her love of good stories and fancy dress with her ability to stare out of the window and make stuff up.

CHAPTER ONE

WHILE SHAKESPEARE CLAIMED that April was the cruelest month, Danyl Fitzhugh would have argued for December. He flipped the top collar of his Garrick up to protect his face from the chill and knotted the muffler to hold it in place. Even at this late hour, the streets of London were cold, muddy and crowded with people rushing from one place to another to no apparent purpose. They wasted their money on excesses of food and drink and gifts to celebrate the season. To Danyl's mind, far too few of them were going to the theater.

There would be even fewer at the Pageant Playhouse, now that he'd lost another actress to the Theatre Royal. He had trained that wench, Maria, from her first step upon the boards, shared his knowledge of the craft, and then used all his skills as a director to set her like a jewel in the crown of his productions. In return, she had stabbed him in the back. And right before Christmas.

If he'd been in the habit of celebrating that particular holiday, it might have been worse. But she had used his mixed-blood heritage as an excuse to defect to Grimaldi for his seasonal pantomime. It stung the pride to be treated as some sort of godless infidel by a woman who had been only too happy to share his bed when she wanted a better role.

As she left, he had shouted that he could turn any whore in Drury Lane into her equal, nay, her superior, if he so chose. And now, it appeared he might have to do just that, if he did not want to cancel the next night's performance. He'd searched London from one end to the other and could not find an actress that suited him.

But Covent Garden was busy with people seeking entertainment of one sort or another—drink, gambling, the theater, or diversions of a carnal nature. In a place like this, whores were thick on the ground, loitering in the alcoves and blocking doorways when the weather turned cold. It sometimes seemed that if a girl meant to fall from grace, she could find no better place to do it then right outside the door of his theater.

If he intended to carry out his threat to Maria, he could not afford to be too particular. A courtesan would never stoop to becoming an actress. The women in brothels were too busy to discuss a change in career. Nor did he wish to pull one from bed, only to have her recognized and jeered by some buck who had lain with her just a night before.

He could tempt a streetwalker with his offer. But he needed someone new, fresh, and without the tarnished and shabby glamour that affected women after time on the street.

He needed *her*.

The poor creature huddled by the wall was small, as

Maria had been. She would fit the costumes without alteration. But where Maria had been a match for his own dark coloring, this girl would be a foil. Fair of skin and hair with wide, innocent, cornflower-blue eyes in a heart-shaped face. When he played Othello, he would tower over her. In response, the audience's heart would break for poor Desdemona.

But he would have to feed her first, and thaw her out. Her dress and shawl were fine, but too light for the weather. Her lips were almost blue from cold. The garments were beginning to hang loose, and her lovely face was gaining the pinched look of one who had missed more than one meal. Everything about her cried that she was out of options and might be agreeable to anything that might ease her suffering.

As he approached, she looked straight at him and then away. Was it the color of his skin that put her off? He'd had women, both English and Indian, refuse him because of it, not wanting to be bedded by some half-caste bastard. But tonight he did not have the time to be angry.

Then she looked up again. It had not been a personal affront. She was simply terrified of the task before her. "Please, sir…" She stopped as though she hoped he would understand the rest.

Wordlessly, he reached into a pocket and gave the coins in his purse a jingle.

She wet her lips again and forced herself to speak. "Fancy a tumble?" She was trying to make her voice sultry but coarse, to give him the impression that she had done this many times. But she was obviously educated, and green as spring grass to the ways of the street.

"How much?" It was unfair of him to toy with her, but he could not resist seeing how strong her nerve might be, and how long she would carry out such an obvious farce.

By the look she gave him, it was clear that she had never done this before. Even an inexperienced whore would have some idea of her worth. "A pound?"

He laughed. "I would not pay a pound for the ladies in the Kama Sutra. But for the nerve to suggest it, I would give you a shilling."

"Done." Before he could make his offer, she had grabbed him by the scarf and hauled him into the shadow of a nearby pillar. She had to stand on the tops of his feet to reach his mouth, but she did so, and planted her lips on his, pushing back with her body to pin him to the bricks as she kissed.

Far be it from him to correct her form. But she would not let him catch a breath to tell her that streetwalkers were never so eager as this. If they kissed at all, it was not with such desperate enthusiasm. It seemed that, if this was her first step on the road to ruin, she meant to run the rest of the way down it before losing her nerve. Her mouth was open, and his tongue played along the straight, clean teeth, and bit the lips that were ice-cold but barely chapped by the weather.

Oh Mother, but this was sweet. He squeezed her breasts through a gown that was fine enough for a drawing room, and felt her shiver. But it was more from the cold than anticipation. His own body was answering, ready. Perhaps, if he had been a gentleman, he'd have refused her. It should be beneath him to take this unfortunate against a wall.

If things went as he expected, she'd be his leading lady

soon enough, and that inevitably lead to a situation much like this one. If they got the first intimacy out of the way before he negotiated her salary, there would be no questions later about what he might wish from her.

He took control, and pulled aside his scarf so that he might open his greatcoat to wrap it around them both. Then he turned their bodies so that she was the one braced against the bricks, and lifted her skirt.

Her shivering ceased and he could feel her fumbling with the buttons of his breeches. But either she was still frightened, or her fingers were numb with the cold. He lifted one hand to his lips and kissed it, breathing the life back into it. With his other hand, he touched her *yahni,* trying to tease some warmth to it as well.

She might be inexperienced, but clearly she was no virgin. She did not seem surprised by his touch. Her breathing quickened and then stopped in fear as voices passed within a few feet of them on the other side of the pillar.

He used her fear against her, pressing into her and increasing his teasing, pulling on the lips of her body, tracing the place between them, and thrusting a finger into the wet center of her, in and out as the strangers on the other side of the pillar discussed whether it would be better to go to Ma Brown's for a girl or to a hell to play faro.

She clenched her body against his hand, fighting the excitement. He added a second finger and increased his speed. And then he guided her warm hand back to his buttons, helping her undo the flap, guiding himself to the body that was wet and ready to receive him, and filling her.

If this act was any indication of how they would fare on stage, he had chosen well. She was responsive to him, sensing his desires almost before he knew them, twisting her hips, pushing back in rhythm with his thrusts, sucking his tongue into her mouth and raking it with her teeth as he took her.

The strangers had moved on, but he did not know or care. He could think of nothing now but the climax, bracing her hips with his hands and hammering into her, losing his control in a tide that seemed to pulse in time to her cries of pleasure and the spasms of her body.

Dear God, he was almost too weak to stand. If it hadn't been for the wall, he'd have dragged them both down to the ground in a heap. As it was, it would take a few moments to recover sufficiently to get her back to his apartments above the theater, and to explain the real reason he had accosted her.

But for now, he fumbled in his purse and pushed a crumpled pound note into the tiny hand that rested against his side.

CHAPTER TWO

SARAH BRANFORD WAS appalled with her own behavior. She had made love to a stranger on the street. Worse yet, he was a foreigner. He had caught her staring at him, as though she had cast off her ladylike manners the moment she had made the decision to fall.

But that was only because she had seen very few men like him. He appeared to be a Punjabi: strikingly handsome, with thick black hair and skin dark as well-tanned leather.

But he was, for want of a better word, elegant. His clothing was almost foppishly well tailored, and his voice as clearly English as any gentleman of her acquaintance. He seemed as at home in Covent Garden as a Londoner.

And she flattered herself when she thought of what had occurred as love. She had whored herself in the street, against a wall, with people walking scant feet from her. The dark-skinned stranger had teased her until she was wet, and then thrust his considerable manhood into her and used her shamelessly.

Perhaps she was as bad as her husband had said. He had accused her of wanting this often enough, calling her whore and worse for no reason at all. He had treated her as though she deserved punishment, until she had feared for her life and run from him.

And now she had done the worst thing she could imagine doing. Worse yet, she had enjoyed it. She had been aroused and climaxed along with her partner. She would do so again, if she thought too long on what had occurred, for the memory of it was exciting her all over again. He was still inside of her. His mouth pressed little kisses against the skin of her throat. But the movement slowed until his head rested on her shoulder, as though his ardor was fading along with his erection.

She calmed herself by thinking of the pound note, and the fact that it was more than enough money for a bed and a meal. It was cold tonight, and she was so hungry. The smell from the vendor down the way had been driving her mad all evening. She could be in her own parlor right now, with a bowl of those chestnuts in her lap, planning her Christmas house party.

She put the thoughts firmly from her mind. There would be no Christmas for her this year: no house party, no chestnuts. And the activity she'd just engaged in had not required mistletoe. When the money in her hand ran out, she would likely have to do this again, and the next man might not be as pleasant.

But at least she would not be hung for it, as she might have if she'd attempted to cut purses. And it would be quite some time before she was downtrodden enough to beg. Three days on the run had not broken her dignity to the point where she was a convincing object of pity. Those she had asked for help had suggested she do just as she had done: offer the only thing of value that she had.

It would be better to be a courtesan, she was sure. But the word would surely get back to the Earl of Sconsbury that his wife had accepted an offer of protection from another man. The consequences to that gentleman would be swift and brutal. Then Sconsbury would haul her home and make sure that she did not escape again.

She had needed to disappear completely. Anonymity would be her salvation, and what better place to be lost than on the street?

But her first customer did not seem to be in any hurry to leave. It was just as well, she supposed. He had given her sufficient money so that she did not need to seek another. And wrapped in his coat she felt warmer than she had felt in days.

He gripped her shoulder, and muttered something under his breath that sounded like approval of her height. Then he asked, quite clearly, "How much do you weigh?"

"I beg your pardon?"

"I asked you how much you weigh. If you are not sure, an estimate will be sufficient."

Less than she had, after several days without food. But she could not think what it might have to do with the present situation. Did he mean to eat her? The thought of his teeth on her body raised scenarios that were terribly wicked. And before she could help herself, she giggled.

He ignored it and ran hands quickly over her body, as though measuring her girth. "Between eight and nine stone, I should think," he supplied, since she had not answered. "That is just about right for my purposes." His fingers closed on her arm, pulling her away from the wall and letting her skirt fall back into place. "Come with me." He was pulling her farther into the darkened alley, and her excitement changed to panic.

She set the heels of her shoes into the slush and muck of the cobbles, trying to stay him. "Why?"

"I wish to talk with you."

"Here is good enough," she insisted. She had thought him...well, not exactly a gentleman. But he had not seemed particularly dangerous. Now she was not so sure.

He ignored her hesitance and smiled at her, releasing her arm to do up his trouser buttons. "I mean you no harm. And I have money. I wish to talk with you. In a warm room. It will take, perhaps, an hour of your time to hear me out. Then you can stay or go, as you wish." He glanced down at her, as though he could see how empty she was. "Either way, I will give you dinner."

Her stomach rumbled in response. Her mouth watered. Her mind ran wild with thoughts of roast goose, stuffing, sprouts and Christmas pudding. It was foolish. He'd said nothing about a feast. But any food would do. Even if he killed her, how much worse could her life become than what it had been a few days ago? When he turned and walked away, she followed him without further argument.

He led her through a doorway, up the back stairs of the theater she had been standing in front of. They passed through the gallery that led to the boxes, and higher still to a set of apartments that must be almost on a level with the cloud-painted ceiling.

He produced a key to the plain door, so she assumed the

rooms were his. They were small, clean and serviceable, and quite clearly empty. Though he did not have a servant, at least he did not seem to share them with anyone. And it was good to be out of the weather. Resting on the thick rug, her feet felt much better than they had on the wet cobbles.

He lit several candles, chasing away the last of the shadows in the room, and returned to her, standing back to observe her and placing his hand thoughtfully upon his chin. "Strip, to your shift."

She hesitated.

"If you please," he added. "And put this on." There was an ornate gown hanging over the back of a nearby couch, and he thrust it in her direction. "We must see if it fits you, before we go any further."

It was a strange request. But he did not seem aroused by the idea of her nakedness. He was staring at her expectantly, as though the change in garments was some obstacle to be overcome before they got to whatever truly interested him.

What right did she have to pretend modesty, after what had just happened between them? She dropped her shawl and pulled awkwardly at her gown, letting it fall to the floor and standing before him in stays and stockings. She took the one he had indicated and dropped it over her head. "If you would help me with the lacings?" She turned her back to him.

He did them up efficiently, and then turned and admired the results. "Can you read?" he asked. And then said more to himself than to her, "I should have asked that first. For if she cannot…" He closed his eyes for a moment, as though praying that she would not disappoint him.

"Of course," she interrupted, slightly offended that he would doubt her literacy. "What language do you wish me to read in? I can manage three, at least."

"English will do," he said, chastened. "And your memory. How is it?"

"I can remember that you promised me dinner," she said, glancing around her. There was a little space in the corner of the room that he seemed to treat as kitchen, but she saw no sign of a meal laid for company.

He went to it and rummaged in a cupboard, removed an apple and a dry bit of cheese, and placed them on a plate along with a half loaf of bread and a boiled egg. "It is not much, but it will hold you until we can finish this discussion. Can you recite, from memory, if I give you the words?"

She grabbed the plate and ripped off a bite of bread. "I can manage well enough," she said, around a mouthful. It felt as though she'd not eaten in ages and was extraordinarily good for something so simple.

"Do you dance? Sing? Juggle?" He was pouring her a glass of wine.

She took the goblet and drank deeply. In her present condition, it would probably go right to her head. But the current situation was already quite mad. She doubted it would be any worse should she be foxed. She thought back to his question. "Yes. Yes. And no."

"You fit the costume." Now he was grinning at her as though he had entirely forgotten what they had done in the alley, and who she might be. He reached out to her, and she tried not to flinch as his hand came up to her chin, tipping her face so that the firelight struck her profile. "And you are a comely thing. Indeed you are."

Was that meant as a compliment? It was raw and horrible, and she'd have slapped him for the presumption, had she her old life back, even for a moment. But it seemed that the rules of etiquette did not apply to her now. So she waited for an explanation.

"Allow me to introduce myself," he said, bowing as though to remind her that she was the one honored. "Danyl Fitzhugh, at your service, madam." He waited, as though she was supposed to recognize the name.

"How do you do," she said, politely.

"I am the proprietor of the theater below," he prompted. "The director and lead actor as well."

She waited, still unsure of what she was expected to say.

"You were almost blocking the doorway, just now."

And she had seen his name on the playbill, which was why he must think she would know it.

"I could have run you off, you know," he added. "It does not do to have girls hanging about the doors, accosting the patrons. The gentlemen do not mind it, of course. But it gives ladies the assumption that our entertainment is on the rough side. And above all else, we must fill the seats."

"I am sorry," she said. "It will not happen again." Of course, she doubted that her absence would improve the traffic. There had been but a thin stream of people entering the door she'd sheltered in. She had been there but one night and could hardly be blamed for that.

He nodded, as though her assurance satisfied him. "I will not hold it against you. When all is said and done, everyone must eat. I understand that need sometimes drives one to extremes. Does this explain your current situation?"

She finished the boiled egg in two bites and reflected for a moment on his question before nodding in agreement.

"Would you be open to other employment, should it be offered to you?"

She would be able to make the fresh start that she had hoped for and finally be free of her past. "Oh, yes. Anything honest," she added, in case he meant something worse than walking the street. "Cooking, cleaning, anything at all, really." Not that she had any skills in those areas. It was quite possible that they would be more physically demanding than leaning back against a wall and giving up all hope. But it did not do to announce one's weaknesses when one sought a position.

He laughed. "Speaking as your last customer, it might be more diplomatic to be less enthusiastic in your desire to do something else. Men are funny creatures. I am likely to take your change of heart as a reflection on my performance."

"You were my first," she said, not sure why she was moved to admit it. But it seemed important to be honest with him, as he seemed to be with her. "Well, not…I mean…not the very first," she amended. "My first customer. And I hope you shall be the last. As you said, I was quite desperate."

He smiled as though it did not bother him one way or the other the depths to which she had been willing to sink. "Then let me explain my predicament. My lead actress has recently left the company. This limits us in the performances we might give. And I noticed, in the alley just now, that you seem to be of a similar size to her."

"You wish me to become an actress?" She took a bite of the apple, still a little surprised at the turn of events. But thus far her whole life had been a lie, hiding bruises and pretending that her husband did not terrify her when they were seen in public together. How difficult could acting be?

"I am fully capable of training you in the craft."

He would have her up on the stage for all to see. Sconsbury would find her in a heartbeat, and it would all be over.

Her expression must have turned grim at the thought, for he hurried to encourage her. "There would be payment, of course," he said, smiling to coax her back into good humor. "The Earl of Spayne is our patron."

And no friend of her husband, thank God.

"He has secured us the building and is responsible for the costumes, the sets, the space and so forth. But any profits are split equally amongst the company."

Perhaps she could try it for a time, and escape with her pay before she was discovered. There were no friends or family to appeal to, no one who would side with her against the earl. But neither were there many who would recognize her. She had been little more than a cipher in her marriage, recognized at functions for the husband at her side and the jewelry he gave her to wear. Without those, how much of her existed to be found?

Mr. Fitzhugh was continuing his reassurances. "I would not expect you to exhibit any gratitude to me," he assured her. "Nor make demands on you based on what has recently occurred between us. The past is in the past."

That was too bad, really. It had been the one nice moment in recent days. She had felt young and desirable again, though she did not wish to admit it. She waved her hands again, as though denying the thought. "I thank you for your assurances, and I will take you at your word. But the thought of going onstage is...well...it is very public. And I do not wish my family to know what has become of me. I doubt they would approve." It was an understatement, but it would have to do. "You mentioned costumes?"

"And makeup, wigs, all manner of disguises," he encouraged. "Once you are prepared for a role, I doubt your own mother would recognize you. Or father, or bailiff, or whatever it is that you are running from." He looked steadily into her eye. "I do not care to hear of it, nor will I question you, as long as you do not mean to go running back to it as soon as there is gold in your pocket. As I said before, the past is the past."

Above all else, that was what she wanted. If the past could be forgotten, then maybe it would be possible to be free. The idea was more warming than a fire, and more satisfying than a Christmas dinner. It was the only present she wanted, this year. Her heart longed for it. But her mind could not let go of its fear so easily. "This payment you speak of? When would it occur? Because—" she bit her lip nervously "—I have nothing but the clothes on my back and the pound note you gave me."

The facts did not seem to bother him. He had an answer for everything. "I will see to it that you have an advance sufficient to outfit yourself for the job required. There is a rooming house nearby where other members of the company stay. Tonight you may remain here, out of the cold. And tomorrow, I will see that you are situated."

"Remain here?" Suddenly, despite what they had done in the alley, she felt shy.

He made an expansive gesture, as though deeding her the space. "As my guest. Take my bed, and I will take the couch you are sitting on. It will all be quite innocent."

It was a bit late to claim that their relationship was innocent. But perhaps he wished to prove to her that his intentions were just as he claimed, and that he needed a performer, not a mistress. "Thank you. You are most kind."

"You accept my offer, then, Miss..."

She could not very well be herself in this. She grasped for the first name that came mind. "Sarah...Simmons."

He snorted in derision. "Actresses frequently take stage names. You can be whoever you wish, and I will not inquire further. But you must come up with something more original than that, with Sarah Siddons performing just down the street at the Royal."

"Anything will do, then," she said, not wanting to blunder again. "Who do you wish me to be?"

He looked at her again, as though appraising her worth and announced, "I would take you for a Sally. It is rather like Sarah, but saucy and impertinent. Sally. Sally. Sally." He was thinking, and then snapped his fingers. "Miss Sally Howe. It is easy to remember, and will fit on the playbill. Fewer letters will mean larger type. Someday you will thank me for that. But for now? Off to bed with you, Sally. Rest tonight. And tomorrow, the real work shall begin."

CHAPTER THREE

HER BELLY WAS full and it was the first time she had been warm in days. But more than that, Sarah woke from a deep sleep in a strange bed with an optimism that had not been present since the first days of her marriage nearly three years before.

Just as he had promised, Mr. Fitzhugh took her to a rooming house and introduced her to the other members of the company, fifteen in number. They ranged in age from a boy of ten, who could pass for a girl in gown and bonnet, to an old man who played fathers, grandfathers, ghosts and kings, as they were needed. It did not take long to settle her. How much time was needed, to be shown her empty room? She had nothing to put in it; nor would she until such time as she had received her pay and the time to spend it.

Payment. How strange was that, after having had servants, and not even an allowance to manage? Her husband had provided all things for her. At first, it had seemed like a privilege to be so cared for. But she had come to view it as a trap, once she realized how dependant she had become.

And now, she had a job. When they returned to the theater, Mr. Fitzhugh handed her a text and hastily marked the bits that she was to read, then put her through the paces of the performance, which he called blocking. She stumbled about on the raked stage, feeling ready to pitch forward into the audience with every step. She always seemed to be in the wrong place with the wrong words, looking in the wrong direction for the people who spoke to her. And all the while Mr. Fitzhugh was shouting that she must keep her face pointed downstage, which was the same as downhill, but to speak her lines up and not down into the boards.

By evening, she was in another woman's dress, painted, wigged, and reciting hurriedly memorized lines before a houseful of people. She dared not look too closely at the faces in the boxes on either side of the stage. If she did, she might know some of them. The game would be up in a flash of recognition.

And at the end of it, there had been applause. She returned to the tiring-rooms with the other actresses who shared her space: an older woman called Kate, and a stout, young girl named Maggie.

A moment later, Mr. Fitzhugh stuck his head through the curtains that served as a door, oblivious to the fact that they were wearing nothing but stays and shifts, and announced gruffly that her performance had been "Fair. For a first attempt." Then he disappeared again.

The other two women shared a glance and a laugh and went back to removing their rouge.

"Did I do something to displease him?" Sarah looked at the velvet drape still swinging from his abrupt exit. "He seemed quite angry, just now. And he shouted at me much of the afternoon." He had been much friendlier the night before. But then, they had...

She scrubbed carefully at her cheeks, hoping that the friction would account for the scarlet blush. They had been intimate. But he had not spoken of it again, and so neither would she.

"Angry?" Kate laughed again. "He is overjoyed. He just does not want to show as much. Especially not to you."

"Why ever not?" An encouraging word would have been helpful. Since she had nothing to compare it to, she had no idea if she had succeeded.

Maggie giggled. "He's afraid you'll run off, like the others."

She had run off. But if she was to run from here as well, where would she go? "He said that the last woman in this part was no longer with the company. But there were others?"

"Marie is off to Grimaldi's troupe to do a Christmas pantomime," Maggie said, her face growing dark. "And the one before that, Caroline, is touring with Kean. Danyl trains 'em up right. But once they are good, they leave for fame or money."

"Or love," Kate reminded her. "The one before that, I hardly remember her name, is a mistress to a gentleman. Does her best work flat on her back."

Maggie laughed again. "She had more looks than talent, bless her. But now?" Maggie pounded the table and moaned in the throes of feigned passion. "Oh, milord. You are a stallion. I am overcome." She stopped suddenly and winked. "I hope her acting has improved. She'll need all of her talents to keep up that ruse. The old goat who took her was as limp as a noodle."

"And not half the man of Danyl Fitzhugh," Kate added, loud enough to be heard in half the theater.

"And still not man enough for you, Katie!" he shouted back from somewhere down the hall, as though women openly discussing his sexual prowess was a common oc-currence.

Sarah thought of the way she had groaned the previous evening, as Danyl Fitzhugh had moved in her. Did he think she was acting? Did he care?

Maggie nudged her companion. "We've made her blush. You are new to this, aren't you, dearie." Then she added, more quietly. "Do not worry. Danyl Fitzhugh might be black as treacle, but he's twice as sweet. The blustering means nothing. And he won't trouble you about other things, if you don't wish him to. He is a perfect gentle-man. And I suspect he's sweet on you already."

"We will know when he decides to do Othello again," Kate added. "Not one of them survived the first rehearsal as Desdemona without giving up to him. Not that they complained," she added. "But no hearts were broken, when they left."

"It is the bedroom scene, I am sure," Maggie said with a sigh. "And a pity it is that I always play the maid, in that."

There was a heavy step in the hall, and the two fell silent as Mr. Fitzhugh parted the curtains again. He barely looked at Sarah, but thrust a package in her direction. "It begins."

She stared at it in confusion.

"You have an admirer already." Kate nudged her arm. When she did not reach for it. Maggie snatched it from

Danyl's hand. "Sometimes it's flowers. Sometimes it's sweets. But this young buck wants to get a jump on the competition." She tore at the paper and displayed the contents. "A gold bracelet. Very nice."

"What am I to do with that?" Sarah said. She did not wish an admirer. Especially not after yesterday. That had been an aberration. But she would not have Mr. Fitzhugh thinking that she was willing to go away with any man who asked.

"Do not look to me for an answer," Danyl said roughly. "Whether you meet the man or no, it is no concern of mine. Time that is not rehearsal or performance is totally your own."

She thrust the bracelet back at Fitzhugh. "Send him away. Please. I am not interested."

Kate snatched the bracelet back. "Dearie, you have much to learn, as does the young man who gives such tokens without a guarantee of affection." She glared at Danyl. "Miss Howe is not at home to visitors. But she thanks the gentleman for the lovely gift."

Danyl laughed, his white teeth showing bright in the dark face. "Very well, then. I will relay the message."

Strange. Was that relief she'd seen, when she had tried to refuse the bracelet? Had he actually thought she would consider leaving so soon? Of course she had been nothing more than a whore when he had found her. Why should he expect loyalty from her?

Because she wanted him to. If this first performance was an indication, she would enjoy her new life and her new companions. She was grateful to the man who had given it to her. That he would ask no more of her after what had occurred in the darkness was a source of both relief and confusion. She did not want to be a whore. She certainly did not want to be his whore.

But she could not seem to stop thinking of him.

CHAPTER FOUR

THE APPLAUSE WAS deafening.

Sarah picked up the rose that struck the toe of her slipper, raised it with a flourish and blew a kiss in the direction of the thrower. She was rewarded with a loud cheer from the audience, and a mutter of disgust from the man at her side.

It was professional jealousy. Nothing more than that. On the previous evening, Mr. Fitzhugh had remarked that, though she had been with the company but a week, she had already learned to upstage him. He had been frowning, as he always seemed to be, and remarked that she would most likely be gone as the last girl had, once she found a tempting enough offer amongst the many that she received.

But she sensed a kind of grudging admiration beneath it, as though he was proud of what he'd accomplished with her in such a short time. He had every right to be. Though it felt quite natural to put on paint and pretend, she would not have had any idea on how to go about it if it hadn't been for Danyl Fitzhugh. It was his direction that made the plays the successes they were.

It had been his idea to add a kiss at a climactic moment when they'd played Beatrice and Benedict. And she had silently cheered. The audience would love it, of course. But more importantly, it would be an excuse to kiss him. Not often, of course. They did not do the play every night. And he'd seemed to think that a rehearsal was hardly necessary, rushing through the scene each time they practiced.

She lived for that scene. And any others where they might pretend to be lovers, trading barbs onstage or exchanging soft words. Even a touch was welcome. For when the lights had burned low and the audience had left, he avoided her as though she had some sort of horrible disease. Perhaps it was as Kate and Mags had said, that he had not want to waste his affections on an actress who might be gone in a few months.

He had promised, after the first night, that their relationship was to be professional, nothing more than that. And she had not wanted to be reminded of how low she had sunk in the days after she'd left home. But now she was feeling much better. There was no sign that Sconsbury was even looking for her. And she had seen more than one old friend in the audience, but none had recognized her. She was safe. She was happy.

And at night, she dreamed about the feel of Danyl Fitzhugh, as he had moved in her body. It was scandalous, of course. But there was no denying that the physical act of love had been more satisfying than any stage kiss. The few moments spent with him had been a revelation.

Was it the risk of discovery that had excited her? Or was it the man? She had to know.

He could not avoid her forever. She would beard him in his den and brazenly engage him in conversation. She would be flirtatious, coy and charming. And of course she would pretend that her unusual request had nothing to do with him. She merely wished to hang a kissing bow back-stage, since it was almost the season for it. Would he mind?

Or did this violate some theatrical superstition she had not yet learned? There seemed to be many of those. Do not wear green on stage, for that was the color that killed Molière. Do not whistle. And never say "Good Luck!" But was there anything about kissing? Even if there was, mistletoe was a pagan thing. Perhaps she could argue for an exception.

But she could not barge into his dressing room as casually as he did hers. As leader of the company, he had the luxury of a door. She stood outside it for a moment, pacing nervously, twisting the sprig of leaves and berries in her hand. Should she knock? Suppose he refused her? If she simply called out a warning and entered without waiting for an answer, she would have no time to lose her nerve and he could not put her off.

She took a deep breath, turned the knob and pushed. "Mr. Fitzhugh…"

She fell speechless with embarrassment and dropped the mistletoe, her fingers numb with shock. He was sitting at his dressing table with his back to her. But the mirror in front of him gave her a clear view of what was happening. His breeches were undone and he was taking a hand to himself.

His eyes met hers in the reflection. "Devil take you, woman. Come in and shut the door."

Without thinking, she picked up the kissing bow and did as she was told. Then she turned back to him, resting her shoulder blades against the wood and wishing that she could sink back through it and pretend that she had never come in.

He had paused in what he was doing, his hand still upon his member, and he stared at her with a tight smile. "Best lock it behind you, Sally Howe. We do not need more company."

She reached behind herself and shot the bolt, unable to take her eyes off the scene in front of her. She had not seen him in the darkness of the street. She had been far too afraid to look. But aroused, he was magnificent, long and hard. And he was slick enough to glide into her body as he had before. She could almost feel him there, now.

He stared back at her and his hand began to move lazily again, then more vigorously. He smiled as if to prove that it was her he had been thinking of, all along. "Say my name."

It was a simple request, but she stumbled on it. "Mr. Fitzhugh…"

"You know that is not what I mean, Sarah." His voice was amazing, as it always was. Rich like sherry, dark and sweet. "Call me by my given name."

"Danyl." It was a relief to say the word. She had been afraid to use it without permission. But she thought it each time she saw him.

He groaned and closed his eyes.

"Danyl," she said more softly, and saw him twitch.

"Danyl," she said one last time on an ecstatic sigh and

felt her body readying itself for him. He could take her to heaven with a single thrust.

He finished. Then he matter-of-factly cleaned up the mess did up his breeches and turned to stare at her as though nothing unusual had happened.

She stared back, unsatisfied and confused.

But he'd recovered quick enough. Suddenly he was all business, as he had been on the first night. "You wished to speak to me?" She saw his lips twitch as he noticed the plant in her hand. "What is it about, then?"

It was probably very wrong to announce that she had wished to help him, with her mouth, her hand or her body. So she kept on staring.

He glanced down, as though to acknowledge his own arousal. "That was a perfectly natural response, after being onstage with you. I swear, woman, by the final curtain, half the men in the audience are rock hard. It only makes them harder when you will not pick a favorite. You should have mercy on us all and select a protector."

Was he honestly suggesting that she leave him? Did he not understand that he was the one she wanted? And why could she not manage to find the words, now that he might listen.

He shrugged his indifference. "Very well then. Stand in my doorway like a mannequin. But make yourself useful." He tossed her a script that waited on the table next to him. "You might as well learn the words to this, as it is a perennial favorite. Your part is marked. We will rehearse it tomorrow evening, when the house is dark."

She glanced at the title. *Othello*. "The death of Desdemona." They were the same words he had used to seduce her predecessors. And while further proof that he wanted her, there was no reason to feel that she was different from any other woman to him. "Is not this a rather heavy subject, for the season?"

"What season are you referring to?"

He could not claim that he did not know. "Christmas, of course."

He laughed. "And you expected something special for it? A gift perhaps? Or to hang that silly thing in your hand in the doorway of your dressing room. Next you will be telling me you want to take the day off. It is for us to entertain the revelers, Lady Sarah, not the other way around."

It took a moment for her to realize that the lady before her name was nothing more than a mockery of her ignorance. If he had known the truth, he would have called her Lady Sconsbury. To cover her confusion, she looked away. "I do not expect privileges where none are offered." And then she tossed her head in defiance. "But if you have us working every day of the year, you will prove yourself as heartless as I suspect you are."

"Not heartless," he replied. "Merely practical. A theater makes more money at Christmas than it does at Diwali. My father did not stay long enough to ingrain the Christian holidays in me. But if you wish, you may have *Lakshmi Puja.*"

"I do not know when that is," she admitted. Nor would I know how to celebrate it if I did."

"Next year?" He calculated quickly on his fingers, "It is on All Hallows' Eve, and five other days around it. And do not give me nonsense about evil spirits, for there is nothing evil about it. It is the triumph of good." He looked distant for a moment, as though seeing into the past. "There should be new clothes, and ghee lamps, and firecrackers. And Mother would draw on the floor with colored sand, and make sweets…" His expression had changed to something soft, hopeful and utterly human.

Then he remembered where he was and who he was speaking with. His indifference fell back into place as quickly as a shutter hiding a house lit for a holiday party. And whether Christian or Hindu, she was not invited to it. "My mother is dead for many years now, of course. I do not celebrate her holidays, either. I am, as you say, heartless."

"I never said…" But hadn't she? Or implied something very much like it.

"It does not matter what you think of me," he said, in the usual gruff tone he used when they were rehearsing. "As long as you learn your lines. You may think the murderous Moor is too dark for Christmas, but it is a part that I am well suited for. And I have no intention of letting you, or the audience, or anyone else, choose the bill for me."

"Of course, Mr. Fitzhugh."

"And as for that thing in your hand?" He stood and walked toward her.

She could feel her knees begin to quake as he neared. Onstage, when she could pretend she was another person, it was so much easier to be near him. Now, he was coming closer, moving with a sense of purpose.

He took the mistletoe from her, glancing down at it, turning it over in his hands. "How does it work?"

Surely he must know that. He was torturing her for his own amusement. She was so nervous she could hardly speak. She wet her lips. "You hang it from the ceiling, or in a doorway. And couples that pass under it must kiss and remove a berry."

"Interesting," he said. "But hardly necessary." He reached for her suddenly, pulling her forward into his arms and crushing the thing between them. His mouth was on hers, and he opened her lips with one horizontal lick at their seam. Then he took them, filling her mouth with his tongue with slow, deep thrusts. His hands were immobile, pressing into her spine low on her back, locking her hips to his.

She'd imagined herself the brave, saucy girl that strutted across the stage. She would steal a kiss from him, intriguing him enough to want another. But in one move, he conquered her, ravishing her mouth as he had her body on the night that they'd met. And that one deep kiss had her trembling to the core, on the brink of surrender.

Then she remembered the scene she had just witnessed: his erect manhood, and the way he'd lost control of it at the sound of her voice. But that had been for the girl on the stage, and not her at all.

The tension drained from her, leaving her unsatisfied. He sensed the change and pulled away. But he was looking at her with a knowing smile and took the mistletoe from her hands. In a single casual gesture, he pulled it through his fingers, stripping all the berries from it at one go. He handed the bare twig back to her. "You'd best get another. If there was any magic in that one, I suspect we have used it all. But let us be clear on one point. You are free to kiss whoever you wish. If you feel the need to cloak desire in English superstition, be my guest."

He stooped to retrieve the script, which she had dropped

while they kissed. "In the future, do not bother me with foolishness. Learn your lines. Be on time for rehearsal. Beyond that, I do not care what you do. And if there is anything else I want—" he reached out a finger and stroked her lower lip, which was still wet and full from his kiss "—we will discuss that at another time."

He was lord and master, here. And for now, at least, he desired her. But it was nothing more than that. He did not care. And since she could not manage to talk five minutes without angering him, she should be lucky to have that. She shifted the script in her hands, not wanting him to see the nervousness that left her damp palm prints on the cover. "Of course, Mr. Fitzhugh." She unlocked the door, turned and left.

CHAPTER FIVE

SARAH LOOKED NERVOUSLY at the bed in the middle of the stage. It seemed very white compared to the boards beneath it, or the drop and wings on the stage. The space was dark, with only a few of the floats lit at the foot of the stage to give them enough light to work by. The painted Forest of Arden, from tonight's production of *As You Like It,* loomed just outside of the glow, like a forbidding wood worthy of Macbeth. Now that the chandeliers had gone out, the darkness filled the house like wadded black velvet, leaving little room for the two of them on the stage.

Danyl did not seem to notice, moving easily in the darkened space as though it were his home. And she had to admit, with the doors locked and the last person gone from the huge building, the feeling of security outweighed the desolation.

If she was afraid of anything, it was Danyl Fitzhugh. She had no reason to be. He would not hurt her. Although he was not always polite, he had never been anything but gentle in his treatment of her.

The intimacy she longed for was the inevitable outcome of this scene, but she could not shake the feeling of unease. He did not read this play as she did. For him it was a tragedy no different than any other he might choose. And for her? It was a chance to die at the hands of a man who should love her, and to do it over and over again while the world watched and did nothing.

He glanced back at the bed, and her shifting uneasily beside it. "Make yourself comfortable."

As if that would even be possible. She removed her robe and sat on the edge, feeling the pitch of the mattress, toward the place where the audience would be. She would be displayed like an offering before them, stripped to her shift, all disguises gone.

But it would be all right, she reminded herself. Later, there might be mistletoe and chestnuts, and parlor games with the others at the rooming house. She could divert herself with ordinary pleasures. Or perhaps she would be lying sated beneath the dark man who had called her here. But there was nothing to be afraid of. This was only a play.

Outside, the winter wind howled. She could hear it rattling in the roof. She shivered against it, drawing the sheet of the prop bed up to her shoulders.

And now Danyl was at her side, instructing her in the scene. "You know the story? The Moor is tricked by his underling into believing that his wife is faithless. He confronts her. She denies, of course."

"Because she is innocent," Sarah whispered, wetting her lips. But when had protestations of innocence ever saved her? It was why she'd run.

"He will not listen. And in a rage, he kills her." He said

it simply, as if it had no meaning outside of the text. Of course, he was not the one who had to die.

"Very well, then," she said. "Let us begin." She was not the director or the lead. It was wrong of her to suggest. But she could not bear to wait a moment longer, before continuing this most unfunny of farces. Once they were through with the business, she would lie back on the pillows and he would come to her as he had the others, and reward her for her performance.

She lay back on the bed and feigned sleep, just as Desdemona must.

He admired her pose for a moment. "More vulnerability, if you please. Do not hide yourself. Throw back the covers and throw an arm across your eyes." She did as she was told, feeling the costume pull across her breasts, outlining her body for the audience. It was an illusion, of course. She was fully clothed. And yet she felt naked.

Danyl did not seem to notice, slipping easily into the character with a shake of his shoulders. Through her slit eyes, he seemed larger and more menacing, a black silhouette against an even blacker room. He approached the bed, muttering words of love for her even as he plotted her end. "When I have pluck'd the rose, I cannot give it vital growth again. It must needs wither: I'll smell it on the tree."

He knelt at her side now, and cradled her body in his arms. His words were sad and gentle. Had she not known where the scene must go, she'd have found them romantic. She threw back her arm as he raised her head to his lips and kissed her.

This was better. She would happily do this again and again over the course of an evening, until the results sat-

isfied him. There was little wonder that the others suc-
cumbed. She did not blame them for it. She was only too
happy to join their ranks.

As Othello, Danyl poured his passion into her, smoothing her hair, kissing her mouth and her temples, lingering,
withdrawing, and returning to kiss again. He was more
tender than he had been in the dressing room, but no less
passionate. And through it all, she must pretend to sleep
and lie unresponsive, though her body screamed to return
his affection. She wanted so much to believe that the kisses
were real that she forgot to speak her part until she felt the
prod in the ribs to remind her.

She opened her eyes and tried to look sleepy and confused. "Who's there? Othello?"

"Ay. Desdemona."

"Will you come to bed, my lord?" She held out a hand
to him, drawing him closer, stoking his cheek. And for a
moment, she saw the character falter, as the actor forgot
his lines. He came forward to meet her, rising slowly from
his knees and letting her draw him toward the bed.

His shirt was open, displaying a vee of smooth, dark
chest, and she put her lips to it, licking once, over the
heart, feeling the gasp as her tongue rasped the skin. His
hand touched one of her breasts through the linen of the
gown, flat palm circling before sliding between the ties
to cover skin.

Around them, the darkness changed from threatening
to comforting. The only secret it held would be theirs as
she seduced him. She tugged the hem of his shirt out of
the breeches he wore and stripped it over his head, running
her hands along the muscles revealed. They had been in-

timate, but not like this. He was beautiful and she wanted to kiss every inch of him. But she would begin with his chest. She tried eagerly to draw a nipple into her mouth.

He took a breath, caught her hands and pushed her away, shaking his head. "If you keep going thus, they will close us for indecency. A touch on the cheek only, please. Your upstage hand, so as not to block my profile. And then I will say my line."

The scene. She must remember that this was all in play. If they could get through to the end of it, he would start again. And each time she would break down a little more of his resistance.

But first, she must die. She lay back in his arms and prepared.

"It strikes where it doth love. She wakes."

His hands were on her throat. She was ready. She could do this. She steeled herself for what she knew was to come, the tightening grip, the fear and the sudden lack of air, ordering her brain not to confuse the actions on the stage tonight with the reality of her past.

He paused in the action and withdrew, and shook her by the shoulder. "What is the matter with you this evening? You were quite enthusiastic, only a moment ago. Suddenly you are as stiff as wood."

Was that it, then? There had been no pain. But then, why would there be? It was only a game. "You are doing it wrong," she said softly.

"I?" He gave a sarcastic laugh. "And what would you know of how this scene must be played."

"More than you might think." Now, when she most needed to dissemble, the actress had left her, leaving nothing but memories of the past. She reached up and rear-ranged his hands on her neck. "Grab me so. As it is, you would have to shake me to death. But if you meant to kill me, your hands would be here. Now, if you squeeze, I shan't be able to make a sound. If I struggle, you have but to slap me until I still."

And now, he was the one who was silent. "Sarah."

She looked up into his startled face. "Did you not won-der why it was that I ran away?"

"I did not think it my business."

"Perhaps it is not," she agreed. Her eyes were foolishly wet. She wiped away the tears with the back of her hand, vowing that she would not sob. Crying and carrying on only made the punishment worse. "I am sorry. But I do not think I can play the scene you have chosen for me. I have played it too many times before, with my husband."

Danyl was still quiet. She wondered, did he think her to blame? Or was he simply thinking of other women that might fill her part just as well but with far less bother. Fi-nally, he asked, "And this husband. What became of him?"

She laughed bitterly. "Nothing at all. At this very mo-ment, I suspect he is drinking at his club. Now that I am gone, he might take out his anger on the servants when he returns to the house. But when one is the Earl of Scons-bury, one does not fear justice for little bouts of temper."

"An earl." Now Danyl's hands fell away from her as though he were afraid to touch her. "But that would make you..."

"A countess," she replied, sitting up and straighten-ing her gown. "But I was quite happy to walk away from the title, once I found the nerve to do so. If you'd had a good look at me, those first weeks, when the bruises were still fading, you'd have understood. I hid them with paint and powder. And I hid myself as well." She smiled triumphantly, for it had been most fortunate to land here, of all places.

"Surely you had friends…"

"None that were brave enough to face the wrath of my husband by sheltering me. When you found me, I had nowhere to turn."

He looked away from her and sat on the edge of the bed, clearly shocked. "You were helpless. I took advantage of the fact."

"You paid me back a hundredfold. You gave me a new life. And I am very grateful." She knelt behind him and stroked the arms that had held her, praying that just once she could coax him into doing her bidding with the offer of her body. "But this scene? I cannot do it. If you mean to make love to me tonight, Danyl, do it without pretense. You must know that I am yours. But do not sully it with violence. I cannot bear to think you would hurt me. Not even in jest."

"And this is why you did not wish to do *Othello*?" He still would not look at her, so she laid her cheek against his back, and kissed. "Why did you not tell me?"

"You told me not to bother you with foolishness." She put her hands around his wrists and left them there, leaning forward to kiss his shoulders. "Can we not do *Twelfth Night* instead?" It suits the season. Or perhaps a pantomime. I know that it is not dignified. It is probably quite beneath your talents. But it is almost Christmas."

"Fairy tales and magic," he said dismissively.

"The audience likes them. And so do I. When Columbine runs away with her lover, I always imagined…" From her husband's theater box, she silently applauded the girl's escape, and dreamed of the moment that she would have such courage.

She kissed him again, playfully, on the ear. "But I shall not run away from you, to Grimaldi or Kean, or anyone else." Then she stripped the linen gown over her head and pressed her naked body against him so that he might know she was his. He had but to turn around and accept her.

His shoulders slumped. "I never thought of myself as a Harlequin, able to right wrongs with a wave of my sword."

"That is how I think of you," she said, realizing that it was true. "I met you, and everything changed."

He said nothing in response. But he slid off the bed, turning as he did so to kneel below her. Then he wrapped his arms around her waist and dropped his head to kiss her thigh.

He might not think himself capable of magic. But surely this must be it. She had never felt anything so wonderful. He nudged her legs apart and settled himself between them, hands stroking up her body to cover her breasts. But his mouth was traveling up her leg to the place she most wished to feel it. His kisses on her sex were firm but gentle as were the fingers tugging at her nipples. The pleasure seemed to ripple through her at each touch. She cradled his head, running her fingers through his wavy black hair, and stroked his face. There were tears on his lashes. *For her?* How strange.

She could feel the water running down her cheeks as well. But for once, it was not from pain or fear or sadness.

They were tears of gratitude for the gift he was giving her. They turned to tears of relief as he traced the very heart of her with the tip of his tongue. Then he pulled her into his mouth, sucking greedily, as the fluttering torture of her core continued.

Lord, if she had to die tonight, let it be this way, at the pleasure of his kiss. She released the last of her fear and let the next wave of sensation sweep her away. And she was reborn, and her cries echoed through the silence of the theater.

When she was silent again, he rose without a word and removed the last of his clothing, then crawled into the bed beside her, stretching out on his back and reaching for her hands. He was directing her, as he always did, setting the scene.

She straddled him, facing out toward the empty house, displayed as though she were a set piece in some erotic drama, and she stroked his erection as he had done himself before lowering herself down on it.

He shuddered, fighting for control, and then moved gently under her, cupping her bottom with his hands, kneading the flesh possessively.

She rocked back and forth in rhythm with him, taking him deeper on each thrust. She had feared that it had been her imagination on that first night, that she had tried to turn something common into a romance for the sake of her self-respect. But everything about Danyl was perfect: his smooth, dark skin, the lithe muscles hiding beneath it, and the slow, precise way he moved inside of her. She was at home here, with her lover, on the stage.

Every sense peaked in awareness at the new world he

offered her. A candle floating in the trough at the foot of the stage guttered and died. She watched the shadows change. She listened to the creak of a board, the squeak of a mouse, and the slow increase of her own breathing as she fell more deeply under the spell of his body.

He drew his knees up so that he could increase the strength of his thrusts, and she hugged them to herself, touching his calves, pressing her hands over his feet and bracing herself so she could meet him with her hips. And as they had that first night, they broke together, and it left them as spent and helpless as puppets with cut strings.

She kissed his knee.

He patted her hip with his hand.

With a groan of feigned exhaustion, he pulled himself from under her and stood. And then he took her hand and they walked in silence to the steps that led to his rooms.

CHAPTER SIX

DANYL KISSED THE woman that slept in his bed, marveling at how peaceful she looked, after the strenuous evening they had shared.

She did not wake.

He smiled. The others at the rooming house would tease her tomorrow, and remark that she had not returned from rehearsing with him. If he did not clear the stage before they arrived, the rumpled bed and strewn clothing would tell the rest of the story.

Let them laugh. She would not be returning to those rooms, ever. For however long he had her, she would stay here, just as she was, so that he could enjoy every last moment of their time together.

She did not belong with him. She would realize it soon enough, and he would let her go. But now there was something he must do. Better that she did not know what he planned. She might run again. And he had no intention of turning back, now that his mind was set.

He let himself down the back stairs that led down into

the theater. First, he went to the tiring-rooms and opened his makeup case, selecting paint and powder to lighten his skin convincingly enough to pass in candlelight. It would be necessary to do something with the hair. The black was always a problem when he sought a disguise. But he settled on oil of Macassar, which tended to leave a dark red glint to the slicked-back locks. A touch of powder at each temple made for a creditable gray. A rough, salt-and-pepper mustache complemented it nicely.

And then to the costumes. He chose a black suit that was far too large for him, and a bit short in the sleeves, so that he would remember to hunch. Then he strapped a millet-filled bag about his waist, making a pendulous belly that swayed more realistically than a pillow ever would. Over it he stretched a garish silk vest, and a cravat tied with unseemly haste. He splashed himself liberally with cologne, and topped the lot with a pair of thick, round spectacles.

He glanced in the mirror. The effect was superb. He pocketed a small stack of engraved calling cards, with a false name, should he be called upon to provide identification.

And then he set out for Pall Mall. Brooks's first, for some speech or other he'd read in *The Times* made him think his quarry was Whig.

He was right in one. He put his request to the doorman there, in a northern accent so thick that they'd likely remember him as a Scot. The man returned, requesting the reason for this interview, and Danyl assured him, it was "too private matter for any but one set of ears." And that it concerned "the location of a certain person that the earl was likely seeking."

The servant returned again to lead him to a reception room. Shortly thereafter, Sconsbury appeared.

He did not look like a brute. But in Danyl's experience, the real bad ones seldom did. The earl looked him up and down as though trying to take his measure. "Do I know you, sir?"

"You have no reason to," Danyl admitted. "But I have learned of you. From your wife."

The man's eyes narrowed with suspicion, but also with covetousness. "What would you know of her?"

"I know that she has run away from you, and tells the most interesting of stories."

"And I suppose you mean me to pay you, to silence her?"

Danyl gave a hearty laugh. "On the contrary, sir. What need would there be to silence a woman? They do nothing but talk, of course. But no sane man listens to them."

The earl laughed back, as though he felt this was quite true.

"But I thought to myself, MacGruder, if the woman was to be silenced, it would be her husband who wanted to do the job. Perhaps he wants her back. Or at least to know that she is well."

"That is true," the earl admitted. "And is she well?" But the man's face did not look so much concerned as annoyed.

"That would depend on your point of view, I am sure. She has fallen in with rough company. And her behavior?" Danyl gave a half shrug as though he did not wish to speak of it. "Shall we say that it is unfitting?"

"She was always a wild one," the earl agreed. "Fractious. Disobedient. And in need of correction." His hands fairly itched at the thought. He was flexing his fingers, as though trying to decide between a slap and a punch.

"I suspected you would say such," Danyl agreed. "And that you would like to do the job yourself, that it might be done with discretion. If, after what I have shown you of her whereabouts, you would think the information worthy of reward?" Danyl shrugged modestly. "That is up to you to decide."

The earl smiled. "You can take me to her?"

"Now, if you like. In a plain carriage, so as not to arouse the lady's suspicion. If she sees you coming with full livery, she will most assuredly run."

The earl smiled, and Danyl felt a chill that made him long for his coat and muffler. "You are right. She must not get away again. A moment only, I will get my hat."

Danyl waited for the earl's return, and then led him to the hired carriage outside. They rode in silence. But what would the great man have to say to him? And he was quite sure that he had nothing he wished to say to the earl.

He only wished to get this over with, and get on with his life.

A short time later, they drew to a stop, and Danyl waited respectfully for the peer to exit the carriage. Then he signaled the driver to depart, leaving them alone in the mist.

"The docks?" the earl said suspiciously.

"I believe her plan was to leave the country. But alas, an insufficiency of funds…" Danyl gave a leer. "To gain money, she has been forced to resort to the sort of behavior that, well…you can imagine."

"The whore." The earl's voice was devoid of passion, as though announcing that his wife was young, or blonde.

"She has always been a filthy whore. And the moment she escapes me, the truth will out."

"I see." And Danyl did. Now that there was no reason to hide the truth behind a polite facade, Sconsbury was every bit as ugly as he'd feared. "If you will but follow me, the place she waits is just a bit farther on. If we are quiet, we will take her unawares."

He gestured down the boards and set off toward a pier in at the far end. It was a quiet night, if one did not count the noise from nearby taverns, and the occasional drunken stevedore. The earl followed happily, silently behind.

When they were as distant from the last sign of humanity as they could be, Danyl stopped suddenly and peered into the fog. "There, that is her."

"Where? I see no one?"

"Because you are looking in the wrong direction," he said, as though being patient. "She walks the jetty looking for clients. I led you past her, and you said nothing. Turn and look behind you."

"Where?" The earl turned obediently.

Danyl removed the cosh from his pocket and swung. As the man went limp, he lifted his purse, then gave a shove and heard the satisfying splash of the body. He sent the blackjack after, and began walking away. By the time he heard the plunk of the weapon hitting water, he had pocketed both glasses and false mustache. An industrious rub with the handkerchief brought his face back to a healthy dark complexion. And the stab of his pocketknife to the false stomach sent the seed to trickling away to be pigeon feed. He dropped the earl's purse off the next pier, for it would not do to be caught with it.

It was not until he was safely seated in a cab and on his way back to Drury Lane that he allowed himself to speak. "Merry Christmas, Sarah," he said, so softly that none but he could hear. "Merry Christmas."

CHAPTER SEVEN

SOME DAYS LATER, Danyl awoke to find his lover on the bed beside him, wrapped in his dressing gown staring at the early edition of *The Times*. Her expression was difficult to read. It appeared that she could not decide whether to rejoice or mourn.

She looked over at him, blinking in confusion. "Edgar. My husband. Is dead."

"Are you sure?"

She blinked again. "The body has been positively identified. He was a victim of robbery on the docks." She frowned. "Although what would have taken him there, I cannot imagine." And then she shrugged. "In life I would not have dared question his comings and goings. Is it wrong that in death I do not much care? I am simply glad that he is gone." Then she looked worried. "You must think me a terrible person.

Danyl laid a hand on her shoulder and gave it a protective squeeze. "I think you are too nice by half, to be worried at all."

She continued to read. "It says that the servants have remarked on my absence."

A thought suddenly occurred to him. "They do not suspect you had anything to do with this."

She shook her head. "He was last seen with some strange man at his club…." She set the paper aside with a shake of her head. "It is all very mysterious. But the servants heard us arguing…"

"Him beating you, more like," Danyl corrected.

"And they suspected that I might have met with foul play as a result."

"You have nothing more to fear, then, from this latest development. Who will take the coronet?"

"His nephew, Albert." Sarah smiled. Now that the conversation no longer involved her husband, her relief was obvious. "He is a very nice young man, as I remember. He will make a fine Sconsbury."

This was not what he wanted to hear. Danyl did not regret what he had done, for if a man could not be brought to justice, then vengeance would have to do. But he did not want to think that this nice, young Albert, who could make her smile, would be the recipient of the gratitude.

He thought of the gift he had hidden in the drawer of the bedside table. He'd waited a day too late to give it to her. Now that it was safe for her to go home, he had no right to hold her. "You could return then, if you wished," he said, resigned. "Explain to him the reason you left. He will not punish you for your absence, I am sure."

"Return?" She blinked again, her blue eyes as wide and innocent as they had been on the day he'd met her. "I suppose I could. He would let me have the dower house, for as long as I needed it. I doubt Edgar thought to provide me with a widow's settlement. But I am sure the family suspects what it was like to live with him, and would take pity."

It was all but settled then, and nothing left but goodbyes. For a change, he would not lose his ingénue to a rival company. This one would take his heart with her when she left. But there was nothing to be done about that.

If he could not put a brave face on this, he was not much of an actor. "And so, my dear, farewell." He drew her into his arms, tenderly, sweetly, kissing her on the forehead.

She pulled away from him in surprise and slapped at his arm. "Why ever for? Are you going somewhere?"

It was his turn to blink in surprise. "I had thought, given the opportunity, you would go back to your old life." His mind raced ahead, trying to find a facial expression to suit the conversation. And then he remembered that he was facing the Dowager Countess of Sconsbury. Suddenly humbled, he gave up and stared at the floor, unable to meet her gaze.

Her touch on his arm was gentle, but her voice had all the petulance of a slighted diva. "Do you have a problem with my work, Mr. Fitzhugh?"

"Quite the contrary." Now that he could play the director again, it was easy to face her, and to put her in her place. "You have a quick mind for the script, and a natural talent for stage business. I suspect that, given a few more lessons, you will tumble and dance as well as any clown. And yet, you…" He felt shy again. "You are the loveliest Columbine I have ever seen. You were right, you know. Christmas is no time for tragedy."

"There should be nothing but games and fun," she said, smiling again. "We will be having a party in the theater, after the last show on Christmas Eve." She glanced at him, as though trying to decide. "If you will cease shouting at me during rehearsals, I shall invite you to it. The rest of the company assures me that there is nothing more diverting than playing charades with actors. And I have promised to show them a bullet pudding."

"If you think pudding is made of bullets," he said, "you are too daft to be let loose."

"It is another game," she said, laughing at his ignorance. "You put a bullet on a pile of flour, and then we all take turns spooning away at the mound until the bullet falls. The loser must root about in it and catch the thing in their teeth and get all covered in flour…. It very comical. I have not played it in years. Not since before I met Edgar." She frowned. "If I return home I will spend Christmas in mourning for Sconsbury. And I vowed that I would not spend another bleak holiday on his account, ever again."

That was good then. If she at least stayed in Covent Garden, he might not lose her altogether. He pretended to brood again. "I have no intention of moderating my behavior to gain admittance to a gathering in my own building. Nor will I give you a raise in pay, if that's what you are after. I am not blind, you know. Grimaldi has been trying to steal you for his troupe." He pointed dramatically at the door. "Go to him, if you mean to do so. You will not see another penny from me."

She dropped the paper and put her arms around his neck. "And where would that leave you?"

Alone, as it always did. It was hardly a surprise. People

died or they left. It was a fact of life. It happened so often that he must eventually grow used to it.

Then she kissed him on the cheek. "Despite what you may expect for me, I am not going anywhere. I like things just as they are."

He turned his head and watched as the dressing gown slipped from her shoulder, revealing a tantalizing expanse of bare skin. "But now you are a widow. Free to do as you like. Do you not think to marry again?"

"Not if it is likely to be as it was," she said firmly. "I have no wish to sit waiting for my husband's family to choose a man that is at all like Edgar was." She considered. "And I do not think that the men crowding the stage door wish to offer me marriage. If any do, they are in love with an illusion, and too foolish for me to even consider."

"But if the right man were to ask me, I suspect I should be tempted." She tightened her grip upon him as though prepared to shake sense into him, should he not take her hint.

Danyl Fitzhugh had never thought of himself as being the right man for anything. Other than running a theater, of course. And training up actresses so that they could abandon him. He'd made a damn fine Othello as well. But of late the Moor seemed more foolish than tragic, and he was tired of playing the fool.

He slipped his hands inside the robe and pushed it off her shoulders and to the floor. "I might know of just the fellow," he said, burying his face in her shoulder and kissing her on the collarbone. "But for now, it is hours until curtain, and I have no desire to leave my bed. Perhaps, once I am rested, I shall remember his name."

"If you mean to sleep, you do not need me," she said, pretending to be hurt.

"And if you leave this bed, I will not give you your Christmas present."

Now he had her attention. Her eyes sparkled like a child's, and she held out her hand. "You shall not have a moment's peace until you give it to me."

"Very well then. Close your eyes." When she did as he asked, he pulled the mistletoe from the drawer and set it in her hand.

She opened her eyes and laughed.

"I spoiled the last one," he reminded her.

"We used it up," she corrected. She kissed him on the cheek again, then plucked a berry and threw it to the floor. "I suspect we shall need another fresh one after I am through with you this morning."

"I think I am learning to like Christmas," Danyl said, settling back into the pillows as the former Countess of Sconsbury climbed into his lap. "And I have heard there are some countries where they bring a whole tree into the house for it. I wonder what you would do for me then?"

"Anything you wish, Mr. Fitzhugh," she said with a smile. "Anything at all."

* * * * *

An Invitation to Pleasure

MARGUERITE KAYE

Born and educated in Scotland, **Marguerite Kaye** originally qualified as a lawyer but chose not to practise—a decision which was a relief both to her and the Scottish legal establishment. While carving out a successful career in IT, she occupied herself with her twin passions of studying history and reading, picking up a first-class honours and a Master's degree along the way.

The course of her life changed dramatically when she found her soul mate. After an idyllic year out, spent travelling round the Mediterranean, Marguerite decided to take the plunge and pursue her life-long ambition to write for a living—a dream she had cherished ever since winning a national poetry competition at the age of nine.

Just like one of her fictional heroines, Marguerite's fantasy has become reality. She has published history and travel articles, as well as short stories, but romances are her passion. Marguerite describes Georgette Heyer and Doris Day as her biggest early influences and her partner as her inspiration.

CHAPTER ONE

August 1815
London

'JILT HIM!' Susanna Hunter repeated the stranger's demand in utter disbelief. 'You wish me to end my betrothal to Sir Jason Mountjoy!'

She eyed the soldier seated on the edge of one of the gilded chairs which were set in carefully casual clusters around the large drawing room of her parents' London town house. Captain Lamont's uniform was ragged, hanging far too loose on his large frame. His boots were much patched and covered in a film of dust, as if he had marched here all the way from Waterloo, for goodness sake. His hair was cropped, auburn and what there was of it stood up in short, angry spikes. Aside from the vivid red welt of the scar on his forehead, his skin had the ashen pallor of suffering, stretched so taut over his cheekbones as to give him the look of a cadaver. His eyes though, a strange colour between tawny and gold, burned with the light of a man on a mission.

Susanna peered nervously over her shoulder at the drawing room door. Charles, her father's footman would be hovering just outside it, she knew, for he had been loathe to leave her alone with Captain Lamont in the first place. Was he dangerous? He had obviously been grievously ill. In fact, he looked as if he should be on his sickbed still. Despite the outrageous demand he had made of her, she softened. 'May I get you some refreshment?'

'I did not come calling to take tea, Miss Hunter,' he replied, drawing her a scornful look. 'I came to tell you...'

'Not to marry the man to whom I have been betrothed for two years,' Susanna interrupted tartly. So much for compassion.

Surprised by the sharpness in her tone, Fergus Lamont surveyed the young woman afresh. In her pale yellow gown, with her dark hair scraped back from her face, she had seemed to him every bit the prettily insipid debutante Mountjoy implied. He was no expert of feminine furbelows, but even he could see that the colour of her gown made her olive skin seem sallow, and now that he looked more closely, it looked as if her blue-black curls were fighting to escape their pins. There was, however, nothing at all insipid about her eyes. No longer demurely downcast, they were her best feature, a grey that was almost silver, thickly fringed with black lashes. And right at this moment, flashing fire. Perhaps after all he could rile her into the defiance he so badly needed in order to exact his longed-for revenge on Mountjoy. 'He calls you his sweet-tempered heiress, did you know that?'

His tone was deliberately insulting, and Fergus was rewarded with a flush which might well be temper, staining Susanna Hunter's pretty neck. His hopes rose as her lip curled, but fell as it just as quickly straightened. 'Jason says it is one of things that he loves most about me, that I am not the type of female who must forever be hearing my own voice.'

''Tis a pity he does not feel the same about his own,' Fergus responded bitterly. Those big grey eyes had lost their spark. He was losing her. 'Do you love him?'

'Jason is handsome and charming. Mama assures me there could be no better match.'

'Don't you care that he is marrying you for your money?'

'It would be foolish of me to pretend that my fortune is not significant, but men like Sir Jason Mountjoy do not marry for money,' she replied with a dignity that would have impressed Fergus were he not certain she was simply parroting her mother. She smoothed the folds of her gown, once more refusing to meet his eyes.

The flush had crept up, staining her cheeks now. Her eyes were bright, not with defiance but unshed tears that under any other circumstances would have given Fergus pause. But not today. Fergus thumped his fist on his knee, and leapt to his feet. 'Do you know what he's really like, this man you intend to marry? An *aide,* he calls himself. A messenger boy is what he actually is, and a damned poor one at that. Do you have any idea of the carnage he wrought? Och, but why should you care any more than he that his carelessness cost God knows how many lives! By God, lassie, if I could shake sense into you I would.'

Susanna flinched, only just resisting the desire to flee.

Far from the walking cadaver he had been a few moments ago, Captain Lamont now seemed lit from the inside. There was something both intimidating and magnificent in the way he threw those caustic words at her. His Scots accent broadened as his temper took hold. As he stood there, shoulders back, glaring at her, she saw the ghost of the man he had been, proud and bold, with a natural authority and a rather barbaric charm.

Awareness of this hit Susanna with a shocking jolt. Under different circumstances, she would have found him extremely attractive. Mortified, she straightened her spine. 'Captain Lamont, I can see that you have suffered much....'

A harsh crack of laughter greeted this remark. 'Not half as much as some, and not near as much as that blackguard Mountjoy deserves.'

Susanna's temper, a very small and timid creature which rarely saw the light of day, began to stir. It irked her that Jason insisted that the war was no topic for a lady, but that did not mean she wished Captain Lamont to educate her. She took a deep breath and got to her feet. 'It is obvious that you hold some sort of grudge against my betrothed. However, I fail to see what it has to do with me, and more importantly, I cannot understand what possible business of yours you think my marriage is. I am sorry for your suffering and wish you a sound recovery, but I must ask you to leave.'

She turned towards the door, upon the brink of congratulating herself for having managed such a difficult situation, when he grabbed her by the arm. 'I haven't yet told you why you must rid yourself of the scoundrel.'

The sleeves of Susanna's gown were long, beribboned

and fitted tight to the wrist, but she could feel the burning heat of his fingers as if her arms were bare. Captain Lamont's grip was tight enough to bruise. Close up, his eyes had a golden rim around them. His stubble too had a golden glint to it. Despite his grubby appearance, he smelled of soap. She was acutely conscious of him, not as a soldier but as a man. 'Release me at once.' Her voice sounded pitiably unconvincing.

'You have to listen to me.'

Whatever lies he wanted to impart, he obviously believed them. The desperation in his voice made Susanna even more convinced that she must quiet him for her own peace of mind. She tried once more to shake herself free, only to find herself in what felt shockingly like an embrace. 'If you do not release me, I will call a servant.'

He ignored her. 'It was a bloodbath, you know.' Captain Lamont swallowed compulsively. Sweat beaded on his brow under the line of the bandage. 'He blamed me for it all,' he continued harshly. 'Said *I* was the one who had misinterpreted the orders, not him. But it's not just on the battlefield he avoids responsibility, that's what you need to know. If it was not for your being promised to him, he'd have been clapped in the debtor's prison months ago, and what he owes to the tradesmen is doubtless nothing to what he has lost on the tables. He's counting on you to make it all good, his sweet-tempered heiress.'

'Stop it! Stop calling me that. All gentlemen have debts. Jason loves me.'

Another of those harsh cracks of laughter. 'You and a hundred others.'

Susanna froze. 'What do you mean?'

'He has a pretty way with compliments, does he not? He uses it to very good effect, charming the officers' wives and making their daughters sigh over him. Of course, he saves his most intimate of favours for those who cannot complain when they are left dealing with the consequences of his passion. As they must, Miss Hunter, for Mountjoy will not.' His grip on her arms tightened. 'Mountjoy left at least one of his side-slips on the continent when he returned to London, did you know that?'

'How dare you! Stop it. I will not listen.'

'You *must* jilt him. You *have* to make him pay. Mountjoy has hurt too many innocents already. Don't let him make you his next victim.'

Disbelief, shock and outrage sent Susanna's head spinning. She could not think straight. All she wanted was to rid herself of this man who for reasons best known to himself seemed bent upon her destruction. Unwilling to admit to the horrible premonition of truth underlying it all, she turned her anger upon the bearer of tidings. 'Do not insult me by trying to pretend that you give a—a *damn* about me. All you want to do is to hurt Jason, and if you have to use me, trample over me or any other innocent party in the process, then you will. Spare me the noble gesture, if you please. I am simply a pawn in your game, and I have absolutely no intentions of changing the course of my life because you wish me to.'

Her visitor looked genuinely aghast. 'You cannot possibly mean to marry Mountjoy after what I've told you.'

'What do you suggest I do instead? Marry you?' Susanna spoke without thinking, caught up in the wholly unfamiliar and strangely heady fire of fury which possessed her. The need to hurt this man in return for the hurt he was inflicting made her reckless. 'Judging from the sad state of your clothing, Captain, you are obviously in dire need of funds. Marriage to a *sweet-tempered heiress* might be just the thing for you.'

To her surprise, the jibe made him smile faintly. 'Not so sweet-tempered now though, are you? Don't do it, Susanna.'

His tone had a sense of urgency which gave sickening credence to his accusations. His use of her name made her abruptly conscious of the intimacy of their stance. She could feel his breath on her cheek. There were muscles of steel under that gaunt frame of his. The smile gave her another fleeting glimpse of the man he must have been. Powerful. Confident. Charismatic. Attractive. Extremely attractive. Her mouth went dry. Her skin prickled with heat. 'You are being ridiculous.'

'Susanna, don't do it. You could do so much better than Mountjoy.'

His hand slid down her arm, snaking round her waist and pulling her against him. Hard body, surprisingly solid. His thighs brushed hers. She felt hot, cold, giddy. Jason had never held her so close. She looked up, trying to think of something to say, and met Captain Lamont's eyes. Tawny and gold, no longer despairing but something else, something that made her heart beat faster, that made her belly clench. She opened her mouth to speak, felt herself jerked tight against him.

He was going to kiss her. She was certain of it. Her heart hammered in shocking anticipation. His mouth hovered over hers. Too late, she realised she should be protesting, but there was no need to struggle, for he had already cast her from him, his expression all the more mortifying because it reflected what should have been her own horror. Susanna pointed at the door. 'Get out.'

The captain stood his ground. 'If you marry him, you'll regret it for the rest of your life.'

'Get *out!*' Realising that she had covered her ears like a child made Susanna even more furious. How could she have allowed him to take such liberties? She would have allowed him to kiss her, had he not stopped. Jason never attempted to kiss her, not like that. This man did not even know her, but he had made her feel as Jason never had. No. She would not think about it, and she would certainly not listen.

Susanna strode over to the drawing room door, startling the footman by throwing it wide open. 'I wish you a complete recovery from your wounds, Captain Lamont. Let me assure you once and for all, that those you have attempted to inflict upon me have missed their mark. Good day.'

She slammed the door in his face before he could reply, leaning back against it and breathing deeply, listening to the two sets of steps retreating down the marble staircase. It was lies. He was quite deranged, and it was all lies. Or perhaps gross exaggeration would be more accurate, for it was to be expected that a gentleman set up a few flirts before he settled down. Marriage would put an end to such minor indiscretions, for Jason was an honourable man. Everyone said so.

Her heart was beating like a wild animal seeking escape. She would put this last hour to the back of her mind. Tonight she and Jason were to attend a victory ball. Tomorrow, she and Mama would be shopping for bride clothes. The wedding date was set. There was no question of doing anything other than going through with it, Susanna told herself firmly. No question at all.

CHAPTER TWO

December 1818
Argyll, Scottish Highlands

THE CROSSING YESTERDAY, from the bustling port outside the city of Glasgow across the River Clyde to the head of the Holy Loch, had been tempestuous, but at least the boat, like its six brawny oarsmen, had been sturdily built. This morning, when Susanna had first laid eyes on the frail craft which was to take her on the last leg of her journey, through the narrow stretches of Echaigh waters to Loch Eck and finally Loch Fyne, she thought the landlord of the Cot House ferry inn was making a joke at her expense.

It was snowing as the boatman cast off. Susanna's travelling pelisse of royal blue kerseymere with its elaborate satin scrollwork piping, the matching poke bonnet and the chinchilla muff which her mother had lent her, had seemed more than warm enough when she set out from London. Five hundred miles north, she wriggled her numb toes inside her kid boots as she balanced precariously on the narrow plank of wood which passed for a seat on the boat, and wondered if she would ever feel warm again.

The boat scudded and bumped over the waves. Excitement and apprehension made Susanna feel slightly sick. *Fergus, Laird of Kilmun,* Captain Lamont had signed himself in his letter. These past three years had seen his star rise if the title was aught to go by, while most would say that hers had reached its nadir.

Three years. So much time for her to regret her marriage to Jason, to dwell upon the consequences and to count the cost. She had done so many times, castigating herself over and over for failing to listen to the captain's words of warning as she discovered, in those early, most disillusioning months as a bride, that all Jason wanted was her money and her compliance. Until that morning, their first anniversary, watching Jason stagger up the stairs, looking every bit the drunken debaucher that he was, she resolved to be done with regrets.

Her husband refused to countenance the shame of a formal separation. They continued under the same roof, he continued to work his way through her inheritance, but the "sweet-tempered heiress" who neither thought nor acted for herself was long gone. That very morning two years ago, Susanna had extinguished the naive and dependent creature who was Jason's wife. From her ashes emerged a woman who prided herself on her strength in the face of adversity. Destitute widow as she now was, she was looking forward to her independence. She would never again allow a man to shape her life.

Susanna smiled to herself as she imagined Captain Lamont's —goodness no, the Laird of Kilmun's—surprise at the changes in her. His unexpected invitation to spend Christmas in the Highlands had arrived out of the blue. She could not deny it had piqued her curiosity, and was all the more welcome since the alternative was to spend the festive period with her parents in London. Her parents mourned their son-in-law as his wife could not. Susanna had abandoned her widow's weeds after three months. She would not be Jason Mountjoy's relic.

How astonished her host would be when she told him, as she had often wished to, that his harsh truths had eventually found their mark. True, she had still become that most absurd of clichés, the heiress wed by a feckless and charming fortune hunter, but in the same circumstances she doubted very much that any gullible girl would have done other than opt for the path of least resistance. She had married, and for a while she had been miserable, but she had no doubt at all that her misery would have lasted a great deal longer had she more illusions to cling to. There was even a chance that she would be clinging to them still. Her widowhood could easily have been the ending most seemed to think it, instead of the beginning Susanna was eager to embrace. For planting those first seeds of doubt, she owed the Laird of Kilmun a debt of gratitude, and so she would tell him.

The boat scudded its way towards a tiny jetty, and Susanna's thoughts turned to her host. The Laird of Kilmun, indeed! She hoped the husk of the man had managed some sort of recovery, but he had been so far gone, she doubted it was possible.

The wind let up and the snow eased, laying the landscape open as if a curtain had been drawn. She gazed around her with the disoriented feeling of one who has travelled too far in too short a time, catching her breath at the unexpected beauty of the place. Wild the Highlands were, but they were also staggeringly lovely. The village, with its white-washed cottages, their thatched roofs glistening with snow, lay in a crescent around the harbour, the church taking the slightly raised ground at the northern end. In the distance, gently rolling hills gave way to craggier peaks, snow-frosted and sharply defined against the pale blue of the winter sky. The waters of the loch had calmed to a gentle lapping onto the pebbled shore. A gull soared high above the fishing nets which were hung out to dry on the beach above the line of the tide. The air was salty, clean and painfully cold, unlike anything Susanna had ever breathed. Everything in view seemed to be painted with the crisp, clear lines of an amateur painting.

As she clutched the calloused hand of the ferry man to climb ashore, she saw him striding towards her. A tall, broad man he was, who exuded strength and vitality with every step. Long, muscled legs clad in tight trews covered the distance between them so quickly that his hair, worn long and loose to his shoulders, flew out behind him. Auburn hair, it glinted fire in the weak sunlight. A rough growth of stubble gleamed the same colour on his chin. Tanned skin he had, and a mouth curled into the hint of a welcoming smile.

Susanna's stomach did a little flip-flop. It was the eyes. Though the lines at the corners seemed less pronounced, and the hard edge of pain was no longer there, they were *his* eyes, a strange colour that must be hazel but looked amber. Was it really him? The man she had known had been tense to the point of breaking, as if he were held together by wires, his face hollowed out by suffering. She had forgotten, but it came back to her vividly now, the way he had looked out at the world, as if from a long distance away.

This could not be him, this wild-looking, vital Highlander. Nerves, a faltering of her hard-won confidence, surprise, admiration and a sharp twinge of attraction wrestled for dominance. She was still trying to form her thoughts when her hands were clasped in his, a rough cheek pressed to hers, and the scent of wool, leather and man enveloped her.

'Lady Mountjoy,' Fergus said.

'Captain Lamont?'

'Aye, but it is actually Laird Kilmun now.' She looked dumbfounded. Fergus wanted to laugh, but he was fair dumbfounded himself, for she seemed quite transformed. The female he remembered had been coltish, unsure of herself. He recalled downcast eyes and clasped hands, a mouth prim with the effort not to cry. The woman before him had a distinct air of confidence about her. He remembered her as a pretty wee thing conventionally turned out. Now she stood on the jetty, looking nothing like. Memorable rather than beautiful, she was all high cheekbones and wide-open grey eyes. Those he did remember.

The wind had whipped several wispy tendrils of hair out from under her bonnet. Her skin was very pale, her lips very red, her hair blue-black, the starkly contrasting colours giving her a touch of the exotic. A most unexpected stirring of his blood made him remember something else from that first meeting of theirs. He had kissed her. Or he had only just stopped himself from kissing her. It was the way she'd stood up to him, challenging his tirade, that had roused him. For a demure wee thing, she'd packed quite a punch. Now she was no longer a demure wee thing, but quite clearly and very delectably grown into her skin, it would be amusing to see if he could stoke her fire. It had been a long while, too long a while, since he'd had either the inclination or the opportunity for a bit of verbal sparring, but damn, there was something about this woman that made him want to forget all about taking life seriously and do just that.

Fergus smiled. 'Has the cat got your tongue, Lady Mountjoy? No, I can't call you that, it sticks in my craw. Since our acquaintance is of such long standing, perhaps you would allow me to call you Susanna, and you may call me Fergus?'

She simply stared, as if he had asked her to call him the devil, and damn, if it didn't make the devil in him react. 'I wonder now, though you would not kiss a mere captain all those years ago, have you a kiss for the laird?'

She looked as if she was torn between slapping him and doing as he was bid. Then, to his astonishment, she laughed. It was a wonderful sound, like the gurgling of a stream. 'You are quite outrageous, Captain—Laird! And in one sense, wholly unchanged, for you must still be taking enormous liberties. In every other sense, however, I barely recognised you.'

Fergus laughed. 'You've no objection then, to a Highlander over a soldier?'

'Laird Kilmun, you may assume the guise of a Russian peasant for all I care. It is no business of mine.'

Her voice remained cool, but he could see the smile lurking in her eyes. Such a serious business duty was, it had not occurred to Fergus that the doing of it would be enjoyable. But then, the woman he'd pictured in the role by his side was a poor wee soul filled with gratitude. A destitute, put-upon widow, he had imagined. But this widow, who was patently not in mourning, did not at all look as if she was in need of saving. He had thought it would be as simple as putting his proposition to her and awaiting her eager and delighted acceptance. His conscience would finally be quieted and his tenants reassured by the sight of the woman who would bear the future laird. Faced with a witty and exotic creature biting back her laughter, Fergus felt a distinct twinge of doubt.

He cursed himself for having made his plans public—though who would blame him, with so much pressure from so many sides to settle down and secure the future for his lands. He was sick to the back teeth of being introduced to Highland misses, all of them eligible, and, to his eyes, wholly interchangeable. Which had led him to conclude that that side of him was dead. Until now.

Fergus put his arms around his visitor's shoulder and steered her towards the path which led to the castle, thanking his stars that her lack of the Gaelic would keep her in temporary ignorance of his presumption. 'You've had a long journey, and there are a good few people who are eager to welcome you to the Highlands,' he said. 'Let me take you home.'

'Home' was a castle. Built of grey stone, it sat square to the loch, though its facade was hidden from the village by a carriageway bordered with oak trees. A round tower with a high conical roof like a witch's hat sat at each corner of the edifice, and although it had no moat, there looked as if there ought to be one to serve the drawbridge which led up to the studded front door. Gothic and baroque, pretty and flamboyant with its buttressed roof and tower windows formed to look like arrow slits, Castle Kilmun looked as if it had been lifted straight out of a children's storybook. The backdrop of snow-capped mountains, the picturesque village and the loch in the foreground added to the fairytale image. Susanna was enchanted.

From the gatekeeper's lodge to the mighty front door, the carriageway was lined with people. Old women in black, younger women in full skirts that stopped well short of the ankle, men in the kilt, which Susanna had never seen before save in paintings. Other men wore trews. 'The shawl the women wear is called an *arisaidh*,' the man who insisted she call him Fergus said, 'and you can tell which of them are married, for they wear the kertch or kerchief tied over their hair.'

Susanna listened to his commentary of names and roles without taking much in save that he had an impressive memory for every face. Bemused by the dropping of curtsies, the dropping of eyes which she could feel raised to stare the moment she passed by, she was very conscious of her clothes, her accent, which marked her out as not one of them. It was all so foreign and so unexpected and quite exhilarating. She smiled in bewildered acknowledgement of the murmurs of 'mistress' and 'my lady', and allowed herself to be beguiled, telling herself it was the people, the scenery, the castle, and nothing at all to do with the man at her side.

In the great hall, where a positive armoury of broadswords and daggers and foils and pistols were displayed on the walls in intricate designs, there were more curtsies and bows and nudging and whispering from a cluster of servants and ancient retainers, whose scrutiny was beginning to make her feel uncomfortable. Who on earth did they think she was?

In the huge stone fireplace, a fire consumed what looked like half a tree. Food was taken, Susanna's health was drunk, and then speeches were made, all in the soft, lilting Gaelic which she could not understand and which Fergus made no attempt to translate. The sense of unreality took hold. Her head began to buzz. She needed to sit down in a quiet room, take off her hat, and gather her thoughts. The whisky burned her throat and made her cough. The heat was overpowering. The flagstone floor seemed to tilt up at her. She slumped back in her seat, and found herself suddenly scooped up into her host's arms.

It felt rather nice to be picked up so effortlessly, to be held against such a broad chest, to be forced to surrender to him, just for a few seconds, so Susanna felt obliged to struggle. 'Put me down.'

Fergus ignored her. 'You will excuse us,' he said to the gathered household. 'My lady is overcome by the warmth of your welcome.'

Laughter greeted this remark. '*My* lady?' Susanna hissed, grabbing hold of a fistful of his auburn hair and yanking hard. It had no effect. Fergus's arms tightened around her as he carried her, ignoring her protests, up the wide sweep of stairs, along a long hallway to a dark panelled door, which he managed to open without letting her fall, and finally he set her down.

CHAPTER THREE

THE ROOM WAS at the rear of the castle, with a view out over parkland where deer were foraging in the frosty grass. Dusk was falling outside. The fireplace was of carved stone, but the smouldering flames indicated a chimney in need of sweeping. It would have been a pleasant room, with its faded damask hangings and its worn rugs, cosy and comfortable like the pair of chairs angled towards the fire, were it not for the fact that it was dominated by a large four-poster bed.

Fergus was leaning against the door. Tall, broad, a bit dishevelled, a bit out of breath, a lot of man. He was looking at her in a way that was far from gentlemanly. His eyes had a wicked glint. And his mouth…

Susanna turned her back on the man and the bed, confused by how sharply she could recall that might-have-been kiss. She had blocked it so completely from her mind that she thought it forgotten. She remembered the way his body felt against hers, recalled precisely the fluttering anticipation as his lips brushed hers. She tugged at the knotted strings of her bonnet. The relief, when she pulled the dratted thing from her head, was enormous. She ran her fingers through her tangled curls with a sigh.

'Have you the headache? I'm not surprised, all that bowing and scraping, I've a headache with it myself.'

She had expected him to bid her goodnight and leave, yet here he was, standing behind her. His strong fingers on her temples were gentle and soothing. His being here was most improper. Perhaps things were different in Scotland. Susanna closed her eyes as the pain surrendered to his touch until it veered from soothing to something more unsettling. Different customs or no, this could not possibly be right. In fact, now her thumping headache was gone, none of it seemed right at all.

She pushed his hands away and turned to confront him. 'What is going on? Why did all those people make such a fuss over me? What were all those toasts about? And what are you doing here, in my bedchamber? I am five-and-twenty and perfectly capable of undressing myself.' Almost before she had finished speaking she started blushing. 'I beg your pardon, I did not mean to imply that you would—that I would—what I mean is, Fergus, you should not be here.'

Fergus ran his fingers through his hair. 'Aye well, actually, Susanna, it's expected that I stay here, under the circumstances.'

He should not have attempted the smile. He'd meant to try for endearing, but Susanna, Fergus was fast realising, was not a woman who could be manipulated, even if it was for her own good. She stared at him in astonishment. 'What circumstances?'

'We need to talk.'

He sat down, and indicated the chair opposite, but Susanna remained rooted to the spot, crossing her arms across her chest. 'Then talk.'

'Will you at least take off your coat?'

'Provided you understand that is all I'm removing. And before I do even that much, let me inform you that I don't care what kind of customs of *droit signeur* prevail in these parts, I will have nothing to do with them.'

He couldn't help it—he laughed. 'Faith, woman. This is the nineteenth century, not the dark ages. Though if the notion of me as a brawny Highland laird in plaid carrying you off to my lair pleases you, I'll do my best to oblige.'

'I would not have you go to such trouble on my behalf,' Susanna replied primly.

She did not laugh, but the sparkle in her eyes gave her away. That biddable wee lass he had imagined would not have been half as much fun as this woman. Though fun, Fergus reminded himself, as Susanna cast her pelisse aside and sat down facing him, was not the point at all. Fergus drummed his fingers on the arm of the chair, struggling for a subtle opening. Looking up, he met a pair of wide-open grey eyes, and decided that bluntness would serve him best. 'They think we are betrothed,' he said baldly.

'Betrothed!'

'There's no need to screech.'

'I did not screech. And if I did, it was your own fault. "I would consider it an honour if you would join me over Christmas," your letter said. "I am sure that you will enjoy the way we celebrate the new year here in the Highlands," you wrote. At no point did you mention marriage. My God,

I've only just escaped the hell of one union. Do you think I'm so stupid as to repeat my mistakes?'

Which at least answered the question of whether or not she had been happy, Fergus thought. He grabbed her before she reached the door. This was not going well. 'Susanna, listen to me. You cannot know how deeply sorry I have been these past three years, knowing how unhappy I made you. I would have written, called on you, but what would be the point when the damage was done? Hearing from me, your nemesis, would only have caused you more pain.'

Susanna frowned, shaking her head in confusion. 'Nemesis? What are you talking about?'

'You were right. I had no thought at all for you—all I cared about was getting at Mountjoy. I didn't think of the damage I was doing to you, the hurt I was inflicting on you. It didn't occur to me, you see, that you might have feelings for the man.'

His remorse startled her, but his misplaced pity was insulting. 'Fergus, my marriage to Jason was a mistake, but it was mine to make, and...'

It has been the making of me, is what she intended to say, but he interrupted her. 'Let us not talk of the past. It is done, I cannot undo it, much as I would wish, but I can make it up to you, Susanna.'

Now he was smiling again, but there was something not quite right about that smile. It made her edgy. His determination to take responsibility for her was really quite annoying, especially since one of the reasons she had come here was to show him how very able she now was to take care of herself. She tried to free herself, but his grip on her tightened. She was not in the least bit frightened, but she was perturbed by the fervent light in his eyes. 'Fergus, you have nothing to make up for.'

But Fergus seemed bent on a speech which sounded bizarrely well-rehearsed. 'I'm no Adonis, but I'm sound in body and in mind, too. Now. The title I hold is an old one, and the lands extensive, though they have been sadly neglected. As for Castle Kilmun, the roof is watertight, and it was Robert Adam himself who designed the main rooms, though they lack a woman's touch, for my cousin never married. In fact, the lack of a woman—the lack of a Lady Kilmun, more precisely—is something I'm under great pressure to address, wish to address, I mean. I never thought to inherit these lands, but I intend to do my best by them and the people, so I need a wife and bairns. My conscience is in your debt. And what's more, you're in need of a home. Our marriage solves all of that. It's the perfect solution. Absolutely perfect.'

Fergus beamed. Susanna's jaw dropped. If he had not been so patently sincere, if there had been one scrap in her make-up of the pathetic relic that he seemed to imagine her, she would have been furious. Instead she was…she was… she didn't quite know what she was. Bewildered, confused, amused, flattered? Endeared, maybe. But tempted? Not one whit of it! 'Fergus, it is very kind of you, but I have absolutely no wish to be married under any circumstances.'

'Kind!' Fergus felt as if the floor had shifted under his feet.

'And generous, too,' Susanna said graciously. 'I am sure when the right woman comes along…'

'But *you* are the right woman.' She could not mean to refuse him. All his plans depended upon her agreeing.

'You have to marry me,' Fergus said, not caring how desperate he sounded.

'I do not *have* to do anything of the sort.'

Her very determined tone completely threw him. 'It is admirable,' Fergus said, clutching at straws, 'your being set upon standing on your own two feet. It's admirable. But foolish. And—and quite unnecessary when I am offering you an alternative. I ruined your life, Susanna, there is no need to pretend I did not. You must let me make amends.' He raked his hands through his hair. Could she not see that he needed to rescue her? By heavens, did she not realise that if she wouldn't have him he would have to marry one of those other milk and water lasses! He had been planning this for months, ever since seeing that death notice. She could not possibly be refusing him. Perhaps if he put it in different terms?

Fergus struggled to conjure a conciliatory smile. 'Susanna, let us face facts. You need a home. I have a home to offer. You are without resources. I have plenty, and I'm more than willing to share them, for I owe you. This place needs a woman. I need a wife.' She could not possibly refuse such a practical offer.

It seemed she could. 'But I have no wish for a husband, Fergus.'

He could have roared with vexation. Did she not know what was good for her? More to the point, what was good for him. He owed it to his conscience to marry her. He was set on it. If he could just persuade her to stay, she would see that. Fergus yanked his temper back onto its leash, and changed tack. 'I can see I've been presumptive.'

Susanna's eyes narrowed. Had she noticed he spoke through gritted teeth? Certainly, she was no fool. Fergus took her hands in his. 'It seems a shame for you to come all this way and miss out on the festivities. From what you've said, Christmas in London with your parents would be a driech affair.'

'They are mourning Jason as if he was their son. I think Mama believes he would not have contracted the fever which killed him if I had been a better wife.'

'I would not expect you to play the weeping widow, if you chose to remain here.'

'But that is impossible.'

What was impossible was her leaving, and it had nothing to do with the fact that his blood stirred at her proximity. He stroked her palms with his thumbs. Soft skin she had. His hands engulfed hers. In for a penny, Fergus thought ruthlessly. 'You could stay,' he said. He pulled her closer. Her figure was much fuller than he remembered. Decidedly curvier. He liked the way her hair tumbled like a live thing over her shoulders. He liked the way she smelled, of cold and salt from the journey, and flowers and lemon. He hadn't really thought about enjoying the wooing, but wooing Susanna would be no hardship at all. 'What if we pretended,' he said. 'Made the best of it?'

She made no effort to pull free from him, so Fergus pressed on. 'What harm is there in saying that we are betrothed, until Hogmanay? That's the night before the new year, when the formal ceremony takes place. All you have to do is refuse me then, make a public break. You'll have had a holiday from London, I'll have saved face.' That was three weeks away. A lot could happen in three weeks. Fergus slid his arm around her waist. 'Say you'll stay, Susanna. It will be…entertaining.'

'Entertaining.'

She said the word as if she did not understand its meaning. Fergus pressed home his advantage. It was underhand, but he was desperate.

'You understand, I have no wish for a husband.'

'You mean you'll stay?'

'Only until this Hogmanay ceremony. A public falling out, did you say?'

Or else she would fall in with his plans. Fergus nodded, but was careful to make no promises. 'After all, you'll not likely get the chance again to see the beauty of the Highlands in winter.'

'It is very lovely here.'

'And I'll do my very best to make your visit unforgettable.'

Susanna laughed. 'Oh, why not? I did not heed you three years ago, Fergus, but I have learned my lesson. I'll stay.'

And she looked so adorable, and Fergus was so elated at having persuaded her that he pulled her into his arms. 'Now,' he said, 'do you think I can finally have that kiss I've waited three years for?'

Soft, his mouth was, with the scrape of his stubble a tantalising, arousing contrast. He smelled nice. Soap and wool and leather. This close, she could see the gold rim around his iris, the faint trace of a scar along his hairline, a bump in his nose where it may have been broken.

Warmth enveloped her as Fergus wrapped his arms around her. Susanna felt the thump of his heart. He kissed her again, softly still. And again, lingering a little, licking into the corner of her mouth, so that she opened to him, and he sighed and kissed her again. She grasped his shoulders to stand on tiptoe to kiss him back. Her eyes fluttered closed. Heat and soft skin and scraping bristle and the sweetly arousing lick of his tongue on her lower lip. It was delightful.

Fergus's hands slid down her arms, only to rest on her waist. He smiled, a slow curl of his lips which took its time forming. 'I have to tell you, lass, I'm very much taken with the changes in you.'

His chest rose and fell rapidly under the soft cambric of his shirt. His fingers were playing up her spine in the most delightful way. One of his hands tangled in her hair. She could feel the warmth of his palm on her scalp. Susanna shivered. She liked the way he looked at her. Wanting her. Jason had never looked at her in that way. Lustfully. The word made her skin prickle. There were golden glints in Fergus's hair. It was surprisingly soft to touch. 'I have to tell you, Laird, that I am very much taken with…the Highlands. And your people, and your castle, too. I feel as if I've been transported to another world.'

Susanna turned away to hide her smile, and came back down to earth with a thump as she caught sight of the huge, looming four poster bed. 'You *were* jesting when you said that it was expected you stay here in this room with me, were you not?'

Fergus too, turned his attention to the bed. 'I was not, but one thing is for certain, board or no board, I'm *not* sleeping in that with you.'

His vehemence should have been reassuring, but Susanna decided she found it insulting. 'What board?'

Fergus strode over to the huge bed, and pulled back the top cover. Sure enough, a huge plank lay down the middle of the mattress, neatly separating it into two. 'Your side,' he indicated, 'and mine. You'll notice that it's a very rough bit of wood. Anyone who tries to cross it will be sure to get a skelf. A splinter,' he explained, seeing her confused look. 'Walking out leads to bundling, in these parts. It's our way of courting, allowing a couple to get used to each other on the understanding that if they get too used to each other then the wedding will take place forthwith.'

'But we are not courting,' Susanna said stupidly. Except, of course they were. Or they were pretending to be.

'Don't take this the wrong way now, but before you arrived here this afternoon, I didn't think the bed would be a problem at all. I'll sleep on the chair.'

Susanna eyed Fergus's large frame sceptically, unsure how to react to this most backhanded of compliments. 'You will be very uncomfortable.'

This time, his grin was positively wolfish. 'I already am. At least we've proved we can put on a persuasive show when we need to.'

She did not blush delicately, but turned a fiery red. 'Will we need to?'

'It will be expected, you're the laird's affianced bride.'

'Until Hogmanay.'

'Until Hogmanay, aye. Do you think you'll mind a few kisses, lass?'

Susanna stuck her nose in the air. 'If it keeps your tenants happy, I expect I shall be able to force myself to bear them. What else have you not told me?'

Fergus chuckled. 'Isn't Christmas the time for surprises?'

CHAPTER FOUR

THE STIRRING OF the pudding which would be eaten on the night before Christmas was the first of Fergus's surprises. 'It's called Clootie dumpling because it's cooked in a cloth. This is the same recipe as belonged to Mrs MacDonald's grandmother,' he translated for the cook, who beamed and nodded at Susanna. 'We stir six times one way, and six times the other.'

'Together,' Mrs MacDonald, the doyenne of the huge stone-flagged kitchen, said in English, handing Susanna the wooden spoon.

It was very hot, down in the basement, thanks to the huge open fire with its collection of spits and cauldrons, one of which contained the pudding ingredients. Fergus put his hands over Susanna's. 'Don't ask me why it is six times and not five or seven. I'm sure there is a reason for it but I'm not sure that I want to spend the next hour listening to it. Are you ready?'

She nodded, and they began to stir the thick mixture of suet and flour and dried fruit. She was fascinated by the contrast of their hands, his tanned, wholly covering hers, which seemed so pale. Perspiration beaded at her hairline, and trickled down the small of her back. There were surely enough ingredients in this pudding to feed an entire village. She very much doubted she'd have been able to move the spoon without Fergus's help.

Two times, three times, clockwise they stirred. Already Susanna's arm ached. She braced herself, bending over the iron pot. Before she could straighten, Fergus put his free arm around her waist to hold her there. This time when they stirred the pudding, their bodies rotated together. Five times, then six. They paused to change direction, but he did not let her go. They stirred, and their bodies moved together, her bottom nestled into his thighs. Slower, round again, and she forgot about her aching arm and thought only of the way he felt against her skirts.

His hand tightened on her waist. His breath was sharp and shallow on her neck. Was he as enthralled by what they were doing now, in front of the kitchen staff, as she was? Their stirring slowed to a mesmerising, arousing rhythm.

The applause startled them both. Susanna dropped the spoon, Fergus dropped Susanna. His cheeks were bright with colour. 'I had not thought a pudding could be so captivating,' he whispered amid the cheering. Handing the spoon back to the cook, she caught the woman's knowing glance. Mrs MacDonald said something to Fergus which made him laugh, but he would not translate it. Instead he bowed, Susanna curtseyed, and the crowd dispersed.

'Those kitchens were hotter than hell,' Fergus said to her as they made their way through the warren of still rooms and pantries to the green baize door which marked the end of the servant's quarters. 'Though not as hot as the company.'

'Indeed,' Susanna replied with eyes downcast.

'I doubt I'll be able to eat a slice of Clootie dumpling again without thinking of you, now.'

They were in the great hall, which was deserted save for the four sleek deerhounds snoozing at the fire. Susanna turned, trying hard to bite back her smile. 'If that is meant to be a compliment, Laird, allow me to tell you that it is one of the most backhanded I have ever received.'

'Aye, but it has the distinction of being the most unusual too, you'll admit. And a mite more respectable than telling you what I was really thinking.'

He had a wicked gleam in his eye. Susanna had not thought herself the type of woman who enjoyed flirting, but this was flirting that could lead nowhere. She liked the edge of it, and she liked that the edge held no danger, so she surrendered to the teasing look in his amber eyes and his curving smile. 'What then, were you really thinking?'

'That you have the most delightful curve to your rear. I was wondering if it was even more delightful without all those petticoats between us. That is something I'd dearly like to find out.'

'A rounded rear being an absolute requirement for a laird's wife?'

'Such a necessity, I think I should maybe just see whether you fit the bill,' the laird said, putting his arms around her waist.

'Fergus, we are in the great hall, someone might see us.'

'Isn't that the point?' he whispered wickedly.

His hands slid down to cup her bottom. Susanna's back

arched of its own accord as his hands buried deeper into her skirts. Something that sounded shockingly like a whimper escaped her as his lips brushed the sensitive flesh just behind her ear. It was delightful. Too delightful. She wriggled free from his embrace. 'Well, do I pass the test?'

'With flying colours. But you are quite right,' Fergus agreed, 'we must not waste our act playing to an empty house. A walk in the snow will do us both good, and they are expecting us in the village.'

Over the passing days, there were many customs and rituals, plenty occasions for public shows of affection. Kisses under the mistletoe that stopped only when their audience cheered. The throwing of the lucky horseshoe made by the smithy which, like the pudding stirring, seemed to require Susanna to be twined in Fergus's arms, her bottom pressed to his thighs.

Such a contrast to the nights. At first she could not sleep for the rustle and thump of Fergus trying to make himself comfortable. For several nights she listened to him shift about on the chair, then the floor of their chamber. Finally, telling herself she was simply being practical, she had ordered him to share the bed. 'It is big enough to sleep an army,' she'd said, 'and I for one have no intentions of risking a skelf by crossing that bundling board thing. I am astonished that any courting couple do so.'

Now, the mattress sagged when Fergus joined her, and it took her even longer to fall asleep. For some reason, she liked to listen to him breathing. She liked the solid weight of him beside her. But he made no move to cross the board, for which she told herself she should be grateful he seemed interested only in their public performance. As for her, the thrill she got from his kisses, from the brush of his hand, his thigh, the outrageous things he whispered in her ear, that was because she too was enjoying the performance. It had nothing at all to do with the man himself. Nothing.

Lust fed on deprivation, that's what she was feeling. Though never, not even in the first months of her marriage, had Susanna felt this tingling sense of anticipation. Even as she said her vows, she had withheld a part of herself. Jason's expertise in the marital bed brought her no satisfaction, for it confirmed that these most intimate of caresses had been shared with any number of other women. Duty forced them to share their bodies, but there had been none of this constant urge to touch for the sake of touching. None of this wanting to know how would this feel, and this, and this.

It was all delightful, this Highland Christmas, beguiling, like the scenery and the people and yes, like the man who was laird of it all. But it was not real, and soon it would be over. She may as well enjoy it while it lasted.

Day after day of passionate kisses and bodily contact were taking their toll on Fergus, as night after tortuous night he lay there beside her in bed, with only a bundling board and a nightgown between them. He feigned sleep, and he was pretty certain Susanna did too. Her breathing was too even. She lay too still.

The night before last, he had woken near dawn to find he had worked his way over the damned board to drape an arm around her waist. Last night, it was his leg that had breached the barrier to lie over hers. He had the skelfs to prove it. She had slept through his incursion. Or pretended to.

He had not forgotten his purpose in keeping her here, but he no longer believed in it. The more he knew of her, the more he realised that she meant it when she said she had no need of his rescue. She was witty, attractive and more importantly she seemed happy enough in her own skin. If he thought it a waste that such a woman should be so very set upon being alone, that was her business, not his. Where that left him, he had no idea, save that he was pretty certain Hogmanay was approaching far too quickly, and he was pretty sick and tired of the frustration he had to cope with as each night fell, and the day's kisses left him like a pot of water kept continually simmering and never allowed to boil. There were times, usually towards dawn, that Fergus wished he could be just a bit more unscrupulous.

Tonight was the feet washing. In the cottages and crofts, this was a ritual involving soap and scrubbing brushes which took place separately for the bride and groom, but in the castle the tradition had evolved somewhat. Fergus smiled to himself as he tried to picture Susanna's reaction. His imagination moved on, to anticipating her slender feet in his hands, and once again, his blood rushed to his groin, as it seemed to do so often these days in her company.

They dined formally in the great hall. After dinner was cleared, those of his villagers and tenants who wished to witness the ritual—and drink his whisky—arrived. Susanna, looking even more luscious than ever in a gown of her favourite midnight blue, turned to him questioningly as the crowd formed a circle.

She stared in puzzlement as a large porcelain bowl was filled from a stone pitcher and placed at the foot of an ornately carved chair. 'Is that wine, Fergus? Is this another toast?'

He smiled at her, one of those wicked smiles of his that sent her pulses racing, and warned her to expect the unexpected. 'It is wine, but it is not for drinking,' he said, taking her hand in his. 'This piece of whimsy is known as the Dooking Throne. You must curtsey to our audience, and place that most delightful rear of yours upon it.'

She did as he bid her. Another of his surprises, this was. Was she to be crowned? But no, Fergus knelt at her feet, and to her utter astonishment and no little embarrassment, he removed first one, then the other of her evening slippers. 'Fergus!'

Another of those smiles. Cheers and stomping from their audience. His hand slid up her calf under her skirts, his fingers tickling the back of her knee. 'Fergus, what on earth…'

'It is called the feet washing,' he replied, casting her a mischievous glance as his fingers untied her garter. 'I do like these stockings. Are they silk?'

'Yes.' Susanna bit her lip to catch the tiny sigh that escaped her as his fingers left a trail of sensitised skin, unrolling her stocking back down her leg. He held the delicate item up for the audience to see, causing a burst of laughter when he draped it around his shoulder. She took a deep breath as he cupped her other foot, trying to ignore the shivering sensation as his fingers trailed up her stockinged leg, untied her garter, then went back down her bare skin.

The second stocking joined the first around his neck. He took one of her feet in each of her hands.

'Lift your skirts just a little, if you please. I would not like to stain them.'

Her feet looked pale and narrow in his hands. What was it about a naked foot that was so intimate? Susanna cast a nervous look around the circle of the audience, but they all seemed to be finding the ritual amusing. She hoped they put her blushes down to maidenly modesty. Modesty was the last thing she was feeling as Fergus dipped her feet into the wine and his fingers worked their way over her toes. She no longer heard the laughter and shouts of encouragement which were probably inciting him to scrub harder, as he took a large cloth and began instead to stroke her instep in little circles.

Her eyes drifted closed. There seemed to be no purpose to this ceremony, but she did not care. When Fergus finally lifted one of her feet out of the wine, Susanna jerked awake from her delightful daze. Her eyes flew open, meeting his. Dark, lambent and blatantly aroused, his gaze was. There was no doubting now, the purpose of the feet washing. She was hot and tingling herself, and it was not just her feet which were damp.

The large square of linen turned pink as Fergus dried her feet. He surprised her once more when he fished in the bowl and what she had taken for a piece of wine sediment turned out to be a ring. 'You must throw and whoever catches it will be the next to wed. Aim for Eilidh Fraser over there. I know she is courting, and there's no harm in having it said that the laird's lady has great foresight.'

Once again, she did as she was bid, and was rewarded

by a beaming smile from the girl, and a great cheer. Fergus made a sweepingly theatrical bow. From the doorway, a pair of bagpipes gave their warning groan before bursting into a skirl, and Fergus scooped Susanna up into his arms, leading the way to their bedchamber.

CHAPTER FIVE

FERGUS LEANT AGAINST the door, clutching Susanna's shoes, her stockings draped around his neck. In the corridor, the skirl of the pipes was replaced by raucous singing. It was as well they sang in the Gaelic, though judging from her expression Susanna had a very clear notion of its bawdy content. She was laughing as she sat on the edge of the bed. 'Is it over, or are they going to burst in and strew us with—I don't know—herbs to encourage potency?'

'Dear God, I hope not. I assure you, I need no encouragement. Since you arrived here at Kilmun, I have been made aware of my potency on a daily basis.'

'I am sure you meant that as a complement, but let me tell you, Laird, it is not one fit for a lady's ears. What's more, I am very sure that *any* lady—with the appropriately curved rear, of course—would have the same effect on you as I do.'

She had a way of blushing and smiling provocatively at the same time which he adored, all the more so because he knew that *her* delight in teasing him was something new.

As it was for him, too. He had started it as part of their game of flirting publicly, but it had become a habit he did not want to break.

Her hair was escaping from its pins. At night, it spread across the pillows, over the bolster that separated them. It smelled of flowers, and it tickled his nose. He took a long tendril, winding it around his finger. 'For nigh on two years after the wars, I was in no fit state to look at any woman. To tell the truth, I thought I'd lost interest for good until I set eyes on you, all dark hair and red mouth and grey eyes, on the pier at Kilmun village.' Susanna looked as surprised as he felt at this confession. It was the truth, but he had no idea why he'd told her.

He unwound her curl from his finger and made to get up when she caught his hand. 'Until I came here, I was fairly certain I had no such feelings either,' Susanna whispered. 'Do you think the wanting is stronger for having been asleep so long, Fergus?'

'It's an idea. Like a creature who has slept the winter over, and worked up an appetite, you mean?'

Susanna's laugh had a breathy quality that made his own breathing quicken. 'When I'm lying on this bed, with that horrible plank of wood between us, I sometimes feel as though I've been feasting my eyes all day on a banquet I'm not allowed to eat.'

'When I was washing your feet, I wanted to lick them dry, but I fear that would have been a step too far for our audience. If you'll forgive the pun.'

'They still smell of claret.'

'Most likely they taste of it too. It was the very best claret, I'll have you know. I wonder if it travels well.'

Before she could ask him what he meant, Fergus dropped to his knees before her for the second time that night, and did what he had wanted to do the first time, cupping one of her slender feet in his hand, and sucking on her toe. He was rewarded with one of those telling intakes of breath, and with a widening of those speaking grey eyes of hers. He licked his way along each of her toes, then sucked his way back.

'And does it?' she asked. 'Travel well?'

'I'll need to make sure.' He picked up her other foot, licking each of the toes before kissing his way up to her ankle to the fluttering pulse there. Susanna slumped back on the bed with a soft sigh, and Fergus continued kissing, up her calf, to her knee, his hand following the same route on her other leg. Her petticoats rustled seductively as he pushed them aside to expose the lacy edge of her pantalettes. The salty, vanilla scent of her arousal was as unmistakable as his own urge to keep kissing his way up, until he could taste her.

He hesitated, stroking the soft flesh of her thigh through the thin linen of her undergarments. Susanna gave another of those unbearably erotic little moans, stirring restlessly beneath him. Her pupils were enlarged. Her face was flushed. All these days spent in what seemed like a perpetual state of arousal, nights spent in aching frustration, were suddenly too much to bear. Fergus pushed up her skirts, he parted the legs of her pantalettes, cupped her bottom to tilt her towards his mouth. There was, after all, more than one way to heaven.

Susanna cried out in surprise, then cried out in pleasure as Fergus kissed the soft flesh at the tops of her thighs.

Then the creases at the tops of her legs. And then inside her. A slow, languorous lick it was, parting her, and then another, sliding up and over the swelling nub of her. She shivered, her muscles tensed, heat pooling between her legs.

Fergus licked again, and she felt the familiar tightening, save that it was not at all familiar because it was much more, a stronger, deep pull. So quickly. And so much. It was not at all what she was accustomed to. She tried to think, to hold on, to hold back, to prolong. Not yet, she thought, as he licked again. And then he kissed her. Or suckled her. She did not know what he was doing, but she lost the power to concentrate because what he was doing was so, so, so…

Hot, wet, tight, she felt. She could hear his breathing, ragged. His fingers dug in to the flesh of her bottom, holding her when she arched and bucked, wanting more, wanting to wait, wanting more. She moaned. He did something else with his tongue, a swirling and licking at the same time, she could feel herself tightening, tightening, and tried to clench hold, and he stopped as she cried out, and she heard his low laugh of triumph as he licked her again, there, in precisely the right place, and she climaxed, wave after wave pulsing through her. She clutched at the sheets, at his hair, at his shoulders, pulling him up towards her, thrusting herself unashamedly at him.

He kissed her mouth. She tasted herself on his lips and wrapped her arms and legs around him. She could feel the hard length of his erection through his trews, against the damp between her legs. He still had all his clothes on. What's more, so did she. *What were they doing?*

What was he doing! Fergus hesitated, breathing heavily. This, this woman, what she did to him, it was too much. Too good. *She* was too good for him. Much as he wanted her, what he wanted more was to let her live the life she had set her heart on. He cursed. His timing could have been a hell of a lot better! It took every ounce of resolution, but he rolled away from her. 'No,' he said, more to himself than Susanna. 'No.'

The next day, which was Christmas Eve, saw the lighting of the Yule log in the great hall, where the Clootie dumpling was served to the castle's servants. Custom demanded that the laird and his lady do the waiting, a practice which Susanna took seriously, descending to Mrs MacDonald's domain to lend what assistance she could.

In the kitchens, she rolled up the sleeves of her Turkey-red gown and threw herself into the cooking and setting out of the night's feast. This was much to the cook's surprise and she unwittingly earned herself the approval of the household, who had naturally been suspicious of a London lady likely to think herself above getting her hands dirty. Though the gruff man in charge of the household laughed at her attempts to pronounce the Gaelic, he did not mock her, and the arduous hours of work had the benefit of distracting her from thoughts of the night before. Until she stood, smiling and tired, by Fergus's side in the great hall, as their health was drunk.

'Mrs MacDonald has nothing but good words to say of you,' Fergus said, slipping an arm around her waist. 'I did wonder though, if you worked so hard in those kitchens of hers in order to avoid me?'

She could not look at him. An image of herself, crying out in abandon beneath him, flashed into her mind. Fergus brushed her hair from her forehead and kissed her temple. 'No need to answer. Your silence speaks volumes.'

She shook her head helplessly and caught his hand in hers. His knuckles were scored with small cuts from hacking away the brambles which had been growing around the tree which became the Yule log. She kissed them and slipped away up the stairs, leaving Fergus to socialise and, more importantly, ensure that the whisky did not run dry before the men did.

Susanna lay awake with the bed curtains open, a candle burning low on the night table at the side of the bed. Sick of the bundling board, yet unwilling to cause an uproar by removing it, she had wrapped one of her shawls around it, and covered it with a bolster. When Fergus entered the room, she feigned sleep.

He stood over her for a long moment, looking down, then set about undressing. She watched from between her lashes as he shrugged out of his coat, then sat by the fireside to pull off his boots and stockings. His waistcoat and stock came next. Then his shirt, tugged free from his trews and pulled over his head. His torso was pale compared to the tan of his arms and throat. As he stretched his hands over his head and rolled his shoulders, his muscles rippled. She must have made a sound, for he froze. 'Did I wake you?' The mattress sagged as he sat on the edge of it.

Susanna pushed herself up. 'I couldn't sleep.'

He flashed a smile. 'Tell me about it.'

She plucked at the scalloped embroidery which edged the sheet. 'Fergus, do you regret last night?'

'I wish I could say I did, but if I'm honest I haven't been able to stop thinking about it all day.'

'Nor I.' Susanna began to tug at a loose thread. 'Fergus, why did you stop?'

'Because I knew I would regret it. No, not the way you think.' He ran his fingers through his hair. 'Since we're being very honest, I'll tell you now that I asked you to stay here in the hopes of changing your mind.'

'Change my—you mean make me marry you?'

'Not make you. It was just that I had it in my head—och, I don't know if I can explain. After Waterloo, when I was lying wounded in that field hospital, plotting my revenge on Mountjoy kept me alive. I wasn't right in my head that day I visited you, though I thought I was. I suppose being at war for nigh on ten years takes its toll on the mind as well as the body. Anyway, I blamed Mountjoy because I had to blame someone, and he made it easy for me, being such a callous bastard. I knew the moment you slammed that drawing room door in my face that I'd made a huge mistake, and for the best part of the past three years I've been wishing it undone. When I read his death notice, it was like the answer to my prayers. Finally, I'd get to make it up to you.'

'Had you not called that day, I'd have married Jason in complete ignorance. It would have taken me longer to discover his true nature and his true feelings for me—or lack of them—and perhaps I would have tried harder to be the wife I thought he wanted for longer. You saved me from wasting my time. When I finally worked up the courage to ask him what became of the child—Maria's child, the woman you told me of—do you know, he laughed. "What do I care about one more little bastard," he said. And even after I had traced them, he was not relieved, but furious. I grew up that day, Fergus, and I've been growing ever since. You are not responsible for ruining my life, far from it.'

Fergus eyed her in astonishment. 'You found Maria? You mean you sought out Mountjoy's mistress and child?'

'I did, and I took care of them. If you had not informed me of their existence, I hate to think what would have happened to them. So you see, you played your part in saving them.'

This was pushing it much too far for Fergus. 'I did no such thing. All I was interested in was ruining Mountjoy.'

'Well, he ruined himself in the end.'

'But he did not ruin you.' Fergus leaned over to touch her cheek. 'I can see that. I do see that. And that's why I stopped last night. I wanted you to stay here so I could persuade you to marry me, but I realise now that I know you, that I'm the last thing you need. You've made a far better fist of the hand life has dealt you than I, Susanna.'

'Rubbish. I simply had to come to terms with a drunken libertine of a husband, while you— I cannot imagine what you suffered during the wars. If you do not remember the state you were in that day, I certainly do. You were like a ghost of yourself. I was astonished when I met you again. I did not expect you to recover so completely. Our acquaintance has been only a few weeks, but I only have to look at the way your tenants behave towards you. You're loyal and you're hard-working and you're honest and you're fair. You're a good laird, Fergus, I have no doubt you were an excellent captain. You have made a very good hand indeed of the cards life has dealt you.'

Fergus shrugged. Touched as he was by her defence of him, he was a man accustomed to giving orders rather than receiving praise. Maybe what she said made sense, maybe not, but he was too tired to deal with it right now. 'What I wanted to say was that we should forget all about that stupid idea of mine for us to marry, and make the most of this last week of your visit.' He leaned over to touch her cheek again. 'You're a fine woman, Susanna. Too fine for me.'

'If I wanted a husband, Fergus, I could not do finer than you. But I do not. Now shut up and come to bed.'

He laughed at that. 'An invitation I cannot resist. You should thank the lord for that bloody board, for you are quite adorable.'

She made a strange little sound he could not understand. Until he blew out the candle and climbed into bed after discarding his trews. Instead of splintery wood, there was something soft between them. His palm flattened over soft pillow and something silky underneath. 'Susanna?'

'I was sick of getting splinters. Skelfs.' She leaned over to press a kiss to his temple. 'Go to sleep, Fergus.'

He pulled her over towards him, flattening her palm on his belly. 'I love the way your hair tickles my nose,' he mumbled. And then he slept.

Susanna lay awake, feeling the quiet rhythm of Fergus's breathing reverberate on the skin of her palm. Tomorrow was Christmas Day. A week after that was Hogmanay, and somehow they would have to persuade all the Kilmun villagers and tenants, and all Fergus's neighbours, that they had fallen out, with no hope of making it up. She wouldn't see Fergus again after that. The new year would be the beginning of her new life, whatever that was. It was true, the beauty of this little village had captured her heart, but there were many other little villages in England equally beautiful in which she could live. Once Jason's estate was settled, there would be enough for a cottage, so the lawyer said. Other villages where she could help build a school, just as Fergus planned. And though they would not have anyone like Fergus in them, there would be other friends to make. She did not want a husband. She most certainly did not need a husband. This lust, passion, desire, wanting, whatever it was, that existed between her and Fergus, it was a product of the circumstances, merely. Though it felt so real, it would pass.

He was soundly asleep now. She ran her hand over his torso. Rough hair, smooth skin, the line of a scar. The dip of his belly. The indent of his navel. She hesitated, then ventured further down. Rougher hair. The silky skin of his shaft becoming smoother as her touch roused him. Her fingers curled around him. She felt the pulse of his blood as he thickened in her hold, felt the answering throb between her thighs as she imagined him inside her. She stroked him, and with her other hand, cupped herself. Hot and wet. It would not take much to bring her to a climax. She imagined him, sinking into her, thrusting. She ached. But she would not take what he had made it clear he did not want to give. With a sigh, she let him go and turned her back. He sighed in his sleep, and snaked his hands around her waist. The hard length of him nestled into the curve of her bottom. It was Susanna's turn to sigh as she fell, eventually, into slumber.

CHAPTER SIX

CHRISTMAS DAY WAS cold and bright, the sky a wide icy-blue, the distant mountains melding with the wispy white clouds. The soft shush of the waves on the pebbled shores of Loch Fyne were peaceful, the creels stacked neatly on the jetty, the nets limp on the drying lines, for no one worked this day. They walked to church at the head of the procession from Castle Kilmun, the laird and his lady at the head of their household. Susanna wore a half pelisse over a promenade dress of emerald green with rucked sleeves, French trimming and a winged collar. The high crown of her bonnet was trimmed with an ostrich feather in the same shade as her gown, and her hair had for once obediently allowed itself to be pinned and curled just as she wanted it.

Fergus was wearing the kilt, the tightly pleated plaid held together with a large leather belt and silver buckle into which was tucked a sheathed dagger with a chased silver handle. His hose were also plaid, and he wore another larger plaid over his short jacket, the *filleadh mòr,* which served as a cloak when unfolded. Today, it was formally pleated over his shoulder and kept in place with a jewelled pin. The plaid swung out behind him when he walked, showing off tantalising glimpses of muscled thigh. Though most of the men wore similar clothes, Fergus's were clearly superior, and to Susanna's eyes, the laird had by far the better physique.

Her first glimpse of him as a slightly wild, slightly rough Highlander had been wholly unexpected and utterly beguiling. Fergus had a natural authority, but with the traditional Scottish dress, he seemed also to have donned his heritage. He looked every bit the proud Highland laird, as natural a part of the landscape as the majestic peaks in the distance. 'I feel I should curtsey before you, Laird Kilmun,' she said lightly, for she was feeling just a little overawed.

'Does the sight of my manly calf please you, my lady?'

'The trouble is that I suspect it pleases every one of the ladies,' Susanna told him tartly, for she had already intercepted several admiring glances from village women.

Fergus grinned. 'Then in that we are equal, for I know the eyes of all the men will be upon you.'

'Is my gown too fine?'

'Susanna, the lassies may well be admiring your clothes, but the men are far more interested in what is beneath them.' Fergus pulled her closer, so that her skirts brushed his plaid as they walked, matching their steps. 'I can't blame them for wondering, I think about it myself, far too often for my own good. 'Tis one of the advantages of the plaid over the trews, you know, that I can do so without fear of discovery.'

'Fergus! For shame, we are on our way to church.'

'The things I think of when I look at you, Susanna, I think I might be on my way to hell.'

The sermon in the church at the end of the village was long and incomprehensible to Susanna, since it was given in the Gaelic, but she was content to listen to the soft cadences of the language and to pass the time feasting her eyes on the solid figure of Fergus beside her in the closed pew. When he sat down, the plaid rode up his legs. She only just resisted placing her gloved hands on the exposed flesh. She did not resist imagining the rest of his body under the cloth. Fergus was not the only one destined for hell, she thought guiltily, realising that the closing prayer was finished and that he was perfectly aware of the fact that she had not been paying any attention at all to the black-clad minister.

There was another sermon later in the day in the private chapel belonging to the castle. Christmas in the Highlands was a day for praying, not celebrating. 'We do that at the end of the year,' Fergus told her.

At Hogmanay. When they must break forever. The unspoken words cast a pall over the day.

The days hurtled towards the New Year. At night, Susanna and Fergus slept entwined, though in the morning they pretended they had not. Their daytime shows of affection took on a desperate edge as the calendar moved inexorably on. The temperature dropped. The waterfalls which trickled down the rock faces, and which in the spring would become cascades from the melting snow, now froze into glittering icicles.

On the last day of the year, there was another good luck horse shoe to be cast, this time from a boat in the middle of the loch. Instead of returning to the castle, Fergus led them into the forest. Here, the ground was softer, moss and brown bracken underfoot, for the high Caledonian pines had protected it from the snow. The light filtered silver through the branches, the air smelt of resin and peat and fallen needles, which made the ground underfoot soft and muffled their footsteps. They stopped at a strange pool, the water green, deep, seemingly bottomless and icy cold to touch.

'They say that this belongs to the wee folk,' Fergus told Susanna. 'Faeries,' he explained, seeing her puzzled look, 'and mighty powerful they are believed to be, in these parts. You've no idea the lengths some people will go to, to keep them happy—or to blame them when something goes wrong, whether it's a lost shoe or a changeling child.'

'Do you believe in them?'

He shook his head. 'No, but I'm not daft enough to say so. It is said that if you look deep enough into this pool, you will see your heart's desire. Do you want to try it?'

Susanna gazed down into the greeny water, smiling at the foolishness of it, but aware too of a strange fluttery feeling inside. It was the cold, she thought, even though she was wrapped in a fur-lined cloak which Fergus had found for her. Just the cold. She stared down, and could not for a moment work out what was wrong with what she saw. A reflection, which should be there. Except that it was not hers, it belonged only to the man behind her. She stared again, more intently, but though Fergus remained clear as if she were looking in a mirror, there was no trace of her own face. 'Did you see that?'

'Your reflection,' he said. 'Of course I did.'

'No, I mean...'

She turned, but he was not looking at the pool. 'We're going to have to work awful hard at convincing people at the ceremony tonight, for I fear we've been too convincing in the run up to it,' he said.

'I don't want to quarrel with you.'

'Well, it's that or spend a lifetime with me, and I know you don't want that,' Fergus replied with a wry smile. 'I'm glad you came here. I hope you get whatever it is your heart really desires.'

'Freedom. Independence.' The ideas so long coveted sounded empty. But her heart's desire was certainly not the man who had been reflected in the pool. It could not be. It was not what she had planned. 'And you, Fergus, I hope that you'll get your heart's desire too. I hope you find your biddable wee wife, and I hope she makes you happy.' She meant it, Susanna told herself resolutely. Even if she did sound most unaccountably forlorn. Fergus deserved someone to—to *care* for.

'I'm not sure a biddable wee wife is really for me. I'm too much the soldier still. I'd be ordering her about and making her miserable. I need someone to stand up to me.'

'Send her to me, I will give her lessons.' Susanna stared down at the pool, where the pair of them were reflected now. If you satisfied a heart's desire, could you then leave him behind? She was being foolish, affected by the other-worldly atmosphere of the forest, by the approaching ceremony, by her imminent departure. But once she left, she would never again have the chance. And wasn't that one of her own resolutions, not to let her life pass her by? Relieved at having found, with this convoluted logic, the excuse she did not even know she'd been seeking, Susanna turned away from the pool.

Her heart beat fast, her stomach churned. Was she making a huge mistake? No. Was she sure? No, not sure-sure, but definitely take-a-chance sure. 'Fergus,' she said, pushing the heavy folds of the cloak back over her shoulders and putting her arms around his waist, hooking her fingers into the belt which held his plaid in place to balance herself. 'Fergus, make love to me.'

'Susanna…'

'Make love to me, Fergus. Not because I've changed my mind about us, or because I want you to change yours or because anything's changed, but just because I want you to. That is, if you want to.'

'You know I do. In fact, if you come much closer, you'll see for yourself just how much I do.'

She did just that, deliberately brushing herself against the front of his kilt. She had the satisfaction of seeing his eyes darken, hearing the sudden intake of his breath. She was having trouble controlling her own breathing, which was first fast and then slow. 'Fergus, I mean it.' She smiled up at him, a slow, deliberately provocative smile. 'Call it a farewell present. Farewell to the old year, farewell to the old us. I don't care what you call it actually, I just want you to make love to me, because if you don't I suspect I might regret it, and I hope you might too, and that is another thing we are both done with, is it not?'

Fergus cupped the back of her head, tangling his fingers in the thick chignon of curls which she knew would come undone with very little encouragement. 'A goodbye present. Are you sure?'

'Are you?'

'I am absolutely certain,' Fergus answered.

'Do you think we will shock the faeries?'

She felt the deep rumble of his laughter in his chest, which was pressed up against hers. 'Provided they're the only witnesses, I don't much care.'

He pulled her tight to him and kissed her. Not a gentle kiss, but a ruthless one, which was also exactly what she wanted. His lips were warm over hers, his mouth demanding and giving at the same time. She moaned softly and surrendered to the turmoil of wanting that churned, had been churning inside her since she had arrived here, or so it seemed. She kissed him back frantically, running her hands up his back, clutching at his plaid, his coat, his belt, anything which would allow her the purchase to drag him closer. His tongue touched hers, then plunged into her mouth. She licked into him. Their kisses had an edge now that was not enough.

Fergus unclasped Susanna's cloak and spread it on the soft ground. They sank onto the fur lining together, kneeling, breast to breast, thigh to thigh, kissing, touching, stroking, snatching at buttons and fastenings, tugging at cloth in a frantic desire to find flesh. Finesse was beyond them, they wanted simply to be joined.

Her breasts ached for his touch, and his cupping them through her gown intensified it, but the gown fastened at the back, and there were too many layers of petticoats and stays and chemise to deal with, and the ache was worse lower down. He tugged at her nipples through it all, and set up a searing path of fiery lust straight down to the heat between her legs.

Their kisses deepened as their hands tore at each other. She was lying on her back on the cloak now; her gown rucked up under her. He was over her, between her legs, his hands parting the two halves of her pantalettes, stroking the tops of her thighs, then stroking the folds of her sex, and then stroking inside her. The sound she made was guttural.

His plaid made it easy for her to touch him. His buttocks. Firm. Clenched. The rough hairs of his legs. The softer flesh at the top. The potent weight of his seed. And the thick length of him, velvet smooth and engorged, curving up under his plaid. She wrapped her fingers around it and felt him pulse, felt her own muscles throbbing inside as his fingers slid slickly in and out and over her. She was swollen and ready. And he was swollen and ready. His tongue plunged into her mouth. She released her hold on his shaft and arched under him, desperate, desperate for him to be inside her before it was too late.

He paused, poised above her, his shaft nudging at her, and looked straight into her eyes. Amber and gold his were, dark with wanting, and seeing her, looking right into her. Almost, she did not need any more than that, and then he entered her, and she realised how wrong she was as he pushed up, inside her, and up, and she clung to him.

He paused. They lay joined. Then she put her arms around him and kissed him fiercely, and they began the final ascent together. He thrust, she clung as he withdrew, opened as he thrust again, tilting up to open more, feeling the clenching tightness of her climax claim her. She tried to hold it but it took her over, and Fergus thrust through it, harder and faster now, making the same guttural noises as she, plunging into her, his shaft and his tongue, harder, riding the waves of her orgasm until he reached his own, pouring himself into her with a wild animal cry, and holding her, tight, tight, tight in every way against him.

CHAPTER SEVEN

Susanna bathed in a scullery off the kitchen, for by the time it would take to carry the hot water up to her chamber, it would be cold. Mrs MacDonald herself stood guard at the door. Not even Fergus was permitted through, though she could hear him jokingly remonstrating as she lay soaking in the scented tub. After he was gone, she heard him still in her head, that guttural cry, the harshness of his breathing, the memory of it making her soap-filled hands linger on her breasts and between her thighs.

Dressed for Hogmanay, she wore an evening gown of crimson silk with jet beadwork around the hem. Her long kid gloves left only the tiniest gap of flesh between their ending and the little puff sleeves of her gown. She was putting a simple locket around her neck when Fergus arrived in her dressing room resplendent in his plaid, his face freshly shaved, his hair tied neatly back.

'You look very lairdly,' she told him, striving for a lightness of tone she did not feel. She felt sick to her stomach at the very thought of the pending ordeal. She did not want to deny him. They would hate her for it, all these people she had come to like and respect. They would see it as a betrayal. It felt like a betrayal. Her fingers were icy inside her gloves as she placed them on Fergus's arm.

'You look very lovely,' Fergus said.

He kissed her on the cheek. A cold wee kiss it was, as if he was afraid to do more. Though more likely, he was simply falling into his role of spurned lover. She did not want to spurn him. Too late, as they made their way down the grand staircase, Susanna realised that it was already over. Their goodbyes had not been said, but there would be no more private moments, no more sharing of the big four poster bed with the bundling board, once their betrothal was ended. She panicked. She wasn't ready. 'Fergus...'

But he mistook her meaning, and gave her a reassuring and distant little pat. 'Don't fear, you'll be fine.'

His face was set. Remote. He had already moved on, away, past this fake betrothal, to the time after. For Fergus, their lovemaking had been exactly what she had said it was, a farewell present. And for her—for her— What had it been for her?

The sweeping out of the old year through the huge front door of the castle was just one of the many things which were part of the Highland Hogmanay. Susanna watched and smiled a frozen smile and struggled with the growing conviction that something was horribly, terribly wrong. The faerie pool had shown her Fergus as her heart's desire. She thought that making love to him would put an end to that, but it seemed to have had quite the opposite effect. She did not, could not possibly want to risk her true heart's desire, her freedom, her independence, to take a chance on a man she had known a few short weeks, but she wasn't sure she could leave him.

She couldn't. She couldn't go through with it. But as the clock ticked closer to midnight, and Fergus seemed to grow more and more distant, she thought she had no other option but to do so.

Fergus tried to concentrate his attention on the hanging of rowan for good luck over the doorway, and the hanging of hazel to ward off any evil spirits who might try and get in with the new year. But his eyes kept straying towards Susanna, pale and tense in her crimson gown. In his head, he replayed their lovemaking. A farewell is what it had been. He had no doubt that marrying her to atone for that fateful morning over three years ago would have been a huge mistake, but he was having serious doubts about whether or not he could let her go.

He had to let her go. It was what she wanted. She deserved to have what she wanted, but did she really know what that was, any more than he did?

As midnight chimed, and the first foot, a tall villager with black hair, bearing a bottle of whisky and the black bun, led the rest of the villagers in to witness the betrothal ceremony, Fergus swore softly to himself. He'd thought he needed to atone. Susanna had shown him how wrong his thinking had been, but even after he'd realised he would not try to persuade her, he'd become so accustomed to the idea of her as his betrothed that he hadn't spent any time wondering what it would be like without her.

Susanna wanted to be free. But what was the good of liberty if you were not happy? Then again, what right had he to decide what was best for her? He shook his head, as if that would make sense of the whirl of thoughts going round and round, but it made no difference. Susanna wanted to leave. If she left he would be miserable. Did she really want to leave? Did he want her to stay if that was not what she wanted? Did he even have the right to ask her to stay? On and on it went, in circles and spirals.

When the great gong which stood at the side of the hearth clanged, Fergus was no further forward and beginning to panic. He wasn't ready to say goodbye. Not yet. But his villagers, crofters, tenants and servants with their ancient dependents and their bairns, generations of families crowded round, and any moment now, she would deny him, just as they had planned.

Susanna looked terrified as Fergus took her hand. They stood in front of Alec Fraser, the village elder who would conduct the ceremony. They had rehearsed the words briefly. She knew the Gaelic words which were her cue to tell him *nae*.

Alec chanted the ancient verses which were the prelude to the question. Finally, it came. 'Do you take him?' First in the Gaelic, then in painfully slow English for Susanna's sake.

Silence. Her fingers curled into Fergus's like a vice. 'I…'

'No! Susanna, don't say it. Please don't say it.'

'I…'

'I don't want you to go. I know I should not say it, I know we had a bargain, I know that I have no right at all to interfere with how you want to live your life, but I can't let you go. I can make you promises, Susanna, any number of promises, but I know they won't mean anything to you. So all I ask is that you give me a chance. Give me a chance to prove that I can be the husband you deserve, that I can make you happy, that I'll never want you to be anyone other than yourself. Please Susanna, take a chance on me. Don't go.'

'Fergus.' She was crying. He thought he had lost her, with those tears, until she smiled. 'Fergus, I wasn't going to say no. I was going to say yes.'

'Yes?'

'Yes! Yes! Yes! Because I realised today that I want you more than anything. Because I think, I really do think, that with you I'll be free to be myself. I don't know it, but I think it. And I want you. And right now, that's enough for me to take a chance on. If you will.'

'*If!*' Fergus pulled her into his arms. 'Just try to stop me.'

It was not Susanna, but Alec Fraser who stopped them though, with a sound punch to Fergus's shoulder, when it looked as if the kiss would not stop. 'Here now, we've not actually finished with the formalities, Laird Kilmun,' he said in a shocked voice. 'Keep your powder dry man, for a wee bit longer.'

This sally caused much laughter. Even more laughter greeted Fergus's command to get on with it, which Alec did. The vows were said. The verses were sung. The betrothal ring was blessed with a foul-smelling potion that was, Fergus told Susanna in an undertone, even older than Alec. Finally, the piper struck up a lonesome tune, a pibroch, or lament. 'For the passing of the old, and the beginning of the new,' Fergus told his wife. 'And once it is done, you and I shall quit this party and make one of our own, if you are agreeable. For I wish to make up for my lack of finesse earlier.'

'If you will tell me your preferences, laird, so too shall I,' Susanna replied with a wicked smile which reflected his own.

He gave a shout of laughter. 'By God, do you mean that you've decided to play the biddable wife after all?'

'That very much depends on what you bid me do.' She dropped a mock curtsey, looking up at him from under her lashes.

Fergus took her hand, and led her to the foot of the staircase, where he turned and bowed to the people. He wished them all a good New Year, and Susanna joined him, speaking in faltering Gaelic.

'Is it over?' Susanna asked as he closed the door behind them and turned the key in the lock. .

'I very much hope that it is only just begun. I know this is a bit back to front, but there's a formality we've not yet attended to.' Fergus pulled her into his arms. *'Am pòsadh tu mi?* Will you marry me, Susanna?'

She twined her arms around his neck, and stood on tiptoe to kiss him. 'Yes, Fergus, I will.'

They did not speak of love, not yet, but they made love, slowly and reverently taking off their clothes, tenderly touching, tracing, learning their bodies, skin on skin, lip on lip, coming together in a deeper and more meaningful way than before.

It was later, a year later, when Susanna lay in their bed, their daughter, Brianna, asleep beside her in her swaddling, that they finally spoke their feelings.

Fergus sat on the side of the bed, awed by his new family. 'I did not think it was possible to be so happy. I did not dare hope that it would last, but now I do not doubt it. You are all to me, Susanna, *gràdh mo chrìidh.*'

Her single tear fell on top of the baby's downy head. 'Love of my heart,' she repeated the words in English. 'Always, Fergus.'

* * * * *

His Wicked
Christmas Wager

ANNIE BURROWS

For Aidan again—you really are my hero.

Annie Burrows' love of stories meant that when she was old enough to go to university, she chose to do English literature. She wasn't sure what she wanted to do beyond that, but one day, when her youngest child was at senior school, she began to wonder if all those daydreams that had kept her mind occupied whilst carrying out mundane chores would provide similar pleasure to other women. She was right…and Annie hasn't looked back since!

CHAPTER ONE

"ARE YOU SURE this is the place?" Lady Caroline Fallow-field peered through the window of the hired hack, her nose wrinkling in disgust.

Though from all she had heard, this did look exactly the sort of low haunt Lord Sinclair frequented these days.

"Oh yes ma'am," Arbuthnot assured her.

"And he's still inside?" She could not imagine any-one willingly spending their evenings in a hovel like this. When they'd crossed the bridge into Southwark, she had imagined she might end up somewhere quaint and full of character. Not this ramshackle building, its roof slumped over mouldering piles which looked ready to slide into the Thames should the next tide turn with too much vigour.

"Yes ma'am," Arbuthnot said again. "I've had the nipper keeping a close watch." He pointed to the ragged urchin running up and down outside the Crossed Oars, aggres-sively accosting every passer-by.

"How can he possibly keep watch while he is so busy begging?"

"Easy," he said with pride. "Any road," he added with a shrug, "it's better for him to have a good reason for hanging about the Oars. If he'd just stood in a doorway, watching like, then somebody would have took him for a spy and moved him on. Reg'lars are always afeard of someone laying information."

"I see." She smiled at him. Arbuthnot had turned out to be something of a treasure. The matter in hand was so delicate she had not wanted to employ a private investigator. But Arbuthnot owed her a favour. She had made sure he had medical help, and then compensation for the injuries he'd suffered when her late husband had forced him into the ring against a much younger, fitter opponent. She shuddered at the memory, which was so hard to blot out, of the event her husband had also forced her to attend. It had been sickening to discover that a great many so-called gentlemen could derive so much pleasure from watching one man beating another to a pulp.

"I'll go in first," said Arbuthnot, and rapped on the roof, to get the driver to set the horse in motion. When they'd rounded the corner, Arbuthnot heaved his bulk out of the carriage. "I've told the jarvey to wait ten minutes," he said, leaning back into the carriage, his body almost completely blocking out the bitter wind blowing off the river. "Then he'll go round again, and drop you off right outside. I'll have found his lordship by then. Wherever he is in the place, I'll be standing right near, so you can go to him straight off."

She nodded again. Arbuthnot would stand head and shoulders above whatever crowd might be in there. His plan meant that she would not have to waste time searching for Lord Sinclair.

She pulled her collar up round her throat against the chill which swirled inside as he slammed the door shut. For a moment, she wondered if she could go through with it. But then she reminded herself, as she'd done over and over again on the way here, that walking into a room full of drunken lightermen and mudlarks would be nothing—not after enduring four years of marriage to a monster.

It was just that it hadn't seemed quite so daunting when Arbuthnot had been in the carriage with her. Now he'd got out, she felt very alone, and small, and defenceless.

She glared at the depression in the opposite seat where the gigantic prizefighter had been sitting. That's what you got if you ever began to think you could rely on a man, she reminded herself. He rendered you weak, and dependant, and vulnerable.

She firmed her lips and lifted her chin. There was nothing that rabble could do to her that her husband had not already done. And done with more finesse. She'd survived him, and she would survive this.

The carriage jerked into motion, flinging her back against the squabs and putting her moment of doubt to flight.

Everyone was relying on her.

And so she was jolly well going to make Lord Sinclair see sense.

When the carriage stopped, Arbuthnot's nipper sprang to open the door and pull the steps down. She tossed him a coin from the deliberately meagre supply she'd brought with her and strode into the tavern, head high.

This time it was not just the look of the place that offended her sensibilities. A wave of eau d'unwashed male, topped with a foam of tobacco smoke, with a base note of spilled ale and something she did not care to identify, slapped her directly in the nostrils.

"Ooh, la-di-da," observed one of the men closest to the door as her hand flew instinctively to shield her nose.

She had expected trouble. She had briefly considered donning a disguise and attempting to blend in. But only briefly. In her experience, timidity only made bullies look upon you as an easy target. And so, instead, she'd emphasized her station. She'd donned her newest winter coat of dark green, with its wide lapels and trio of capes on the shoulders. Though it was based on a man's redingote, the profusion of velvet trim, and the matching bonnet with all its ribbons and feathers, made the outfit indisputably feminine, high fashion, and costly.

"Lost, are yer darling?" asked another, eyeing her tightly-fitted bodice, or perhaps the double row of large silver buttons running down its length. "Mebbe I can show yer the way…" He waggled his eyebrows suggestively.

"There's summat I could show yer," said another, lewdly clutching at the front of his breeches.

She lifted her chin a fraction, though that was the only sign she gave that she'd heard a single word. Their talk was all for show. Not one of them would dare do more than throw crude jibes her way, so long as she kept her nerve. She was a lady, and everyone knew the penalties for tangling with a member of the Quality.

Besides, she'd brought Arbuthnot with her, just in case. And speaking of Arbuthnot…she scanned the throng swiftly. Even through the haze of tobacco smoke he was easy to spot, leaning nonchalantly against one of the supporting timbers, away to her left.

Directly in front of him, his booted feet stretched towards a blazing fire, slouched her quarry.

Lord Sinclair.

Her heart squeezed to see he had a woman sprawled across his lap. He was using one hand to stroke her thigh, while the other held a tankard very similar to the one clutched in Arbuthnot's massive paw.

She rebuked herself for minding so much as she stalked across the room toward him. Naturally, he would have had women over the years. But she managed to blank out the catcalls and vulgar gestures that came her way with greater ease than she could deal with the vicious pangs of jealousy. The woman made matters worse by nuzzling at his ear. She could see why the woman appeared so fond of him. Although the Lord Sinclair she was looking at was a far cry from the youth with whom she'd so disastrously fallen in love six years before, he was the kind of customer she would have favoured, had she been a whore. Even with more than a day's growth of beard darkening his jaw, his clothing neither new nor all that clean, and his blue-black hair straggling down almost to his shoulders, he was still the most compellingly virile male she'd ever seen.

So greatly did her hostility mount, with every step she took, that when she reached the table at which they sat, all she had to do was raise one haughty eyebrow, and the woman he'd been groping scrambled off his lap as though he'd turned white hot.

"No, Molly, don't go," Lord Sinclair drawled. "I like

you." Molly had offered a kind of comfort he'd sometimes needed after Caroline had casually destroyed him. And she had the gall to look down her haughty nose at them both.

Lady Caroline gave Molly a hard smile as she sat down on a bench on the opposite side of his table.

"We can conduct our discussion with Molly on your lap, if you prefer," she said. "It makes no difference to me."

"No, it wouldn't," he sneered. "You always do just as you please, and to hell with everyone else."

She quirked one eyebrow. "Really? I rather thought that was your particular speciality."

He could hardly believe his ears. She was accusing him of selfishness?

"Sebastian and Phoebe want you home," she said. "The wedding…"

"Wedding?" Molly took a swift backward step. "I ain't wasting my time with you if you've got marriage to some gentry mort in mind."

"No, Molly, you've got it wrong…"

But it was too late. She'd flounced off.

"Happy now?"

He lifted his drink to a suddenly dry mouth, thanking God he'd suppressed any outward sign of how the mere sight of Caroline had affected him. When she'd walked in through the door, in spite of all she'd done, his heart had pounded, his stomach had clenched, and he'd gripped Molly's leg so hard he'd probably left a bruise.

But she'd only come to deliver yet another message from his brother. So far he'd resolutely ignored all the increasingly impassioned requests to watch Sebastian marry Lady Caroline's younger sister, telling himself he couldn't be bothered. But the way he'd reacted when she'd stalked into this hell-hole was a mocking reminder that his reasons for avoiding the ceremony went so much deeper.

Lady Caroline watched him glaring at her over the rim of his tankard as he drained it to the last drop. Happy? She could not recall the last time she'd applied that word to her state of mind. Before the last time she'd seen him, probably. When she'd had dreams of marrying for love, to a man who claimed to love her too.

What a goose she'd been!

"No," she said bluntly. "But that is beside the point."

"The point being?"

"Oh, don't be so obtuse. You know very well why I've come. You said as much."

"That damned wedding," he snapped. "Do you seriously think there is anything you can say that would induce me to attend that farce?"

"It is not a farce! Phoebe and Sebastian love each other."

"Love," he snorted with contempt. "There's no such thing."

Her heart, which she'd long since thought immune to anything that anyone could throw at it, abruptly revealed she had been wrong. Once, this man had said he loved her. Passionately. Devotedly. Madly enough to defy the world and create a scandal that would have set the ton rocking on its heels.

She smothered the memory before it grew strong enough to wound her, took a deep breath, and said, "Even if that was true, your brother and my sister believe in it."

"More fool them."

She shrugged as nonchalantly as she could. "If you don't

believe in love, what is there to keep you away from their wedding?"

"What do you mean by that?"

"Oh, come. Everyone is saying you mean to stay away because you are still broken-hearted over me. That you cannot bear to see me, especially not at a wedding. But if you don't believe in love..." She leaned forward, her eyes narrowed. "...then what is the reason you have so far refused to attend?"

My God, but she was a cold, hard woman. Every word had been like a dagger thrust to the heart.

But he would be damned if he let her know just how accurately she'd summed him up.

"Perhaps I don't wish to waste my time watching my baby brother making a fool of himself over a female from your family," he snarled.

"And I can see how profitably you normally spend your time," she retorted, casting a swift glance around the shoddy tavern in which he looked very much at home. "From the rumours abounding about your life, of late, one would think your brother would be glad you have so far adamantly refused to answer his invitation. What man of good ton would want someone like you to darken his doors, after all? A notorious womanizer, gambler, drunkard, and even, if the latest *on dit* has any substance to it, a man who is not beyond breaking the law."

"Your point being?"

The lazily lifted left eyebrow made him look every inch the viscount, in spite of the shabby clothing, and the situation in which she'd found him, in spite of the fact that he had not denied even one of the accusations she'd flung at him.

"The point being," she replied, "that no matter how low you have sunk, your family still care about you. They love you, though you would deny the emotion exists. They want you to be there to celebrate the event with them."

He knew that! His brother had done all he could to prevent his downward slide. Even when he'd sunk about as low as a man could get, Seb had taken pains to get word to him that the door would always be open.

And part of him yearned to go back.

If only she weren't going to be there, this wedding would be the perfect opportunity to start mending fences.

"It would mean so much to them if you could just…" She gave him an exasperated look. "…clean yourself up, and pretend, just for a few days, that there is still some remnant of the gentleman left in you."

He glared into his empty tankard—a remarkably apt symbol of his life.

"Oh," she said, in such a way that he braced himself for what was coming next.

"It has not occurred to anyone that you might not be able to afford to purchase decent clothes, let alone stand the cost of travelling all the way to Berkshire. Is that the case Crispin? If so, I can give you the money…"

"Damn you, Caro," he growled, slamming the empty tankard down on the rough table that separated them, his face contorted with fury. "Do you think I would touch a penny of the money that bastard Fallowfield left you?"

"Probably not," she conceded. "But I had to at least try."

"Why?"

"You know why. You would not have gambled away your entire fortune, and be living like this if I had not…" She could not look him in the face, any more than she could end that sentence.

And so her eyes were gazing into the fire as he ended it for her, in a low voice that throbbed with hatred. "Shown yourself to be a mercenary, scheming, deceitful jade?"

She opened her mouth to refute the allegations he'd levelled at her before. But would he be any more willing to hear her side of the story now? She'd been a widow for the best part of two years. If he'd really wanted to know the truth, he'd had plenty of time to find her and ask her to explain. But he had not.

Which meant he didn't really care.

And if he didn't, then neither did she.

"If I am so worthless, then there is nothing to keep you away, is there?" She smiled at him with the smile she had perfected through the years of her marriage. The one that told the world she cared nothing for its opinion—that, in fact, she rather despised it.

"There is no reason you should not be reconciled to your family. Even if the wedding itself is so offensive to you, remind yourself that it is also Christmas. The one time of year when even someone who has sunk as low as you can be justified for attempting to make a fresh start."

My God, but she was patronizing. He laughed harshly. "Did you really think preaching me a sermon would have any impact upon me?"

She leaned back and sighed.

"Not really. But I had to try."

He leaned forward and glowered at her. "You thought

you would only have to stroll in here and crook your little finger, and I would come panting to heel, like some kind of...lap dog, didn't you?"

"No...I..."

"Listen to me, Caroline, and listen well. I am not your plaything. It will take more than a few words and a couple of coy smiles to bend me to your will these days."

She sat forward, too. "How much more? What would it take, Crispin? What could I do to make you consider putting aside your animosity to me, and travelling to Hatton Hall for your brother's wedding?"

Stay away from it. So that he wouldn't have to pretend that the sight of her wasn't wrenching what was left of his mangled heart out of his chest. If only he could think of some way to run her off, without letting her suspect the truth...

And then it hit him.

And he smiled.

"Well, isn't that just what I should have expected from you?"

"What?"

But after only a second or two, the lascivious way he was looking her up and down revealed exactly what he had thought she'd meant. He had assumed she was offering herself to him.

And he was interested. For he had that hooded, hungry gaze men got when they were imagining what you'd look like naked.

The hard smile that followed when they started thinking about what they would like to do once they got you into that state.

It didn't look as though it would be anything pleasant, at least not for her. He was probably thinking up ways he could punish her. For all that he denied believing in love any more, at one time he'd accused her of breaking his heart by marrying another man, after she'd vowed she loved him. And would only ever love him.

No wonder he was thinking up ways he could make her pay.

"If you really want me to come to Hatton Hall," he said, "and play at being a functioning part of one big, happy family, then you are going to have to make it worth my while."

Something shrivelled up and died inside her. Something she had not even known still existed, until this moment. The belief that he was different. That he was not like other men. To be specific, like her husband.

"Am I, indeed?" Years of practice meant her voice showed no trace of her disappointment. She might have been discussing the weather, her tone was so bland.

"Oh, yes. If you want to change my mind, what you ought to do is offer me something that interests me."

"Like what?" Though she knew. And the very thought of it chilled her. What men liked best was dominating and humiliating a woman to compensate for what they considered the weakness of desiring them in the first place.

"A wager," he said.

A wager? That was not what she had expected him to say at all.

"You say I have become a notorious gambler, so what other way did you expect to impress me, but by offering a wager that would interest me? Something…a bit different.

Something that will provide me with adequate compensation for giving up a large portion of my time in order to please our respective siblings. And something to compensate me for spoiling my plans for this evening, too." His eyes flickered across the room to where Molly was draping herself over another potential customer.

She hadn't brought enough money. She'd thought it sensible to bring only a very little with her, so that if she was robbed, at least she would not lose much.

"I…I have little to stake," she confessed.

He shook his head, his mouth slowly widening into a cruel smile.

"I have already told you I don't want your money," he reminded her. "What I want you to stake is just one hour of your time. Upstairs, in the room I would have used with Molly." He lowered his voice and leaned forward. "And just to be sure we understand each other, I would like to remind you of the fact that you never let me see any part of you unclothed. So now you will have to agree to stand before me completely naked."

"Wh—what?"

"You heard." He leaned back, and repeated, in a louder voice, "Your stake is to be one hour," he lifted his index finger, "upstairs," he lifted his middle finger, "in the room I would have shared with Molly," he lifted his ring finger, "with every single inch of you on show." And if that didn't make her run for the hills, he didn't know what would.

The word "naked" in conjunction with the word "wager" not only shocked her, but provoked a ripple of interest throughout the men already intrigued by her appearance in their midst. She could feel them turning toward their corner of the room, jostling one another as they moved closer, forming a natural ring—just like the men who'd clustered round the arena in which Arbuthnot had been reduced to human mincemeat.

Proudly, she lifted her chin, and stared Lord Sinclair straight in the eye.

"You would wager one hour of my time, against your attendance at the wedding of my sister to your brother?"

"One hour of your time, naked," he said, causing the wall of men behind her to rumble their appreciation.

My God, how he must hate her, to deliberately humiliate her in front of this rabble.

"And how do you propose we determine a winner?"

Dear Lord, but she was going to accept his wager. When any decent woman would have backed down.

But then she wasn't decent, was she? Or she couldn't have tossed him aside and let him founder. And no decent woman could have cheerfully married a man like Lord Fallowfield. From what he'd heard, the earl made what went on in a thieves' den like this one look like nursery games.

"I have no intention of sitting here half the night playing cards with you, when we could be far more gainfully employed." He let his eyes drift down her body, to make sure she understood the nature of his insult.

"Besides, neither of us could be sure, given the company we have been keeping of late, that the other would not be cheating."

She shot him a look she hoped he could read as the fury she felt at that accusation. She might have been compelled to marry a villain, but she'd never permitted his vile habits to taint her own soul.

"But we could draw cards," he suggested. "Or toss a coin."

"Cards," she said defiantly.

A buzz of excitement swept the room. She could distinctly hear rough voices making side bets on Sinner Sinclair or the "green goddess." Herself, she presumed. Then somebody slapped a pack of grimy cards down onto the table in front of her.

"Since you are the nearest thing to a lady that has ever set foot in here…" Laughter rumbled through the crowd. "…you may shuffle the pack, and spread them face down on the table. And then we shall take turns in drawing one card each. Highest card wins. Best of three. And," he said, reaching out to stay her hand as she went to pick up the pack, "remove the aces first. So there will be no occasion for argument about whether they count as high or low."

She looked at the deck of cards. She looked at Lord Sinclair. And she looked into her heart.

She could get up and walk out. She could return to her sister and admit defeat.

But when had she ever been ready to admit defeat? Especially when the odds stacked against her seemed impossibly high.

"Very well," she said. "I accept your terms."

CHAPTER TWO

SHE TOOK A deep breath and willed her hands not to tremble as she flipped through the deck, removing the aces. Three draws of the cards, and if she won, he would go to Hatton Hall for the wedding. He might have sunk very low, but no man, not even one of these drunkards and thieves, would dream of welching on a bet.

Men described gambling debts as debts of honour. Her mouth compressed with bitterness as she shuffled the pack. She didn't think very much of men's idea of honour. It certainly did not march with her own. What was so honourable about a man selling his daughter into a marriage that he'd known would make her miserable, just so that he could hold his head up in his clubs?

Realising what her face might be betraying, she forced it back into a mask of hauteur. By the time she spread the cards out in a fan, face down on the table, she was able to dart a challenging smile Lord Sinclair's way.

If he went to his brother's wedding it could well be the first step on the road to restoring him to his rightful place in society. A place he'd lost because of the damage she'd inflicted on him when she'd married the Earl of Fallowfield. So it was fitting that she was the one taking a risk, here, tonight.

And if she lost…

Her heart skipped a beat. She would pay him, of course. Exactly what he'd asked for. Exactly.

"You first," said Lord Sinclair, gesturing towards the cards.

She took a card. The three of spades.

The entire room held its breath as Lord Sinclair slowly leaned forward and drew…a two of diamonds.

She looked into Lord Sinclair's eyes. Eyes that had once blazed with adoration, but which were now cold and hard as chips of wet slate.

The sound of her blood pounding through her veins almost obliterated the babble of men's voices, urging on whichever one of them they'd backed. That had been an amazing stroke of luck. Or had it been luck? Was there something more powerful at work here? Had she won that draw, against all the odds, because she was trying to right the wrong she'd done—albeit against her will?

"Draw again," grated Lord Sinclair, his eyes holding hers. "And let's get this over with."

Her heart pounded. Was she imagining it, or did he, too, think she was going to win? And was there just the tiniest hint of relief in his expression? Then…if she was reading him aright, it must mean he had only challenged her because he needed an excuse to back down about attending the wedding, without losing face. Without admitting that somehow, she had reached him when nobody else could…

She drew the ten of diamonds, convinced she was going to win. It was meant to be. He would go home, and stand up beside his brother.

He drew the king of hearts.

A hubbub of voices rumbled behind her as her heart plunged to her boots.

Why had she thought, even for one moment, that there was such a thing as divine justice? She was not going to win because what she was attempting to do was right! It was just down to luck. The random distribution of numbers.

"Best of three," Lord Sinclair reminded her.

His eyes were hard. But he was breathing just as rapidly and unevenly as she was.

It was all down to this last draw.

The arc of cards spread across the table had grown ragged as they'd pulled out their previous choices. For some reason, she did not want to pick from the ones that stuck out like jagged teeth from the mocking grin that leered up at her from the table.

So she simply turned over the one at the very far end.

The nine of clubs.

Lord Sinclair held her gaze as he turned over the card which had been under hers. He flipped it face up on the table.

The crowd went wild.

They both looked down at the same instant.

And saw the ten.

Lord Sinclair got to his feet and extended his hand to her across the table.

"Upstairs, now," he commanded her sharply.

Was it significant that he didn't look as though he was glad he'd just won? Or was she clutching at straws?

She got to her feet and took his hand anyway. Whatever might be going through his head, she had to escape this room. The atmosphere was suffocating. Most of the men were baying like a pack of hounds in their excitement at seeing her brought down. The rest—the few who'd lost their money on her—jeered as Lord Sinclair led her to the staircase.

She gathered her skirts in one hand, hitching them deftly so she could climb the stairs, pausing only once she reached the landing.

Perhaps, once they were alone, once it was just the two of them, he might relent. Surely he knew that obliging her to strip naked was more of an insult than she deserved?

She abandoned that faint hope as he pushed her roughly along the corridor that lurched drunkenly towards the river. What she could see in his face, whenever she glanced over her shoulder, was chillingly merciless.

"In there," he said, opening a door at the very far end.

The room they entered was pretty much what she would expect to find in such an establishment—apart from a fire which blazed in the hearth, dispelling most of the chill, if not managing to make the atmosphere exactly cosy.

He shut the door and shot the bolt home.

"Is that to keep the rabble out, or me in?" She feigned a light, jocular tone, vowing she would not let him see how sick and frightened she felt. "If the latter, you need not worry. I have no intention of attempting to defraud you, sir. I shall pay you exactly what we agreed upon."

Mustering a smile, she drew off her gloves and dropped

them onto a table which stood beneath an uncurtained window. No fear of anyone seeing in, she ascertained with one swift glance through its grimy panes. The room looked directly over the river.

"Is there no clock in here?" She looked round the room in vain and frowned. "I would rather not have to get into a dispute about the length of time you keep me in this room."

He had to admire her courage. A woman with less pride would be begging for mercy by now. Oh, he was still angry with her. And now he'd got her up here, he was going to take the opportunity the fates had given him to exact some revenge. Didn't she deserve to suffer for so casually breaking his heart? For walking back in here and imperiously demanding he do as she told him? For treating him as though he was just…nothing?

Yes, she did. And so he would make her squirm like a worm on a hook before he offered her, as though it was a compromise, the outcome he'd wanted all along.

But for now…

He settled his features into a mask of vengeful triumph, got his father's gold hunter watch from the pocket of his sadly shabby waistcoat, checked the time, showed it to her, then put it back.

"Very well," she said, undoing the ribbons of her bonnet. "Let us commence."

She tossed her bonnet onto the table with her gloves with what she hoped was an air of insouciance.

He might have won the wager, but he had not beaten her.

And she had no intention of allowing him to do so.

"I am afraid I have not dressed for the occasion," she said, unbuttoning her coat. She slid out of it, looked round for somewhere to hang it up, then, with a moue of distaste, walked to the tester bed and draped it over the footboard. Then she turned round, and shot him a rueful smile as she hitched her dress up, and extended one foot.

"These boots are suitable for the weather, but not for... seduction."

"So long as they come off," he said grimly, "I don't care what the hell you are wearing on your feet."

She noticed a low stool in front of the fireplace. Sashaying over to it, she lifted her skirts to allow some freedom of movement, placed one foot on its surface, and set about unlacing the sturdy calf-length boot. Every now and then she shot him a provocative look from under her eyelashes. His eyes were greedily sweeping the amount of leg she was showing.

She pulled off her left boot, then repeated the performance with the other.

Then she forced herself to walk across to where he was standing, devouring her with his eyes. It was not easy to approach him, for now that she'd removed her boots he seemed much bigger and far more dangerous. So she reached for every ounce of courage she possessed, before saying, "You know, of course that you will have to unlace me."

She shot him her most coquettish smile, then turned her back to him.

He could hardly believe it. She intended to go through with it! And from the looks she was darting him, it did not bother her one whit.

She had the soul of a whore. He'd told himself so, often,

over the years. But it was only now, seeing her willingness to strip for him, that it really sank in.

And this was the woman he'd allowed to destroy him. Because of her, he'd entirely destroyed his good name, whilst deliberately obliterating every last vestige of the boy who'd been soft enough to get crushed by the cruelty of her rejection.

She stood there, head bent, offering him free access to the ties of her gown. And, for a moment, all he could see was his fingers closing round that treacherous neck, squeezing and squeezing until she dropped to her knees on the floor at his feet.

He sucked in a sharp breath, willing the red mists of rage to subside, then reached for her ties and yanked them open.

Her heart sank as he methodically loosened her gown. For a moment she'd begun to hope he was going to call it quits, he'd hesitated about unlacing her for so long. If there had been anything left of the man she'd once loved beneath the bitterness that seemed second nature to him now, he wouldn't be going through with it.

But any last hope that he had shown signs of regretting pushing her this far withered as he undid not only her gown, but her stays.

The swift precise way his fingers worked at her laces was a devastating contrast to the reverent, gentle way he used to touch her.

But then he didn't love her any more.

If he ever really had.

She stepped briskly away from him as soon as he'd finished his task, turned, and gave him another dazzling smile.

He took a step towards her, his face a mask of lustful intent.

She took an involuntary step backwards, holding up one hand to stay him, clutching her dress tightly in the other.

"Why do you not sit down," she said breathlessly, indicating a rather dilapidated wing chair positioned by the fire. "And watch me disrobe. Would you not enjoy that?"

She almost flinched at the contemptuous smile he shot her.

"Yes, why not? You always did like to show off."

He frowned, recalling her love of fine clothes and masculine attention. He'd always made excuses for her, telling himself she had no idea what she was doing. How could he have been so blind?

"Go ahead," he said, strolling to the armchair, flinging himself into it, and stretching out his legs. "But do not think I will let you get away with anything less than complete disrobing." Not now.

"Of course not."

She smiled again. A stretching of the lips across her teeth that hurt the muscles in her cheeks. But she wasn't going to let him see one jot of the pain he was giving her.

Standing completely still, she let go of her gown, allowing the weight of the velvet to carry it down her body and crumple on the floor. She stepped out of it, then turned her back to him before picking it up. She didn't need to look over her shoulder to know that he would be watching her bottom as she bent over, the curves clearly delineated through the remaining layers of clothing. But she looked anyway, just quickly.

Fierce resentment seared through her at the lordly way

he was looking at her, as though she were his slave, and her only function in life was to amuse him.

She grasped the gown that she would never be able to wear again, since it would always remind her of how determined he was to humble her, shook it out, and draped it over the footboard with her coat. Then she hitched up her petticoat, sat on the edge of the mattress, and raised her left foot, pointing the toes in his direction.

"My stockings are not exactly the stuff to make a man's heart beat faster either, are they?" She raised one leg, then the other, as though lamenting over the thickness of the brown cotton coverings, whilst really giving him tantalising glimpses of her knees. "But they are so lovely and warm," she said huskily, bending forward to run her hands all the way down her left leg.

His eyes followed her hands as they caressed her lower leg. Then flicked to the top of her gaping bodice, where the full mounds of her breasts threatened to spill out. Then back to her hands as she slowly slid them up until they reached her garter.

It was a deliberately provocative performance that should have filled him with disgust. Instead, he was powerless to tear his eyes from her hands as they stroked the stocking down her leg. He was as aroused as if he was doing it himself. He could almost feel the satin smoothness of that milk-white skin.

His breath hitched as she reached up to untie her second garter. She stretched out lazily to drop both stockings on top of her other clothes, rolling her body slightly to emphasize the curve of her hip.

When she turned to face him again, his face was

flushed. And even from that distance, she could see that he was aroused. Though he probably had been from the moment they set foot in this room. It was just that the way he was sitting, his legs stretched out straight before him, made it blatantly obvious.

"What next?"

He shifted uncomfortably, hating the teasing note in her voice. Hating seeing what she really was. Hating the discovery that he'd made a wreck of his life for...her. But most of all, hating the effect she still had on him.

"My petticoat, perhaps?"

She tilted her head to one side as she coyly ran her fingers along the drawstring.

"Yes," he grated, his voice hoarse with desire.

She loosened the drawstring, stood up, and shimmied the petticoat off. His eyes fastened on her bosom, still covered, but only just, by her loosened stays and her chemise.

Her nipples tautened in anticipation of the moment they would be bared to the heat of that gaze.

Her heart did a funny little somersault. Her stomach pulled taut.

In dismay, she realized that his excitement was affecting her in a completely unexpected way. It did not repel her, as her husband's lust had repelled her. No—far worse—her body was remembering the times she'd gone to this man willingly, eagerly, and only their joint belief that it would be wrong outside marriage had prevented them from becoming lovers.

She could have wept. Back then, what had been between them had seemed so pure and lovely, even when their bodies had burned and throbbed as hers was beginning to do now. Time and time again he had drawn back, declaring he would not sully her.

And now, now he was intent on doing just that. He was urging her on with his hot eyes, and his heavy breathing, and the ruthless line of his hard mouth.

"W—would you like me to take down my hair for you?" She curled one blonde ringlet round her finger, remembering how he used to beg her for permission to plunge his own fingers through the luxuriant mass. She'd scolded him for dislodging even a single pin, or disarranging one artfully crafted curl back then, fearing that if she went back to the ballroom even slightly dishevelled, people would know what they'd been up to.

"No, dammit," he growled harshly. "Just get rid of the clothes. Every last stitch."

She shrugged as though it made no difference to her. When really his attitude brought an end to her hope that this might have turned into something more...meaningful between them.

She'd been foolish to wish for the impossible. There was no hope of rekindling what he'd once felt for her. She'd destroyed it.

She took hold of the edge of her stays and tossed them aside.

Her chemise was virtually transparent, for she only wore the very finest, sheerest material next to her skin these days. He could see everything as though through a veil. The duskiness of her nipples, the swell of her breasts and her belly. The dark triangle at the apex of her thighs.

As his gaze swept over her, she felt it like a caress. Her breasts ached for it to become a real touch. She imagined

ANNIE BURROWS 161

what his body would feel like, hard and muscular against
the softness of her own. And she grew damp with desire.

But beyond that, came the tiny hope that if he felt anything for her, anything at all, he would surely tell her to
stop now. She knew he felt entitled to some revenge, but
would not this be enough?

"What are you waiting for," he growled. "Pretending
to be shy now?"

She didn't know why she should feel such crushing disappointment. She'd never met a man who had not let her
down, in one way or another. And men were never satisfied until they had what they thought was complete victory.

So be it.

With a hard smile she untied her chemise, lifted it over
her head, and tossed it to the floor.

"There," she said with malice. "Like what you see? Oh,
but wait, you said you wanted to see every single inch of
me." Quivering with rage, she slowly turned round, then
round again, so that he could not say she had not shown
him everything. He got to his feet. With hands that were
shaking, he tore away his cravat, then unbuttoned his waistcoat.

"On the bed," he commanded her, tossing the waistcoat
onto the chair on which he'd been sitting.

She lay down on her side, no longer bothering to con-
ceal her contempt as she watched him stride to the bed.

And it was with total disdain that she said, "What do
you think you are doing?"

"What does it look like? I'm going to take what you've
been offering."

"I have not been offering you anything more than we

agreed," she said brazenly, before he'd managed to do more than get one knee on the bed. "The exact terms of our wager were that I should be naked in this room with you. If you attempt to lay so much as one finger on me I shall scream. And the man I brought with me, who is pledged to protect me, will come in here and pound you to a pulp."

She hadn't really thought she'd need Arbuthnot to protect her from Lord Sinclair—but then, it was downright dangerous to attempt to call a halt when a man was so rampant with lust and hatred. Her heart beat double time as he hovered over her, breathing hard, his face twisted with fury.

"You scheming, cheating jade," he spat. "You deliberately undressed in the most provocative manner, deliberately roused me to a state where I might not have been able to hold back. And all for what? So you could have your man beat me?" He reared back as though she disgusted him.

"N—no." She frowned in confusion. Why would he think she wanted to do anything so vile?

"Don't lie to me! You haven't changed a bit, have you? You deliberately rouse lust in a man just so you can humiliate him when you spurn him."

"That's not true!" It had never been true. "You were the one who wanted to dish out humiliation tonight. You made me strip for you like, like a whore," she cried bitterly.

"Is that not exactly what you are? A very highly paid one," he sneered. "But there's no denying you sold your body to a man for money."

"I did no such thing!" Suddenly, it was too much to be lying there, with him towering over her while she was so exposed. She grabbed a corner of the coverlet and pulled it up to her neck as she sat up.

"Why else did you marry Fallowfield if not for his money?"

"Because I had no choice!"

"I offered you a choice," he roared. "We could have been together. But instead of running away with me, you went willingly to the ball your father threw to announce your betrothal, and smiled at all your guests while you walked round on Fallowfield's arm, simpering up at him as though he was your every dream come true."

"You...you went to that betrothal ball?"

"Yes. I had to see for myself that you were willing. I couldn't believe it when I read the announcement of your betrothal to another man, when you'd professed undying love to me."

"And what would you have done if I'd looked as miserable as I felt? Dragged me out of the ballroom? Carried me off to Gretna Green?"

"Yes, dammit!"

"And then what? Do you think we would have lived happily ever after, like characters out of a storybook? Fallowfield had the power to ruin my whole family. Hadn't you heard about my father's gambling debts? When Fallowfield promised to deal with it all if he would hand me over to him, Papa didn't hesitate. He'd already sent the announcement to the *Gazette* by the time he informed me of the deal the pair of them had made. And yes, I suppose I could have wept and wailed all through that ghastly ball, or run off with you to save myself. But...poor Phoebe...

what had she done to deserve a life of penury? And why should my brothers have had to forfeit their education?"

She shook her head reproachfully. "Do you think I could ever have known a moment's happiness, if I'd abandoned them all? We were doomed from the moment the earl set his sights on me."

He strode to the far side of the room, running his fingers through his hair.

"I cannot believe you have never thought of it from anyone else's point of view but your own," she said with contempt. "You have to be the most self-centred male on this planet. You won't even ease your brother's concerns by putting in an appearance at his wedding."

"Get out," he growled.

"What?"

"You heard," he said, rounding on her furiously. "Put your clothes back on and get out of here, before I…" He turned away again, stalked over to the window and put his hands on the sill. His shoulders hunched as he stared out over the darkened water.

Lady Caroline seized the opportunity, and her clothes, with both hands. Within minutes she was downstairs, and outside, and clambering into the carriage that Arbuthnot had miraculously managed to procure for her at the exact moment she needed it.

She hadn't been able to do up her stays or her gown properly. Underneath her neatly buttoned coat she was half undone.

Which was exactly how she felt. Over the next few days she would present a neatly buttoned-up exterior to the world. But inside, she would be a mess. She had not only failed to persuade Lord Sinclair to attend the wedding but also forfeited any remaining shred of respect he might have felt for her, all in one evening.

She'd thought she would find some consolation in outwitting him over the wording of that vile wager. Instead, she was bitterly regretting not having reached up and pulled him to her on that bed. Oh, how she'd longed to feel his lips upon hers once more.

Only it wouldn't have been like before. His kiss would have been brutally punishing.

But at least she would have held him in her arms, one last time. And to judge by the way her body had melted for him, as though it recognized its one true mate, she might have finally experienced the rapture that women spoke of finding with their lovers.

Instead of which, she was returning to an empty, lonely house, and a future where she would have to deal with not only her own sense of failure but her sister's disappointment, too.

It had all been for nothing.

CHAPTER THREE

"I'M SURE YOU did your best," said Phoebe when Lady Caroline confessed that, although she'd located Lord Sinclair, he'd been deaf to her entreaties.

But something about the tone of her voice implied she'd never believed Caroline's best was going to be good enough. And when Sebastian arrived at Hatton Hall, he looked at her as though he hadn't expected much of her either.

Oh, everyone was polite on the surface, but their lack of faith in her, and her own resentment at all she'd gone through on their behalf, were simmering under the surface, just awaiting the right opportunity to come to a boil.

By the morning of Christmas Eve it was all Caroline could do to sit still while her maid put the finishing touches to her hair.

Phoebe was, after all, getting her wish to be married on Christmas Day in the little parish church they'd attended since childhood. Their father was throwing an immense party, at Caroline's expense, though nobody but the two of them knew it, so that the whole community could make it a Christmas to remember. And the house was crammed with friends and family come to wish the bridal couple well.

But was that enough for Phoebe? No. She kept shooting Lady Caroline little looks of reproach, then sighing, and hurrying to Sebastian's side, and gazing up at him with the air of a tragedy queen, until it made her want to scream.

Didn't Phoebe appreciate the fact that she was free to marry for no other reason than that she had fallen in love with a man who loved her too?

Which was a good thing. Of course it was. It meant that her own sacrifice, in giving up the man she'd loved, to marry Lord Fallowfield, had not been in vain.

Oh, yes—and then there was Crispin. Crispin who was not here in person, but who was very much present in everyone's thoughts.

Especially in hers. She could not stop thinking about the bitterness in his voice as he'd accused her of leading him on. The leap of excitement she'd felt when he'd torn off his cravat and stalked to the bed. The passion in his eyes the moment before she'd stopped him kissing her.

And the fierce quarrel they'd subsequently had.

And her flight home, half naked under her coat. And the sleepless night that had followed. And all the sleepless nights since, when she'd dozed off, only to jerk awake to the feel of his fingers at her back, the echo of her garments whispering to the floor. And the way she'd lain naked, letting him look at her. Shamelessly glorying in the way he'd looked at her.

And the burn of humiliation as the dream faded, leaving her alone and humiliated in the bed she'd chosen over one she could have shared with Crispin.

And then for Phoebe to say, in that injured little voice, that she was sure she'd done her best.

Ooh!

If only she could throw a vase against the wall, or kick a few chairs over, she was sure she would feel much better.

But as it was, there was a house full of guests to whom she had to be pleasant, and a sister whose happiness she would absolutely not dent by revealing one iota of her own turmoil.

And a certain handsome rake to consign to perdition.

If only he had not improved with age. Most men who led his kind of life ended up looking positively raddled. But that slightly dishevelled, degenerate look had only made him more attractive, not less.

"There you go my lady," said Betsy. "All done."

She glared at her reflection in the mirror, knowing she would not be feeling half so cross if she had just allowed him to have his way with her. Her pride might have got dented, but when, over the past six years, had it ever been completely whole?

"Is your hair not done to your satisfaction, my lady?" Betsy sounded anxious.

Lady Caroline forced a smile to her lips. "You have done wonders, as usual. I was thinking of something else entirely."

With that smile fixed on her face, Lady Caroline left her room and went to join the others. At least everyone else appeared to be in good spirits. They were all gathering in the dining room, where a substantial meal had been laid out from one end of the long room to the other, on a succession of sturdy sideboards. From the way they were loading up their plates, one would think they were about to embark on a major expedition, rather than a walk round the grounds to gather the traditional greenery with which to decorate the hall.

She came to a halt just inside the doorway, feeling like a lump of hewn granite forever stuck in the middle of a stream, watching the jollity endlessly babble round while she stayed fixed in one place, unable to move on even if she wanted to.

Which she didn't. It was more than she could do to make her feet carry her forward into that throng. How she wished she'd been as selfish as Lord Sinclair. If only she didn't care about the effect her actions had on others she could have stayed in the dower house on the Fallowfield estate, shut the doors and barred the windows, and spent this season doing exactly as she pleased.

Kicking chairs over, smashing vases, and ruing the day she'd tried to appeal to Lord Sinclair's better nature. For, otherwise, she would not have discovered he didn't have one.

Because she was standing in the doorway, she heard someone pounding on the front door, saw the butler, Chapman, go scuttling down the hall, and knew the reason for the sudden blast of cold air that swirled into the house.

Though she could not believe her eyes when she saw the late, and very unexpected guest handing his hat and coat to the beaming butler.

Lord Sinclair.

While she stood frozen to the spot, Sebastian went

bounding past her, grabbed his brother's hand, and pumped it up and down.

"I did not think you were coming," he said, with a delighted grin. "But it's so good to see you. Come and meet my fiancée."

Phoebe, who never strayed very far from Sebastian, materialized at Caroline's side.

"I thought you said he was not coming," she said indignantly. "I thought you said you could not change his mind."

The petulant voice drifted to Lord Sinclair as his brother tugged him across the hall, making his hackles rise. Caro's bravery in going to that tavern had impressed him even when he thought he still hated her, and this was the thanks she got?

But he gave no sign he'd heard that last remark as he bowed over Phoebe's hand, and said all that was proper. Until he said, "You have your sister to thank for my presence here today. Although at the time I was not receptive to her arguments, after she left, and I had time to reflect, I began to see that she might have had a point."

It had been the utter sincerity with which she'd given her version of the events that had driven them apart, which had done the trick. Up till that point, she'd been hiding behind a wall of pretence. Pretending she wasn't afraid, pretending she didn't care what he made her do. But when she'd told him they'd never stood a chance, she forgot everything but the unfairness of what had happened to them. For a fleeting moment he had glimpsed a pain to match his own before she closed the shutters again. But in that moment, his whole world turned upside down. Or was it the right way up? For even though he'd surely made her hate him, by the way he'd deliberately intimidated and humiliated her, he kept going back to what she'd said about this being the time of year for a new start. That no matter how low a man had sunk, Christmas was a time for redemption. Wasn't it?

His heart pounded as she looked into his eyes.

Could she tell why he'd come? Did she feel it too? The wild hope that they might be able to erase the past, and start again?

But if so, why was she frowning like that?

What was he doing here? After all he'd said? And—her brow puckered—had he robbed somebody? She couldn't think how else he had managed to get hold of such a stylish set of clothes. They all looked brand new. And so well-made that she had a brief vision of him holding some terrified tailor at gunpoint until he'd been furnished with a set of garments fit to go visiting.

While she was still reeling at the sight of him looking so vastly improved, Phoebe was hugging him, and kissing him on the cheek and prattling away.

"Oh, we are so glad to see you. And looking so well. And dressed so well! Caro said you might not be able to afford to come, but you look as fine as fivepence."

"Chapman informs me you drew up in a coach and four," said Sebastian. "So were the rumours that you gambled away your entire fortune false? If so, I am heartily glad of it."

"Rumours have a tendency to be inaccurate, Seb. Or perhaps," he said with a darkling look at Caroline, "my luck at cards took a turn for the better, and I won back everything I thought I had lost, and a bit more besides."

Lady Caroline swallowed. Was he trying to tell her something? She had never been very good at having conversations where people said one thing while meaning another.

"Well however it came about, I am glad of it," said Sebastian staunchly, thumping him on the back for good measure.

"You must come in and partake of some refreshments," said Phoebe.

"In a moment," he said. "But first I would like to have a moment alone with Lady Caroline."

Phoebe's eyes widened. "Oh! Well, if you really must…"

As she and Sebastian went back to circulate amongst their other guests, Lord Sinclair stepped round her so that his back was to the room. So nobody but her saw the way his face changed from congeniality to steely intent in the blink of an eye.

"You are dying to ask me why I have really come, aren't you? I can see questions veritably bubbling up and pressing against the back of your sweet, seductive lips," he drawled softly.

He thought her lips were seductive? All of a sudden they felt seductive. As though they'd been made for kissing.

Kissing him.

"Ask me," he said.

So sternly she daren't voice her hope he might have relented towards her.

"Is it…is it because of what I said about family? That they…they all love you, and miss you?"

He tipped his head to one side. "Partly. Yes, in part that was my motive for coming here. They, at least, have never done anything to warrant my hurting them, have they?"

Meaning that she had. But at least he was acknowledging that he had hurt them unfairly, and that he was sorry and was here to make amends.

Though he'd also said that was only part of the reason he had come. Her heart gave a girlish little skip.

"Ask me," he insisted. "Ask me what you really want to know."

She gathered her courage in both hands. "Is it because you understand, now? Is it because you have forgiven me?"

He shook his head, making her heart sink.

"It had not even occurred to me that you wanted my forgiveness. You were so very emphatic in denying you had done anything wrong," he said grimly. "So I shall just have to tell you plainly what brought me here, in spite of my aversion to weddings."

She'd given him hope, yes—but he was not a green boy any longer. He needed proof that the girl he'd fallen in love with was all he'd ever believed—that he hadn't made her up out of his own fevered imaginings and longings. For all he knew, that glimpse of what he took to be pain might only have been the last desperate attempt of a cunning woman to rouse his pity, so she could escape unscathed from what was becoming an increasingly volatile situation. Had she been clever enough to say exactly what he most wanted to hear—that she'd sacrificed herself to save her family? Or was she really someone with whom he could rebuild his future? He knew what he wanted to believe, but that was just the trouble. He wanted to believe in her far too much.

The only way to be absolutely certain about her was to test her to the limits. Only then would he find out what she was really made of.

And he may as well start by letting her know the kind of man he was now.

"And my aversion to this kind of gluttony, in the name of religion," he said, sweeping a scornful gaze round the room. "Back in London, people shiver and starve in the slums, while all this," he gestured at the laden sideboards, "is provided for people who have no need of it."

Her eyes widened. She had never suspected him of harbouring such radical zeal. But then, during the years since they'd parted he could well have experienced the hardships he'd just been speaking of for himself. The things he'd seen, and suffered, were bound to have changed him.

Well, the same could be said of her.

So when he gave her a hard smile, and said, "I have come, Lady Caroline, to collect my winnings," she barely flinched.

"I paid promptly," she retorted.

"Oh, no, you didn't. You cheated me. And after promising, practically the moment you set foot in Molly's room, that you would adhere to the exact wording of that wager."

"I did not cheat!"

"You could not have been in that room for more than twenty minutes," he said. "When we agreed upon one hour."

"But you threw me out."

"Only after you provoked me into losing my temper, by stripping in that provocative manner, leading me to suppose…all sorts of things. And then calling a halt."

"You…I…"

"You owe me another forty minutes, Caro," he said silk-ily. "Whichever way you look at it."

"What do you mean, whichever way you look at it?"

"Oh, come. I might have been the worse for drink when you played your tricks on me, but I was sober the next morning. You thought you could get away with just spending an hour in the room if you could get me confused enough. That was why you spent so long getting undressed. You hadn't done it to deliberately play the whore. You were playing for time."

"Y—yes…"

She was so glad he'd finally realized she was not the kind of woman he'd accused her of being, that it was a moment before she realized her admission had not had the effect she'd hoped for.

"You admit it? Just like that?"

"Well, yes. I…" She darted a look past him. People were watching their increasingly heated tête-à-tête with beady eyes. Since she had no wish to provide fuel for gossip, she lifted her chin, and gave him a dazzling smile.

"Get to the point, sir," she said through gritted teeth.

"You owe me," he replied with an equally forced smile, "forty minutes naked."

"I cannot believe that you have come all the way here, just to humiliate me all over again," she said. "Was that night at the Crossed Oars not enough?"

"Nobody forced you into anything," he reminded her. "You walked into that tavern of your own free will, and you agreed to the terms of our wager. You swore you would meet them. Are you telling me now that you refuse to pay up?"

"Look," she said in desperation. "You are here now. The breach with your family is healed. By the looks of you, your luck has changed. So surely, that stupid wager we made no longer matters."

"The wager is all that matters," he said fiercely. He could mend the breach with his family at any time. This was about them. And if she could still prattle on about the family, rather than seize the chance he was offering her…

Had he ever meant anything to her?

"If you intend to welch, then there is no point in me remaining." He made as though to move past her, back to the hallway.

"Wait," she cried, seizing his arm. "You cannot go now."

"Oh, yes I can. I have wished my brother well. Kissed his bride-to-be. That is already far more than anyone expected from me."

Oh, no. If he stormed off like this, after arguing with her in the doorway, everyone would think it was her fault. Everyone already knew, or thought they knew, that they had been as good as betrothed before Lord Fallowfield put in a higher bid. Everyone also knew that her marriage was the cause of his spectacular downfall. She'd lived with the blame all these years, but she was blowed if she was meekly going to let him tarnish her reputation all over again.

"What do you want me to do? Go back to that tavern and strip for you all over again?"

"No, don't be so foolish. We would not be back in time

for the wedding if we stuck to the terms of the wager that strictly."

"What then?"

He gave a slow smile.

"I am prepared to be lenient. I will accept your nudity in whatever bedroom I have been given in this house, to-night. I shall even be generous enough not to remind you that you were actually naked for a scant ten minutes of the time you were with me before. Since it is Christmas, I will reduce the tally to just half an hour."

"Oh, yes, very generous," she snapped.

"As I have already altered the location where you will pay me, yes, I think I am being very generous."

She'd taken a breath to call him a rude name when she recalled Phoebe's guests, and shut her mouth with a snap.

"And do not try to cheat me again," he said sternly. He was going to stay in charge of the situation this time. He would turn the tables on her, use the methods she'd em-ployed on him to thoroughly confuse and disarm her. And he would not relent until he'd wrung the truth out of her. "I shall not start counting the minutes until you are naked."

She gave him her most dazzling social smile. "I think I hate you," she said, dropping him a curtsey.

He bowed. "Do you mean, by that statement, that you agree to my terms?"

"Yes, damn you," she seethed. "You have given me no choice."

He gave her a grave look. "There is always a choice, Caro. It is no use blaming others for the position in which you find yourself."

So it was all her own fault, was it? She couldn't possibly have been the victim of her father's failings, or her husband's cruelty, her sister's demands, or his own need to see her humiliated. No, she had somehow brought it all on herself by making the wrong choices.

She turned on her heel and stalked away from him, although as the day progressed, it was hard to avoid him altogether.

He was one of the party that went out to gather greenery. He stayed to watch as the ladies fashioned the branches into swags and bunches, and he helped the footmen dispose them in various parts of the hall. He laughed and flirted with the younger females of the party as they fashioned kissing balls from the mistletoe. And applauded along with the others when the great Yule log was brought in, and set alight.

And every expression of enjoyment he showed only served to remind her what a cold-hearted beast he was. Tonight, she would have to make some excuse for not attending Midnight Mass so that she could go to his room and pay him what she owed.

Only this time, it would be ten times worse. Because she'd spent so many nights wishing she had not stopped him joining her on that bed.

And this time he was going to insist she lie there for a full half hour, naked.

What was she going to do if he made an attempt to touch her, this time? How would she be able to resist him?

Oh, how she hated him.

But how much more she hated herself, for still wanting him.

CHAPTER FOUR

SHE PUSHED OPEN the door to Lord Sinclair's bedchamber without knocking, slid inside and shut it firmly behind her.

He was sitting in a wingback armchair before the fire, his legs stretched out in front of him, reminding her of the position he'd adopted to watch her strip in the Crossed Oars. Only tonight, he wasn't fully dressed. He looked as though he'd started to prepare for bed, removing his jacket and waistcoat, then donned a dressing gown to take one last drink before the fire. A decanter sat on a cluttered table at his side. The only glass was the one he held in his hand, from which he was sipping.

"I approve of your attire," he said as she discarded the shawl she'd wrapped round her shoulders before scurrying along the chilly moonlit corridors to the guest wing.

Pride had made her put on her best nightwear, a confection of silk and lace, held in place by a series of ribbons she could easily slip from their bows herself. She was not going to give him any chance to lay so much as one finger on her this time.

The trouble was, the silk of her gown had already slid over her limbs like a lover's caress as she'd made her way through the deserted house to his room. It had roused her body to want things it had no business wanting. If only he didn't hate and despise her, she would have been hurrying to this clandestine assignation eagerly.

Instead of which, the very fact that they were the only ones who had not gone to church increased her feelings of shame and resentment.

He beckoned to her.

Her heart, which was already pounding from her dash through the house, picked up speed still further. Knowing that if she hesitated, she might never pluck up courage to go through with it, she tugged the ribbon of her robe loose, and let it slide from her shoulders.

The gown she wore underneath was of the sheerest ivory silk, inset with panels of blond lace. It hid virtually nothing, yet she knew he would not even permit her this much to hide behind.

Lifting her chin, she tore open the front fastenings until she could let that garment, too, slide down her body and pool round her feet on the floor.

In the distance, she heard the stable clock striking the half hour.

"No attempt to fuddle my brain with teasing and tempting me, eh? I can only assume you have learned your lesson from last time," he said wryly. "If you play with fire, you risk getting burned. And speaking of which," he said, "you had better come closer."

For a moment, she hesitated. But then, tearing her eyes

from his face, she saw he was gesturing to a mound of cushions and quilts covering the hearthrug.

Head high, she stalked across the room to where he sat. But her knees were shaking so much that she could make no attempt to sit down gracefully. She just dropped to the floor at his feet.

As soon as she'd done so, she found that the way he'd angled the fire screen had created a little nest, shielded from draughts.

"You will soon warm up," he said.

She darted a hopeful glance up at him. Surely, if he'd seen to her comfort in this way, it must be a sign that he cared for her, to some degree?

"The sight of gooseflesh is not the least bit alluring."

Her heart sank. Once again, she'd misunderstood his actions. What she'd thought of as a token of kindness had only been a precaution he'd taken to ensure nothing spoiled his own pleasure. Since he now knew she would not let him touch her, he'd set the scene to derive maximum pleasure from just looking at her. She suddenly felt like one of those slave women depicted in paintings, lying naked at the feet of some Eastern pasha. The fact that he wore a billowing silken dressing gown over his open shirt added to that impression. As did the horrid, superior look in his lazily hooded eyes.

"You look very beautiful with the firelight playing over your…hair," he said, after a few minutes silent contemplation.

She glanced up at him and met a wall of heat. She could not hold that gaze. But as her eyes drifted downward she saw that his whole body was tense, trembling. And that he was very, very aroused. Already.

And it occurred to her that she was not as powerless as she'd first felt. She had set the boundaries—that he could look, but not touch.

She got a reckless urge to tip the scales still further in her favour. She didn't see why she should be the only one feeling on edge tonight.

Keeping her eyes demurely fixed on the fire, she wriggled into the cushions as though to make herself more comfortable, whilst subtly arranging her limbs in as suggestive a pose as she dared.

When she heard his breath catch in his throat she could not resist smiling to herself.

"How long is it," he said, his eyes lingering on the curve of her lips, "since you smiled at a man, the way you used to smile at me?"

"I don't know what you mean."

"Oh, I think you do." He set the glass down on the table, and picked up a glove that had been lying there amidst the clutter.

"And I have decided that tonight I will not permit you to tell me anything other than the complete truth."

With that, he leaned forward and drew the glove down the centre of her torso, starting between her breasts, and ending at her navel.

"Stop that!"

"No. I am not breaking the terms of our agreement. I am not laying so much as one finger on you."

As he drew the glove across her stomach she couldn't help gasping, and clenching her muscles. And resenting him for taunting her with her own words by choosing a facsimile of fingers to inflict his retribution.

"D—don't," she begged him. He just smiled, and ran the glove over her hip.

Oh, but he could do anything with that glove. Flick it over her nipples, or play it between her thighs…and he wouldn't, technically, be breaking the terms upon which she'd insisted.

In an instinct for self-preservation she pressed her legs closer together, but it was too late. Moist heat was already blooming just at the thought of what he might do. And she had only been naked at his feet for five minutes.

Damn him for reasserting his dominance!

He stroked the glove right down her arm, flicking it over her fingers, as though daring her to try taking it.

For a moment she considered doing just that, and tossing his implement of torture into the fire. Only, his reactions were likely to be very quick. He would snatch his hands back. She would be obliged to kneel up and there would be an ungainly tussle. Which he would win, since he was physically stronger.

She gritted her teeth and glared at him.

"I see what this is. You have come here to get your revenge because of the way I deliberately roused and thwarted you," she said.

"Is that what you think? That I am petty enough to want revenge for what you did?" He leaned back and regarded her thoughtfully.

"If this is not some twisted form of revenge, then…"

"Caro." He sighed. "I could not let you get away with

the trick you played on me at the Crossed Oars. You would not respect a man who allowed you to best him."

Respect? How could he be talking about gaining her respect? While he was clearly intent on torturing her?

"Now," he said, drawing the glove repeatedly between his nimble fingers, and eyeing her as though wondering where to ply it next, "to business."

He started at her left knee this time and trailed the glove gently all the way up her outer thigh, then round to trace the curve of her hip.

She didn't know if it was the texture of soft leather or the knowledge that his hand had once been inside the glove,that made the light touch so very…suggestive. If his fingers were inside the leather…

"Tell me the truth," he said, his eyes gleaming with triumph when she shifted and squirmed.

"The truth about what?"

He slid the glove round her waist and slowly up her abdomen.

She caught her lower lip between her teeth as he stopped just beneath her left breast, remembering the time, so many years before, when she'd let him take it in his hand. He'd stroked it gently, palmed it, then bent his head to kiss its upper slope. The sensations he'd provoked had been so pleasurable, so strong, she'd taken fright and pushed him away. She closed her eyes and bit back a moan as those feelings surged through her all over again.

Stronger than ever. For she hadn't been naked then, alone in his room in an empty house. If it was his hand on her breast now, rather than just a glove, would she have the strength to resist him? She'd regretted, so many, many times not having yielded her virginity to him, the man she'd loved. Then the brutish husband she loathed would not have been able to rip it from her.

"Are you going to beg me for mercy?"

The mockery in his voice jolted her from her reverie, and back to seething resentment.

"Never!"

"No, you are far too proud," he said, drawing the glove across to her other breast. "When your back is to the wall, you refuse to let anyone see your fear. You would rather cover it all up with a smile," he said, circling her nipple with one finger of the empty glove. "I was too young to understand it at your betrothal ball, but since then, I've been in some pretty tight spots myself."

As her nipple contracted almost painfully, he mused, "I never touched this breast before. Never sucked this nipple into my mouth and felt it harden against my tongue…"

Damn him! He knew was he was doing to her. The combination of those light, almost-there touches, and his evocative words, were driving her mad.

"I recognized the desperation behind your smiles that night at the Crossed Oars," he said as he slid the glove down into the valley between her breasts, and slowly lower.

"I recalled that it was exactly the way you smiled when your father announced your betrothal to Fallowfield." The glove hovered just above the thatch of curls at the juncture of her thighs. She pressed herself down into the cushions to avoid its touch. Because if he touched her there…

"So when you gave me your version of why you went through with the marriage it all fell into place."

She heaved a sigh of relief—or was it regret?—when he

stopped threatening her with the most intimate touch of all, and drew the glove slowly back up her stomach, between her breasts, up her neck, then gently, oh, so gently, round the outline of her mouth.

"It was exactly the way you smiled in the tavern. Hard, determined, without a trace of real joy. For show, not for real."

Through the haze of lust he'd created, she felt yet another of those irrational spurts of hope. He believed her!

"But you were so angry with me," she said, raising her hand to push the glove away from her mouth.

He let it go with a rueful smile, and she found herself in possession of it.

"You assumed I wanted you upstairs to make up for what I hinted I would have missed with Molly. You turned your back to me, expecting me to be bastard enough to undo your laces. It was what you thought of me, and your willingness to just give in to such demands that made me want to slide my hands up round your neck and throttle you." He looked down at his hands, which he promptly clasped tightly between his knees.

"I could not bear the thought of you playing the whore, confirming my worst suspicions of you," he grated. "You are still the most beautiful woman I've ever known. How, I wondered, could you be so lovely on the outside, yet so full of ugliness inside?"

"I'm not—I didn't…"

"I know. I know now, that is, but that night…" He shook his head. "Yes, I was furious when you would not let me so much as kiss you. But at the same time, it was a huge relief to see something of the old Caro still existed—the one I'd begun to think I'd imagined. Once I sobered up, I began to admire the way you'd played the hand you'd been dealt. That's one of the reasons I came here today. Some men feel threatened when a woman shows she's got brains, but I've always relished a challenge."

With a wicked smile, he turned to the table, and picked up the other glove.

"Which is why I have to demonstrate who is in charge here, tonight," he said in a low, playful voice.

She swallowed. Her brief respite was over. The sensual torment was about to begin all over again.

Only this time, it was not so much the whisper of sensation the glove created, but the look in his eyes as he traced the outline of her body, which excited her.

"It was not avarice that drove you to marry Fallowfield, was it?"

"You know it wasn't."

Slowly, oh so slowly, he trailed the glove down the centre of her tummy.

"How would you describe it, then?"

"Duty…" she just managed to gasp plaintively as those leathern fingers brushed over her feminine curls. She was panting now, her heart hammering in her chest.

"Just as it was your duty to come and find me, and make sure I attended Sebastian and Phoebe's wedding?"

"Yes, yes," she whimpered. She no longer cared that he was subjugating her. She'd never felt this aroused in her entire life. Though she was beginning to hate that glove. She wanted his hand on her. There. She let her thighs fall apart. He dipped the glove between her legs but it wasn't enough. She whimpered, then bit down on a plea that he would stop teasing and really touch her.

"Why don't you value yourself more, Caro?"

His question was like a slap in the face.

"You...you..." She snatched the glove from him, furious that he'd driven her so far, only to mock her again.

"Why did you let them drive you to come and find me, knowing you would have to face my antagonism?"

He did not seem in the least bothered that she was now in possession of both his gloves. He just carried on speaking, his voice low and steady.

"And why did you let me foist that devil's bargain onto you?"

He dipped his index finger into his glass of wine.

"How could you sacrifice yourself for your family, all over again?"

She flinched as he leaned forward, and very deliberately sprinkled several drops of the ruby-red liquid onto her right breast.

"Did you think it would make them respect you?"

She shook her head furiously, not sure whether she was answering his question or trying to deny the feeling of being so completely at his mercy.

"From what I have observed, Phoebe is a spoilt madam, who cares only for herself. And as for your father..." His face twisted in disgust.

Just as the stable clock struck midnight.

"It is Christmas Day," he said flatly. "Our bargain is at an end. You have paid in full."

He sat back, but his eyes followed the droplets of wine

as they merged then slid down the slope of her breast toward her cleavage.

She saw hunger in his face, but what moved her to speak was the sadness she sensed in him. A sadness that matched her own.

"What if I tell you that I don't want to leave?"

His eyes flew to hers. His chest heaved as he sucked in a deep breath.

"It is a new day. Couldn't we agree that whatever happens, from this moment on, can happen because it is what we both choose?"

He dropped to his knees at her side.

"You would choose me? Freely?"

In silent invitation, she held out her arms to him.

With a groan, he bent his head and licked along the trail of wine, laving the side of her breast before swirling his tongue round her nipple, then sucking it into his mouth.

With a wild cry, Caroline arched up off the cushions, and clasped him round his neck.

His mouth met hers then, in a passionate kiss. As their tongues tangled, she pushed the robe from his shoulders, marvelling at the feel of sculpted muscles under her questing fingers. She drew back briefly to admire his body, gleaming in the golden glow of firelight. Then it was her turn to run her hands all over him. She caressed his chest, his taut abdomen. He flung his head back with a groan when she found the fastenings at the waist of his breeches and fumbled them undone.

"Just once, Crispin, just once let us love each other, not because of any obligation, or out of vengeance or...or anything but because we just want each other."

"No!"

To her utter shock and dismay, he reared back as though she'd struck him.

"I won't let you use me," he grated. "You are only acting like this because I roused you past the point of bearing."

He scrambled back to the chair, ploughing his fingers through his hair.

"God knows I have sunk about as low as a man can get, but I refuse to let you treat me as though I am worthless. As though I mean nothing to you. I have had enough of meaningless couplings over the past six years. I tried so hard to blot you out of my mind, with drink and vice of all sorts. But the hell of my own making was no improvement over the hell of imagining you with him…laughing at me…"

"I never laughed at you…"

He carried on as though he hadn't heard her.

"And if you let me into your body tonight, then walk away from me once more, I don't…" He thrust his fingers through his hair again. "I will survive. Don't go getting the idea I will do anything dramatic or foolhardy. But there will be no coming back from your defection, not a second time."

She knelt, and placed one hand on his knee. Tears streamed down her face.

"Crispin, surely you know by now that I would never deliberately hurt you? I—I love you."

There. She had said it. He might say he no longer believed in love, but it made no difference. She could not deny what she felt. What she had always felt for this man.

He seized her hands and clasped them between his own.

"Love isn't always enough," he said grimly. "Not in your

case. When it was tested, last time, you put duty to others first. And don't say you had no choice," he put his fingers to her lips when she was about to protest exactly that.

"There is always a choice," he finished fiercely.

"Well now I choose you. I do!"

"Only because you lust after my body. You would not entrust your whole future to me."

"I would!"

"Would you indeed?" He looked at her intently. "I have seen how far you will go for duty. But how far would you go for what you say is love? I have already told you that I will never touch a penny of that man's money. And I cannot keep you in the style to which you've become accustomed."

"I don't care! Not about his money,or the life he insisted we follow. I hated it. Every minute of it. You have no idea how worthless I felt, how cheap and tawdry, in spite of… no—" she laughed bitterly "—because of the jewels he made me wear. Each one of them was a reproach. They weighed me down like manacles."

"You are not worthless." He stroked her face. "And you deserve better than to live in a hovel with a man like me."

"If only I could believe you loved me, that you really wanted to spend the rest of our lives together, that it would make you happy, I would…I would even get a job in the Crossed Oars!"

His mouth firmed and he flung her hands from him. For one awful moment, she thought it was because he did not believe her. But then she saw he was rummaging through the heap of papers on the table. He stopped when he came to one particular document.

"This is a special licence," he said, handing it to her. "If you mean what you say, we can make it a double wedding with your sister and my brother. "Well," he continued with a nonchalant shrug, "you know I cannot stand weddings, so it makes sense to get it over with while there's already a wedding breakfast organized."

She clasped the licence to her breast. He might feign nonchalance, but she could see through him. After that incident in the Crossed Oars, he'd gone straight out and procured a licence. Which meant that he'd come down here hoping for a chance to ask her to marry him. When she'd reacted to his arrival in that aloof and frosty manner, he'd applied what pressure he could to break down all her barriers.

Until he could discover the true state of her heart.

And only then had he dared to bare his own.

It had not been about revenge at all.

"This is the best Christmas present I could ever have," she whispered. "To know that you still love me, in spite of everything."

"I never stopped," he admitted soberly. "I couldn't. It was what made life so painful. But you understand that, don't you? You hid your wounds behind a smile, while I mostly smothered mine under a mountain of bitterness. But I didn't know what to do with the pain you inflicted by coming into the Crossed Oars and asking me, not to come back to you, but to go to somebody else's bloody wedding! So I lashed out at you. I wanted you to hurt the way I did. Can you ever forgive me?"

"Of course I forgive you. You were hurt and angry, and…a trifle castaway…" She smiled up at him impishly.

And then said, "You aren't really going to make me wait until after the ceremony, are you?"

He looked down the length of her naked body, his eyes hot and hungry.

"God forgive me, but no," he grated, sweeping her into his arms.

They kissed passionately as they fell in a tangle of limbs onto the cushions.

"Perhaps I should just confess," he said, as he raised himself to push his breeches to his knees, "that I am no longer quite so hard up as everyone believes."

"Really?" She pouted, then reached for him. "You look hard enough for my purposes," she purred, stroking along his magnificent length.

"Witch," he gasped, sinking down onto her, and then, most satisfyingly, into her.

His moan of pleasure reverberated through her whole body. She'd never dreamed joining with a man could feel so wonderful. She wound her legs round his waist and clung to him tightly as he went wild. But the harder he pounded into her, the better it felt. He thrust into her so deeply it was as though he wanted to reach the very heart of her. And her joy just kept on building until she could no longer contain it. Bliss ripped through her, radiating outward from that place they were joined, until it seemed to shoot out from the tips of her toes. Her fingers clenched his shoulders as she cried out in rapture. He let out a triumphant roar, shuddering all over.

"I feel…as though I've come home," he sighed as they slumped together, sated, into the cushions.

"I know exactly what you mean," she agreed. "We belong together. We always have. And," she planted a fervent kiss on his throat, "we always will."

* * * * *

A Lady's Lesson
in Seduction

BARBARA MONAJEM

Barbara Monajem grew up in western Canada. She wrote her first story in third grade about apple tree gnomes. After dabbling in neighbourhood musicals and teen melodrama, she published a middle-grade fantasy when her children were young. Now her kids are adults and she writes historical and paranormal romance for grown-ups. She lives in Georgia, USA, with an ever-shifting population of relatives, friends and mostly feline strays.

To Katherine Briggs, author of the delightful children's story *Hobberdy Dick*, about a hobgoblin who protects a house in Puritan times. Dick is the inspiration for the hobgoblin hovering unseen in the background of this story, adding a wee bit of magic to a Christmas tale.

CAMDEN FOLK, Marquis of Warbury, dumped an armful of holly cuttings on the vast dining table at his country estate. A vigorous tramp through the home wood to collect greenery, one of the pleasures of the Christmas season, had heightened his anticipation. Soon Frances Burdett would arrive, and after a year of patience—and no women—he would finally get on with his life.

Not that he'd chosen to be celibate for the past year. He'd merely lost interest in dalliance, but he knew what had caused the problem and what would fix it. Once he'd seduced Frances Burdett and made amends for the past, he would go on his merry way once more. Back to the good old days when he'd indulged himself with many women, made a point of giving them as much pleasure as possible, and then moved on—no harm done.

He smiled at his mother, who was fashioning evergreens into swags to decorate the banisters. 'Here you are, Mama. Tomorrow we'll go to the orchard for mistletoe.'

Edwin Folk, his cousin, dropped a bundle of holly onto

the table with a groan. 'More walking about in this frigid weather?' He stripped off his gloves and went to warm his hands at the fire.

'Think of the reward at the end of it, Edwin,' Lady Warbury said, tying a strip of red silk around a sprig of rosemary. 'We'll make kissing rings, and the house will be filled with lovely young ladies.'

'If they get here,' Edwin said gloomily. 'It's started snowing again. Do you think it will be bad, Cam?'

The marquis shrugged. They were almost certain to be snowed in, probably without some of the kissable ladies, but the only one he cared about was Frances Burdett, who should arrive at any moment. He'd had to resort to subterfuge to get her here at all. She'd made it clear to the Polite World that she didn't blame him for the death of her husband, but she'd refused to talk to him after the accident and still treated him with the barest civility. Most likely, she despised him. He couldn't fault her for that.

But now, after more than a year's mourning, she'd told everyone that she would never marry again.

And Cam knew why.

Not that he could tell her that, or how he knew. But if only he could manage to seduce her, he could prove to her that her husband's cruel verdict—that she was a cold, passionless woman—was entirely wrong. Such a young, desirable creature shouldn't cut herself off from the pleasures of life, and he meant to make sure she didn't.

It was a case of honour. Of living up to the family motto, 'Do no harm.' For her own sake as well as his, he *must* succeed in seducing Frances Burdett.

'What else do you want, Mama?' he asked. 'Hawthorn? Ivy?'

'No hawthorn.' His mother raised her hands as if to ward off evil. 'Thomas says it's bad luck to cut hawthorn except when it's in bloom.'

'Very well—what the Druid says, goes.' Mr. Thomas Lumpkin, whose enormous beard and study of pagan customs had earned him the nickname of Druid, had first come to Warbury Hall to study its history but had soon become his mother's friend and lover. Cam didn't know which lore he believed and which he didn't—lately, he mostly didn't—but tradition mattered at Warbury House, and he didn't begrudge his mother and Lumpkin their fun.

'Dear me, it has started to come down, hasn't it?' said his mother, watching the steadily thickening snow. 'I hope *some* of our guests arrive.'

Cam laid his gloves on the table and wandered to the sideboard to pour brandy for himself and Edwin. 'I could do without most of them.' He'd supported his mother's plans and encouraged Edwin's infatuation with Almeria Dane only because Frances Burdett was the girl's chaperone. He couldn't think of any other way to get close to Frances for long enough to win her over.

'The young people can be counted upon to enter into the spirit of the festivities,' Lady Warbury said, 'unlike some thirty-year-old curmudgeons I know.'

'I'm not yet thirty, nor am I a curmudgeon,' Camden said. 'I'm simply, er, past the age of youthful folly.'

'What nonsense,' his mother said. 'As I have recently proven, one is never too old for folly.'

He snorted. 'I can't argue with that.' Her love affair with the Druid was a matter for much ribald jesting in the ton.

'I'm having fun with dear Thomas. Perhaps one of the lively girls I've invited will reawaken your spirit of adventure, too. Almeria Dane, for example. Such a pretty girl.' She threw a teasing glance at Edwin. 'Don't you agree?'

'She's ravishingly beautiful, as everyone knows.' Edwin, irritable the instant it was suggested he might have a rival, pretended to savour the bouquet of the brandy.

'But so appallingly young,' Cam said. 'And giggly.' Fortunately for him, if not for Edwin, his mother had invited plenty of other men for Almeria to flirt with.

'Are you sure you don't want me to invite someone for you, Cam?' Lady Warbury said. 'Even at such short notice, I can find you a widow to dally with.'

And she would, if he didn't put a stop to it immediately. 'Mama, I suppose you think it's very enlightened of you, but there's a difference between turning a blind eye to my peccadilloes and acting as a procuress.'

Edwin choked on his brandy, but Lady Warbury merely rolled her eyes. 'I want you to enjoy yourself, Camden. A passionate woman in your bed at night will make up for being obliged to play host to a group of people who don't interest you.'

At least she wasn't matchmaking again. For years, she'd introduced him to one marriageable female after another, but he'd succeeded in fending them all off. 'I'll be fine,' he said, and fortunately a bustle from the front of the house prevented her from making any more unacceptable suggestions. 'Perhaps our cousins have arrived.' Or better, Frances Burdett.

He couldn't recall a more tangled mess of emotions than what he'd felt after Timothy Burdett's death: anger, chagrin, guilt… Not that Timothy hadn't deserved a good tongue-lashing. He'd maundered on in the vilest manner about his disappointment with Frances, his wife of only two weeks. Then Cam, in his arrogant, tactless way— what an ass he'd been—had said he could teach Timothy a thing or two about how to please a woman. Angry words had quickly become blows, and when Timothy had challenged Cam to a curricle race, then and there, Cam had of course agreed.

And Timothy, made careless by drink and rage, had overturned his curricle and broken his neck.

In the midst of the ensuing scandal—for everyone who'd heard the quarrel assumed they were fighting over some doxy—a sexually voracious lady, wife of an older man, had approached Cam with the sort of prurient suggestions he'd once enjoyed, and he'd been disgusted with both himself and her. He'd been unable to drum up any enthusiasm for dalliance since.

Maybe he *had* been a bit of a curmudgeon lately, but not for much longer. He put on the smile of a delighted host as he entered the Great Hall. The porter was holding the front door wide open, looking perplexed. A petite blonde stood in the entry, divesting herself of cloak and muff, while a middle-aged abigail and two footmen bustled about with bandboxes and trunks.

'Oh, do come inside, dearest!' the blonde cried, stamping her feet. 'I shall catch my death of cold. You can decipher inscriptions some other time.'

A soft voice carried from outdoors. 'What a pity I don't read Latin.'

No, the pity was that the damned family motto, which he'd so badly failed to live up to, was prominently displayed in every single room of his house.

It's only for a fortnight, Frances Burdett told herself sternly, hovering on the bottom step of Warbury Hall. Snowflakes landed on her eyelashes and nose. She was cold and tired, and after hours in a frigid coach with her prattling cousin Almeria, her head ached abominably. She longed for warmth, quiet and solitude, and the only way to get it was to go indoors, brave the Marquis of Warbury, and ask to be conducted speedily to her bedchamber.

Instead she remained outdoors, peering at the inscription above the door.

It was just so *awkward* visiting Warbury House. The marquis had called on her in London three times right after Timothy's fatal accident, and three times she'd had him turned away. It had been frightfully ill-mannered of her, but she'd been so sickened and angry that she couldn't bring herself to see him. Not for his part in Timothy's death, but because he and Timothy had been quarreling over a prostitute.

She'd written to the marquis to reassure him that she didn't hold him responsible for the curricle accident. Not only that, she'd told the world the same thing over and over—that racing whilst drunk was the sort of stupid thing young men did, and Timothy was entirely to blame. If that didn't make up for her rudeness, there was no help for it.

'Frances, I'm turning to *ice* in here.' That was Almeria again.

'In a moment,' Frances said. Her head pounded wearily, and she frowned up at the inscription, trying to sound preoccupied while she gathered her courage. '*Secundum*...that seems obvious, but...'

Lord Warbury had made no attempt to speak to her again in the little over a year since Timothy's death, so the invitation to the Christmas house party had come as a surprise. Only one explanation made sense—that Lord Warbury was romantically interested in Almeria Dane, the young, motherless cousin whom Frances now chaperoned.

'The porter can't keep the door open forever!'

'Coming, Almeria.' In her opinion, Almeria was too young and innocent for the rakish marquis, but she was a beautiful heiress, and society considered him an excellent catch. Whether she liked it or not, it was Frances's duty to promote the match. She took a deep breath and—

'Welcome, Mrs. Burdett, Miss Dane.' The Marquis of Warbury's voice made her shiver, and not from the cold. He had always had that strange effect on her, as if the warmth of his voice vibrated through her. He appeared in the doorway and came down the steps toward Frances. 'It's the family motto, or at least half of it.' He turned and stood beside her, gazing up at the weathered stone. '*Secundum, Non Nocere*. Translated, it says, Secondly, Do No Harm.'

She pulled herself together. 'That sounds typically motto-like—stern and idealistic. What is the first half?'

His eyes lit suddenly, touched with mischief. It made something swell within her chest, something she didn't un-

derstand. Relief? She'd been rather afraid he would bear a
grudge because of her rudeness.

'No one knows,' he said. 'My cousins and I used to
make up the first part ourselves. Firstly, Eat Beans, and
Secondly, Do No Harm.'

A bubble of laughter escaped Frances, and Lord Warbury grinned down at her.

Instinctively, she stiffened. Since her short, disastrous
marriage, she avoided men with that sort of grin. Other
women might enjoy succumbing to such rakish charm, but
for Frances that would only lead to misery.

Consternation erased the smile. 'I beg your pardon—
that's not the sort of jest one repeats to a lady.'

'I didn't mind,' she protested, instantly contrite. 'It's
just the kind of thing my brothers would have delighted
in.' She didn't wish to do away with his smile—merely
its effect on her.

Once she'd gotten over the shock of Timothy's death,
all she'd felt was relief. But she couldn't say so, nor could
she tell people that she'd hated marital relations. That she'd
cried herself to sleep when Timothy had turned from her
in scorn, saying she was a bore in bed, and had gone to
some doxy instead.

Judging by gossip, other women enjoyed carnal relations very much. That made Frances feel even more of a
failure, but she knew better than to inflict her cold, tedious
self on another man. She would never take a lover, never
remarry, and that was that.

Lord Warbury's warm voice assailed her again. 'We
have no idea how the family managed to lose the first part
of its motto. The second half is found frequently indoors

as well as over all exterior doors and on the turret, so we assume the loss predates the house, which is Elizabethan.' He took her arm and escorted her through the doorway into a vast hall. 'I trust your journey went well?'

She stepped away from him, smoothing her skirts as an excuse. She summoned the vague smile she used to keep her distance from gentlemen as a whole and attractive ones in particular, and murmured, 'Yes, thank you, my lord.'

Almeria launched into excited speech. 'Lord Warbury, how *kind* of you to invite us!' She gazed rapturously up at him. 'We've been in an *agony* of excitement for weeks.' She batted her eyelashes. 'What a *magnificent* estate you have.'

With difficulty, Frances refrained from rolling her eyes. Almeria was only eighteen, so no better could be expected of her. How an experienced gentleman like Lord Warbury could find such youthful silliness appealing, she had no idea. However, if it meant he would turn his attractive smiles on Almeria and leave Frances be, she would muddle through the next fortnight reasonably well.

She couldn't avoid him entirely, though. She had a duty to assess his reaction to Almeria, so she closed her eyes briefly to ward off the headache and then opened them again.

And caught him frowning at her instead. His eyes flicked back to Almeria, but he staved off her babble with a hand and returned to Frances. 'Excuse me, Mrs. Burdett, but are you quite well?'

'Mrs. Burdett has a headache,' Almeria cooed. 'I daresay she needs to rest in a darkened room, like my poor mama used to do. Oh, there's Mr. Edwin Folk.' She flashed

Lord Warbury a wide smile and tripped away to greet his cousin.

Leaving Frances alone with the marquis and inexplicably annoyed. 'I don't need a darkened room.'

'A respite from your cousin's chatter, perhaps?' he asked, and she blinked at him in surprise. 'Ah, here comes my mother. She will know what to do for you.'

Lady Warbury swanned up to greet her. She was an odd figure at the best of times, and now, dressed in a voluminous robe that looked more like a wrapper than a gown, she seemed positively outré.

But so very welcoming and kind. She embraced Frances, and when Lord Warbury mentioned her headache, passed her into the care of a motherly housekeeper who showed her to her room with a promise of a bracing cup of tea.

She had changed. Cam had always liked Frances, always found her an attractive woman—but out there on the steps with snowflakes on her lashes, hazel eyes sparkling, cheeks flushed with cold and her lush chestnut hair framing her face, she'd shone with such vivid life… He'd been hard put to say anything coherent, which was why he'd blurted out that vulgar boys' jest.

Not that she'd minded that. She'd flinched not at the jest, but at his smile. She'd stiffened and her laughter had died, and when he'd taken her arm to escort her indoors, she'd moved away at the first possible moment.

Damn. Usually, that smile beguiled women quickly into bed. This wasn't going to be as easy as he'd hoped.

'Are you all right, Cam?' His mother peered at him in

something between consternation and amusement. 'You knew Mrs. Burdett was coming.'

The last thing he needed was his mother realizing what he intended for Frances. He thrust a plausible lie into the awkward silence. 'Seeing her brought it all back—the quarrel and Timothy's death. Perhaps, for her sake, I should have stayed in London over Christmas.' Hopefully that would stop his mother from drawing the wrong conclusion.

'For heaven's sake, why? She doesn't blame you, does she? As I recall, she never did. She put the blame squarely on Timothy himself.'

'But I felt responsible,' he said. 'I wouldn't want to spoil her enjoyment of the holidays.'

'Nonsense, she'll be perfectly fine. We need you here. No one makes lamb's wool like you do. No one else can crown the King of the Revels. And what about serving treats to the Luck?' She paused. 'Not thatThomas wouldn't love to do it. That's what drew him here in the first place, you know. Houses with their own hobgoblins are few and far between. But I don't think Duff the Luck would take it well. He expects *you* to give him his due.'

Glad of the change of subject, Cam agreed. The resident hobgoblin, also known as the Luck of the House, was one of the Warbury legends. As a child, Cam had seen the little fellow now and then out of the corner of his eye; now, he wasn't sure what was memory and what was imagination. It didn't matter. The traditions about the hobgoblin did no harm, and Cam intended to support and preserve them.

By dusk, so much snow had fallen that the roads would be impassable for days. The expected cousins had arrived, as well as another young man and a couple, the Cutlows.

A half hour before dinner and well after dark, Mr. Lumpkin rode up on horseback, to Lady Warbury's great relief. He had spent a few days at the Rollright Stones, deeming Yule the perfect occasion for a visit to such an ancient monument.

Cam didn't care one way or another about the stone circle. He did care about the way the eldest of his cousins, Alan Folk, was eyeing Frances Burdett's bosom. Alan reminded him uncomfortably of himself several years earlier—except that generally the ladies he'd ogled had welcomed the attention.

'Alan,' he said. His cousin turned, and Cam gave him a look that even an idiot couldn't misinterpret. Alan scowled but immediately turned his attention to Mrs. Cutlow, who welcomed vulgar leers. The unhappy flush drained from Mrs. Burdett's cheeks, and when Cam caught her eye, she nodded her thanks, and her lips twisted into something approaching a smile.

Well, that was a start.

Frances found herself seated next to Alan Folk, whose manners had undergone an abrupt improvement just before dinner. She knew whom she had to thank. She told herself the marquis was merely acting his proper role of watchful and considerate host, but that didn't stop her heart from warming to him. He could have been cold and horrid to her instead, and she wouldn't have blamed him. He'd done nothing wrong in quarreling about a prostitute. He wasn't a newly married man, and he hadn't deserved her anger a year ago.

While she pondered him, she found other parts of her anatomy warming to him, as well.

Horrified, she quelled that unexpected, uncalled for, *completely* unacceptable kindling of desire. Once, long ago… Was it only a little over a year? It felt like a century. Once, she'd believed herself a passionate woman. She'd felt the stirrings of arousal when in the company of an attractive man. She'd dreamed of kissing and lovemaking as every other young woman did.

Until she found out that kissing was mostly sloppy and unpleasant, and that she felt absolutely nothing during lovemaking. After Timothy told her what a bore she was, she'd thought herself thoroughly cured of carnal desire… until now.

It must be because of Lord Warbury's reputation as a skilful lover. More than once, she'd heard a fast widow or unfaithful wife lamenting her inability to lure him to bed. That smile of his had set Frances's imagination moving as if she were a young girl once more.

But she wasn't. She must put a stop to such thoughts straightaway. She gazed about the room seeking something to pretend interest in… There was the Warbury half motto again, over the fireplace. She'd noticed it in the Great Hall as well, and in her bedchamber.

She made polite conversation, avoided looking at the marquis—except to note his mild flirtation with Almeria, who sat next to him, chattering happily—and concentrated on the excellent food, finishing up with two helpings of a truly magnificent trifle. When they adjourned to the drawing room, Frances had her embroidery frame brought downstairs, but her attention kept wandering and so did her stitches, away from the pattern she'd drawn.

Mrs. Cutlow sat next to her on the sofa and made some bland comments about Frances's pattern. Frances knit her brows. Judging by the woman's low-cut gown and roving eyes, Mrs. Cutlow wasn't likely to engage another female in conversation without some ulterior motive.

She wasted no time coming to the point. She leaned close and murmured, 'Has he asked for Miss Dane's hand?'

'Who?' Frances asked, purposely obtuse. 'Lord Warbury, you mean? No, he hasn't.'

'Not yet, then. But there's no other reason why she would be invited.' Mrs. Cutlow pouted. 'She's very young and beautiful. They say he's become harder to seduce lately.'

'I wouldn't know,' Frances said. Perhaps he'd merely learnt discretion, but she doubted Mrs. Cutlow wanted to hear that.

'He can't tup the girl until he's wed to her, so I shan't give up hope. He's the reason we accepted the invitation.' She gazed hungrily to where Lord Warbury played chess with Mr. Cutlow. 'My husband and I both prefer variety in bed. The marquis is so very handsome, isn't he?'

'Very,' Frances agreed, but she couldn't help but be glad when Mrs. Cutlow sidled away, and even gladder when everyone went to bed early to get well rested for the revels of Christmas Eve.

But tired though she was, Frances couldn't sleep. Thoughts of the marquis intruded into her attempts at counting sheep. She dozed and woke, dozed and woke again—this time with her hand between her legs.

She was as bad as Mrs. Cutlow!

Aghast at where her reaction to Lord Warbury had led her, she climbed out of bed and put on her wrapper and slippers. Perhaps a glass of warm milk would put her properly to sleep.

She preferred not to wake one of the servants, who deserved their rest as much as anyone. She lit her bedroom candle and tiptoed downstairs through the cold, quiet house, rendered even stiller and colder by the snowy night. It took a while, but eventually she found the huge, ancient kitchen.

Someone else was already there.

Cam couldn't believe his eyes. He blinked, but the vision in the doorway truly was Frances Burdett in a rose-coloured wrapper, chestnut hair down her back. His long-neglected cock stirred to life.

He ordered it to cease and desist. 'Do come in, Mrs. Burdett. It's only me.'

She let out a soft sigh and took a few steps into the room. Her voice quivered. 'I couldn't sleep but didn't wish to disturb the servants. I should like to warm some milk.'

'A happy coincidence,' he said. 'I was doing just that.' He beckoned to her to come closer, and when she hesitated, put his finger to his lips and indicated a pallet in the shadows. 'We should keep our voices down, as the kitchen boy is asleep in that corner.'

That seemed to reassure her, for she approached, watching him add milk to the pot on the stove. 'You couldn't sleep, either?' Her voice still trembled, which irked him.

'No, my conscience awakened me.' Before she could

read something improper into that, he said, 'I forgot to feed the Luck.'

'The Luck?'

'The Luck of the House,' he said, and then, curiously reluctant to explain, he added, 'Our resident hobgoblin. It's one of our Christmas traditions to offer him treats in return for guarding the house the rest of the year.'

Her smile dazzled his eyes. 'What a delightful custom!'

That was how he'd felt about it during his childhood. Inordinately glad that she hadn't snickered or made an incredulous face, he said, 'He's been with us for centuries. According to legend, it was due to Duff the Luck that we managed to regain Warbury Hall during Puritan times.'

She put out her hands to warm them over the stove. He found himself wanting to fill his gaze with her, to drink in her sweetness, but afraid of disconcerting her, he took a knife and began to slice a small loaf of bread the cook had left for him on one of the deal tables, along with a pipkin of cream. 'Our cook prepares manchet especially for the hob at this season. I don't suppose she believes in him, but she's a great upholder of tradition.'

'But you believe in him?'

He spread cream on a slice of manchet. 'I glimpsed him now and then as a child. That is, I thought I did. At this distance, it's hard to say what was real and what wasn't. Life tends to…oh, drain away one's childish wonder.'

'Indeed it does,' she said, a world of the unhappily unsaid lurking in her voice, sending him back in memory to the day of that fateful race. He'd come to call on Timothy so they could walk together to their club. He'd seen

Frances in passing and remarked to Timothy on her pallor, wondering if she was ill.

To which his friend had shrugged and said, 'Not that I know of, but she might as well be dead for all the pleasure I'm getting out of her.' By the time Timothy finished unburdening himself, Cam was furious.

He still was, just thinking about it. On her wedding day, Frances had glowed with health and happiness, and a mere fortnight later, she'd resembled a wraith. She'd recovered her health and beauty now, but that wasn't good enough.

He didn't expect or even want to regain his own wonder, but he would do his damndest to restore some of hers. He put the slice of bread on a saucer. 'Here, try some.'

She shook her head. 'Oh, no, I shouldn't take the hobgoblin's food.'

'He won't mind,' Cam said. 'Duff's a hospitable hob. In fact, he might take offense if you don't allow him to share.'

She laughed. 'All right, then.' She bit into the manchet and closed her eyes, savouring it as she'd done the trifle at supper. For a long moment—and he prayed no one had noticed—he'd been unable to drag his eyes away. He didn't try to drag them away now.

She swallowed, whispered, 'Thank you, Duff,' and opened her eyes.

A flush crawled up her throat. The expression on his face… oh, it terrified her. The joy drained away. She clutched her arms about herself.

'Oh, hell,' he muttered. 'I've upset you, haven't I?'

'No,' she said quickly, 'no, of course not.'

Skeptically, he raised his brows. 'You looked utterly

blissful a moment ago, as if that bite of manchet gave you great pleasure.'

Pleasure.... The word echoed through her mind.

'And watching you gave *me* great pleasure,' he said, his warm voice curling into her like tendrils.

'Er…' She couldn't think what to say.

'You had that same blissful expression when eating the trifle at dinner,' he said, 'and why not? Food is one of the great sensual delights.' His smile was rueful. 'But now you look as though you're about to be ill.'

She shook her head, shivering, holding herself tighter, fumbling for something, *anything* to say. He was right, of course. She derived great sensual pleasure from excellent food. Just because she was unsuited to one sort of pleasure didn't mean she couldn't experience another.

He huffed. 'I'm an idiot. While I maunder on, you're turning to ice.' He stripped off his banyan and held it out. 'Put this on.'

'But—but you'll be cold,' she whispered, staring helplessly. His nightshirt was open at the neck, and a few dark hairs curled through. He had more hair on his chest than Timothy had.

Why was she *thinking* such a thing?

'No, I'm usually too hot.' Briefly, he covered her still-cold hand with his large, warm one. 'See?' He thrust the banyan at her. 'I'm only wearing this for decency's sake, in case Mrs. Cutlow prowls the corridors hoping to seduce me.'

She didn't know why that frank remark made her feel more comfortable; he was a rake, and house parties were notorious for illicit liaisons. Perhaps it was the notion that

despite his reputation, he didn't hop into bed with just anyone. She put her arms into the banyan and tied it tightly
around herself. It was warm, and it smelled of him.

'Better?' he said.

'Yes,' she whispered. 'Thank you.'

With a faint smile, he turned away to slice the rest of
the manchet. Suddenly overcome with fatigue, she closed
her eyes and took a deep breath.

Desire shot through her, coursing all the way down her
spine.

What was the *matter* with her? Such thoughts and feelings were insanity, and yet his scent in the banyan flooded
her with sensations so fierce she couldn't resist them. She
inhaled again, *deeply,* wishing she could hold his scent in
her nostrils, recall it when alone in her bedchamber once
again, because it made her feel so impossibly *good.* She
breathed him in, over and over.

'Are you all right?' She opened her eyes to find him
watching her again. 'Don't fall asleep on your feet.'

A telltale flush climbed up her cheeks. Hopefully in
this dim light he wouldn't see it. 'I wasn't falling asleep.'

'No?' He raised his brows, and his smile held more than
a hint of mischief. He proffered a cup. 'Your milk is ready.'

'Oh. Thank you.' She took the cup. 'I'd better go.' She
set the cup down to untie the banyan.

'Don't,' he said. 'Come with me to feed the hob, and
then I'll take you upstairs the back way. It's much quicker.'

'Thank you,' she said.

'My pleasure.' That word again. His warm voice caressed her beautifully, unbearably.

He led her to a pantry and set the manchet and milk on the topmost shelf. 'Will it be gone by morning?' she asked.

'No doubt,' he said, 'but skeptics attribute that to rats. It's an insult to poor Duff, who's a tidy eater. Not a crumb will remain behind, nor a drop of milk.'

She didn't know whether or not he was serious, but how sweet to believe for a moment in magic, even if it was childish magic rather than a young girl's dreams of love.

On the way out, she spied writing carved into the lintel over the door. 'There's your motto again.'

'In every room of the house,' he said, sounding irritated.

'It annoys you?'

'I don't need quite so many reminders.' He brought her upstairs by a secondary staircase. At the top, he pushed a door open and peeked through, then shut it again. 'You'd better take off my banyan now.' He took her candle and cup while she complied, then returned them to her. 'Your bedchamber is along the passage to the right, while mine is to the left, third door down. If you should need anything at night again—anything at all—just knock. I'm a light sleeper.'

Was he offering to *bed* her?

No, surely not. He must know she wasn't that sort of woman.

For a moment, she almost wished she were. No, that was lunacy. She sighed.

He pushed the door open again. 'Good night, Mrs. Burdett. Sleep well.'

She tiptoed quickly to her bedchamber, opened the door and turned. The door to the staircase still stood ajar, the light of his candle shining through. She went into her room and shut the door behind her.

She slept, but not without thinking about him far too much.

So far, so good.

Cam felt inordinately cheerful heading toward the orchard the next morning. For the first time in a year, his libido was wide awake, and no wonder. It wasn't merely that Frances Burdett was pretty—he'd had many pretty women—but he liked her. Liked her a great deal, as a matter of fact, and not only that, she'd consented to come mistletoe-gathering. What a relief that he hadn't scared her quite away. Perhaps he'd done something right, or at least was well on the way to it, and life would soon return to normal.

Edwin, his usual morose self, stomped along beside Cam. Almeria had giggled and shied away from the prospect of cold, possibly wet feet, so Lady Warbury pressed her and Mrs. Cutlow into making evergreen rings, to which they would tie the mistletoe. Edwin would have stayed to moon over Almeria, but Cam had ordered him not to be such a bore and come along. 'Everybody moons over her,' he said. 'Be different. Stick out from the crowd.'

Ahead of them, Frances—who had borrowed some old boots from his mother and now trod briskly through the snow—listened to the Druid prose about the significance of mistletoe in pagan rituals. The only significance that mattered to Cam was that he would have plenty of opportunities to kiss Frances.

'Theoretically, we should collect our mistletoe from the oak,' Mr. Lumpkin said, 'but not only does Lord Warbury not wish to risk anyone's life and limb with climbing so high, but there is something different, something special about Warbury Hall.' He leaned close to whisper conspiratorially, 'The house has a resident hobgoblin.'

'So I've heard,' Frances said. 'Isn't it marvellous?'

Mr. Lumpkin nodded his approbation and raised his voice again. 'This thriving orchard is an excellent example of the efficacy of the rites of wassail. Here they celebrate it on old Twelfth Night, which is the seventeenth of January. They frighten the bad spirits away and offer cider to the apple trees.'

'It sounds like great fun,' Frances said.

'What a pity the house party will be over by then, for I'm sure you would enjoy it. The cider from Warbury's orchards is famous hereabouts.'

'So is the lamb's wool, which we'll have tonight,' Edwin said. 'Cam makes the best there is.'

'With the assistance of every member of the household,' Cam said. 'We each take a turn at mashing the apples.'

'Rather like stirring a fruitcake,' Frances said.

'Precisely.' The Druid lowered his voice again, as if he thought Cam wouldn't hear. 'The old lord forbade the communal apple-mashing and the wassail ceremony. Fortunately, the present marquis encourages these traditions. The orchard has done much better since he came into the title.'

Cam came to a halt under an apple tree and took out his shears. 'Come, Mrs. Burdett. You and I shall start here, while Edwin and Lumpkin take another rank of trees.' The others moved obediently away.

Cam eyed the boughs above him. 'Better watch where you stand, Mrs. Burdett. I might feel inclined to kiss you.'

She started and backed away, anxiety shadowing her face. Damn it, had Timothy made her fear a simple kiss?

'Don't be afraid. I shan't do anything you don't want.' He swung himself into the apple tree, which bore a mistletoe plant with plenty of berries. 'Try to catch it when it falls,' he told Frances. 'The more berries remaining on the plant, the better.'

Her cheeks were already pink in the wintry air, but her colour deepened as she stood beneath the mistletoe. She caught it neatly and set it in the basket she had brought from the house. They moved several trees along and repeated the process on a second tree and then chose a third.

Cam brushed off the snow from a handy foothold and climbed. 'But although I can prevent Alan from pressing his unwanted advances on you…' He reached out and snipped. She caught the clipping, but less deftly than before. He jumped down. 'You would draw attention to yourself by refusing a quick kiss, if he or any other man should catch you under the mistletoe.'

'I know that.' Her brows drew together. Evidently, she would rather avoid this subject. Too bad; it had to be addressed.

'Plan to keep your mouth firmly shut,' he said.

'Oh, I shall certainly do that,' she retorted, pursing her lips with distaste.

'Particularly with Alan and Cutlow, who will do their best to take advantage.'

'I heard you the first time,' she snapped. 'Must we discuss this?'

'I believe we should,' Cam said. 'Kissing doesn't have to be unpleasant, you know.'

'I never said anything about it being unpleasant.' She frowned at him, her hazel eyes uneasy. 'I never said anything about it at all.'

Damn. He mustn't let her realize how much he knew about her marriage. She'd already suffered too much mortification. 'No, but you implied it by recoiling from me.'

Her face fell. 'I'm sorry if I hurt your feelings.'

Good God. 'Mrs. Burdett, it's I who should apologize. I don't expect every woman to want to kiss me. I should be ashamed of myself for displaying such insufferable conceit.'

'Doubtless you have good reason,' she said, colouring. 'You are an attractive man, and there is a great deal of gossip about your skill in the bedchamber.'

Was that a point in his favour or against him? Regardless, he could use it to his advantage. 'I am perhaps more patient than other men. More interested than most in discovering what a woman desires.'

Her eyes widened. Good.

'We men tend to be hasty, you know. In our eagerness to achieve our own satisfaction, we are constantly in danger of forgetting that of our lover.'

Her mouth fell open, giving him a glimpse of a sweet pink tongue before she shut it again. She hunched a shoulder and turned away.

Lumpkin and Edwin were several trees behind in the next row, but not far enough away in this stark landscape of snow and bare branches. 'If you allow me to kiss you under the mistletoe, I promise you will enjoy it.'

'You can't possibly promise that,' she retorted.

'And yet, conceited to the core, I just did.' Hopefully, his smile held just the right amount of friendly admiration.

Evidently not; she sent him a fierce, furious glare. 'If you must have it, I don't enjoy kissing.'

'Not at all?'

'No.' She pressed her lips together, as if biting back a stream of complaints.

'Come now,' he teased. 'Surely you're exaggerating.'

Her voice was low, suffused with passion. 'You can't possibly judge how that—that invasion made me feel.'

'That bad, was it?' He spied a likely tree and moved toward it. 'Look at the berries on that one.' She followed him but halted several feet away, and didn't approach until he'd climbed the tree. 'You're right, I can't judge, but the general popularity of kissing tells me you were merely unlucky.' He cut another sprig of mistletoe. 'Perhaps Timothy was clumsy, or maybe your taste in kissing didn't match his.'

He jumped down and led Frances toward a gnarled old tree with a wider trunk than the usual and went round it to the other side.

'There's only one way to find out,' he said. 'Come here.'

Frances stopped dead. 'No.'

'Why not?' His voice drifted seductively around the tree. 'You mustn't let an unfortunate experience ruin you for one of life's great pleasures.' A gloved hand appeared from behind the tree, beckoning. 'The mistletoe awaits.'

She shivered and shook her head, which of course he didn't see. Why had she confessed to not liking kisses?

She'd kept such secrets to herself for a whole year, and now suddenly she'd blurted it out.

He was only flirting. Once, long ago, she would have been able to flirt in return. Now hurt and anger boiled up and got in the way. 'It's not a good idea.'

'Why not? You have nothing to lose.'

No, she had everything to lose. Last night in the kitchen, she'd quite liked Lord Warbury, rake or not. She'd enjoyed talking to him. She'd felt comfortable with him and surprisingly safe. Back in bed, under the lingering influence of his warm, masculine scent, she'd even found herself wondering what it might be like to put her arms around him. To feel his arms around her. To be enveloped in all that warmth and heady aroma.

But she knew better than to think about kisses. Dreams were one thing and reality another. If he kissed her, she wouldn't be able to hide her revulsion, and he would thrust her away in disgust.

'Now's our chance. Lumpkin and my cousin are nowhere near.' He came around the tree again, a sprig of mistletoe in his hand.

What a fool she was; in spite of bitter experience, she *wanted* to kiss him, wanted kissing to be wonderful. How stupid! She was much better off—much safer—as she was.

He kissed the fingertips of his gloves and blew. 'That wasn't so bad, was it?'

She huffed.

He picked a berry from the mistletoe and dropped it. 'We'll make it a very light kiss,' he said, coming closer. 'Short and sweet.'

She didn't trust him; she wanted yet didn't want—

A flurry of snow tumbled from the branches above, distracting her. He swooped in, dropped a swift, cold kiss on her lips, and drew away—but not far. 'Was that too unbearable?' Another mistletoe berry fell to the snow.

'No, of course not,' she said, 'but—'

'Well, then.' He took her hand and pulled her around the tree. 'If you don't want me to invade you—accidentally, needless to say—you'll have to keep your mouth shut.'

'You mustn't do this—'

'Of course I must. No talking.'

She gave up, shutting both her mouth and her eyes. It was her own fault for coming to the orchard this morning, but she'd enjoyed their time together in the middle of the night so very much. It was only a kiss.

Nothing happened. She opened her eyes again. He was contemplating her mouth from under his lashes. 'You have lovely lips.'

Through her teeth, she said, 'Get it *over* with.'

'I've never kissed a martyr before.' His lips curled in a lazy smile, and then he pressed his mouth coolly to hers and withdrew again. 'It requires a more careful approach than we disgustingly hasty men are used to.' He flicked another berry off the sprig.

She couldn't help but watch his mouth. What was he going to do, and when?

'Close your eyes, and whatever happens, keep your lips together.'

This time his mouth lingered on hers a few seconds, then pressed light kisses from one corner of her lips to the other. Kiss. 'One.' Kiss. 'Two.' Kiss. 'Three.'

Bite.

She gasped, and desire shimmered like golden light down her spine. He chuckled and gave his branch of mistletoe a rueful look. 'Can't bring this one in the basket, or they'll know what we've been doing. On the other hand, it would be a pity to waste the one remaining berry.'

She licked her lip where he'd bitten her.

'Such a tempting tongue,' he said.

Anxiety washed over her. All right, it had been pleasant so far—unexpectedly so—but enough was enough. She didn't want anything more, and judging by the darkening of his eyes, he did.

Another shower of snow landed on them both, followed by the sound of approaching voices. From the corner of her eye, Frances caught a hint of movement above. Had a squirrel knocked the snow off a branch? Shouldn't it be hibernating in this weather?

Lord Warbury plucked the solitary berry, stowed it in his pocket, and dropped the sprig to the ground. He retrieved the basket and handed it to Frances.

'More kisses later,' he said.

Christmas Eve passed in a flurry of activity. The ladies made garlands and kissing rings, the men hung them, the servants cooked and baked, and Lord Warbury prepared the apples and syrup for lamb's wool with everyone's participation. Frances couldn't help a tiny thrill of delight when he offered her—and only her—a second turn at mashing the apples.

She also couldn't help wondering when he would kiss her again.

They feasted in the dining room and then descended to

the kitchen, where the marquis crowned his head groom King of the Revels, bent the knee to him, and served him lamb's wool and fruitcake with his own hands. There were games and dancing, a pantomime performed by the three younger men, and roasted chestnuts and apples. She steeled herself to be kissed under the mistletoe by the male guests. Perhaps Lord Warbury had had a word with Alan Folk, for he didn't try to invade her, merely giving her a friendly kiss. So did Edwin, the Druid and the King of the Revels. Mr. Cutlow, who'd drunk too much wine and lamb's wool, put his hand on her bottom and tried to stick his tongue in her mouth. She squirmed indignantly away and warned Almeria not to let Mr. Cutlow catch her under the mistletoe. Lord Warbury bestowed kisses upon several giggly maidservants, an equally giggly Almeria, and Mrs. Cutlow, who tried unsuccessfully to cling to him. He didn't kiss Frances.

Perhaps he didn't mean to kiss her at all. Maybe he'd decided she wasn't worth the bother, and the second turn at mashing apples meant nothing.

Frances licked the foam off a cup of lamb's wool and lapsed into uncomfortable reflections. It was better if he didn't kiss her. If she let herself dwell on Lord Warbury's kisses, she was in danger of forgetting her duty to Almeria. In fact, if he intended to marry Almeria, she shouldn't kiss him at all.

'There you are, Mrs. Burdett.' Lord Warbury strolled up, brandishing a solitary mistletoe berry. 'I've been saving you for last.' He bent and dropped a chaste kiss on her mouth, and then whispered, 'That doesn't count. We'll continue our lessons later.'

Why must he promise more kisses at the very moment when she'd decided she shouldn't allow it? 'It would be better not,' she muttered.

His brows drew together; after a long second, while she squirmed under his contemplative gaze, he merely said, 'Let's see if my mother is ready to adjourn to the drawing room. Traditionally, we take the tea upstairs ourselves and leave the servants to enjoy their celebration without us.'

Soon they all trooped up to the drawing room. Over tea, she sent covert glances at both Lord Warbury and Almeria, trying to assess their attitudes to one another. The girl continued to flirt with the marquis every chance she got, but she toyed with the Folk cousins and their friend, too. As for the marquis, he flirted obligingly back, but he didn't glower like Edwin when Almeria paid attention to someone else. Was he very sure of himself, or too mature to wear his heart on his sleeve? Or was he not interested in Almeria at all?

The younger people gathered about a table to play Speculation, and the Cutlows, Lady Warbury, and the Druid made up a table for whist. Relieved she needn't try to play cards whilst in such a frame of mind, Frances gratefully retired to the sofa with her needlework and her confusion.

'Trying to decide what to embroider next?'

She started; the marquis was looking over her shoulder at her stitchery. 'I drew the design before I left London, but it seems my fingers won't follow the plan.' She gestured to a hodgepodge of stem and chain stitches she'd just made while thinking of other matters entirely. 'That was supposed to be one or two flower stems, but somehow it became chaotic—as if the plant took over and grew on its own.'

'That's what plants do if you let them,' he said. 'If you don't prune them and chop them. Pruning and chopping have their place, but so does growth.' His voice made her shiver. 'Wild, unrestrained growth.'

He wasn't talking about plants anymore. She wasn't ready for anything wild or unrestrained. She wasn't even sure about more kisses.

'I'm Almeria's chaperone,' she said, nodding towards the noisy game of Speculation. 'It's my duty to set a good example for her.'

'You needn't worry about Miss Dane. She may be a little chatterbox, but she is very aware of her worth. She won't do anything foolish or give herself away to just anyone.'

Did he mean she would give herself only to a man of wealth and rank? If he wanted Almeria, why didn't he just say so? He didn't hesitate about anything else, she thought indignantly, and tried another tack. 'She's too young for marriage.'

He cocked his head to one side, watching Almeria laugh merrily at something Alan Folk said. 'Not if she chooses the right man.'

That didn't help, either.

'Just because you didn't like Timothy's kisses, there is no reason to suppose she will have the same experience with her husband.' He smiled. 'It is also no reason for you to decide never to remarry.'

She stiffened, suddenly furious. 'I don't want to marry again, and I shan't, and that's that.' She picked up her needle again and set the first stitch of a rose.

'Then you had better have a passionate affair,' he murmured.

'I certainly will not!' She stabbed the needle in and out, in and out.

'Or at least some more kisses. Deeper ones.'

'Hush!' She glanced about, but no one was close enough to hear him.

'Otherwise, you will moulder away into nothing,' he said. 'What a pity that would be.'

No, what a pity she couldn't storm away and never see him again before she said—or did—something she would regret. She got back to work on what would be a very perfect, very cultivated rose. She would tame the wilderness of her embroidery if it meant unpicking and stitching it over and over again.

'Set an example for Miss Dane by conquering your fear, not by being a Puritan,' he said.

Frances paled so dramatically that he thought she might faint, reminding him unhappily of the day he'd quarrelled with Timothy, when she'd been so sad and wan.... Damn it, what had he done wrong now?

He seated himself next to her. He'd never been known for tact. In fact, his tactless handling of Timothy had proven fatal. 'Are you unwell, Mrs. Burdett?'

'I'm perfectly fine,' she said, but she gazed fixedly at her needlework, and her hand trembled as she set the next stitch. 'Why should you think I'm afraid? I'm *not!*' What a lie. 'And it's none of your business anyway!'

'I don't mean to distress you. Only to...' He couldn't say he wanted to help her. That came close to revealing that he knew too much. She was already beginning to ask questions he couldn't answer.

Ah. Timothy had probably called her a Puritan because she didn't enjoy being bedded. Idiot, he thought, mentally cursing his dead friend, who also hadn't realized that many whores only pretended to enjoy themselves. He'd been both furious and mortified when Cam had explained this to him.

'To what?' She scowled at him with hot, uneasy eyes.

To prove to her that Timothy had been wrong. He couldn't say that. To show her what a passionate woman she truly was. He couldn't say that, either.

He wished he could tell her everything. She was so comfortable and easy to talk to—but she wouldn't be if he blurted out the truth.

Instead of answering, he stood. 'I want to show you something.' He put out an imperative hand.

'What?' she demanded, still suspicious.

'Something my great-great-grandmother embroidered,' he said. 'I think you'll find it interesting.'

She plucked at her stitchery with agitated fingers. 'Damnation,' she muttered under her breath. She wove her needle into the fabric by the edge of the frame and stood, as well.

'It's hardly that bad, is it?' he murmured, holding the drawing room door open for her. 'At the very worst I'll drag you under the mistletoe and poke my tongue in your mouth.'

'That's not what I meant,' she said.

'Good, because you're not meant to be a Puritan.'

'I'm *not* a Puritan,' she snapped. She shouldn't have reacted so strongly, but that word had brought back the last horrid night with Timothy and all the shame and misery she'd kept to herself for the whole past year.

'That's what I just said.' The marquis lit one of the oil lamps that stood on a side table in the Great Hall. 'So why not have some fun?'

She trod beside him up the wide staircase, trying to decide what to say. That it would be morally reprehensible? That certainly sounded puritanical. Anyway, she wasn't a prude. She didn't approve of rakes or unfaithfulness in marriage, but there had to be some leeway for single men and widows. There was the question of whether he wanted to wed Almeria, but when she tried to frame the words, they wouldn't come.

Besides, one other reason overshadowed them all. Damn him, he was entirely correct. She didn't know how he could tell, but she *was* terribly afraid.

A faint smile curled his lips. He led her into a paneled room with family portraits on the walls. 'Why not indulge your natural passion?'

Fury, sharp as lemons, roiled up inside her. 'Why should I? I have the right to avoid carnal passion if I so choose!'

'As long as you truly do choose.'

What if she tried and failed once again? She'd wanted to please Timothy—of course she had—but this was different. She knew too much about herself now. Not only that, the more she saw of the marquis, the more she liked him. The thought of being shamed and shunned once again... She didn't think she could bear it.

He closed the door, shutting them together into the gallery. 'Plenty of those old Puritans made a practice of pretense, too.'

'I'm not pretending!' She was protecting herself. Shielding herself from pain.

His warm voice teased her. 'What they professed was one thing, and what they thought and did behind closed doors, another entirely.'

A hot blush flooded her entire being. She'd had plenty of carnal feelings before marrying Timothy, the sort one enjoyed but kept to oneself. Timothy had snuffed out those feelings like a candle, pinched her flame cold and dead in a few short weeks. She'd felt almost nothing for a whole year. Hadn't thought about love, hadn't touched herself… and now, with his caressing voice and his casual kisses, Lord Warbury had lit that candle again, only it was more like a torch this time.

He winked. 'I'll wager you're the same.'

She swallowed, eyes on the floor, embarrassed beyond words.

He put two fingers beneath her chin and tipped it upwards. 'You're not uninterested in pleasure. I *see* the fire within you.'

'You can't possibly see what's—'

His eyes, half-lidded, burned into her. 'Of course I can.' He put his arms around her and touched her lips with his. 'It may be a small flame now, but it will grow.'

She quivered at his touch, at the light in his eyes. At their closeness, at her breasts brushing his chest and his hands resting on her back just above her derriere. That fire was already growing; desire licked and flickered, flickered and licked through her breasts and belly and thighs.

It would come to nothing. Imagination and reality were horrid worlds apart. She thrust her hands between them, pressing them to his chest. 'How do you know? It could just as easily go out. I don't want—'

He kissed the words away. 'It won't go out if we encourage it.' He blew softly, and in spite of her fear she laughed—uncertainly, to be sure. 'Burn, little flame.' He kissed her again. 'In case you're wondering how much encouragement, there are many, many berries on the mistletoe above us.'

She glanced up. A kissing ring swung gently from a hook in the ceiling. There must be a draft up there.

He licked the tip of her chin. 'I put it there just for us. We're going to kiss and kiss and kiss.'

She groaned and gave in, and his lips captured hers with soft, warm kisses, tempting kisses, making her want to open to the gentle probing of his lips and tongue. Making her want to taste him.

'Feel free to invade me any time you like,' he whispered. She grasped his shoulders and kissed him back, dabbing tentatively with her tongue. His tongue fenced lightly with hers. He licked her lips, and she licked his. She made a small noise of pleasure, shivering again, wanting, *wanting*.

Now his tongue became bolder, but instead of revolting her, the warm insistence of its caresses made her want to open more. To take him into her mouth, to taste and savour him. She couldn't have kept her lips together if she'd wanted to, not when she could run them over the raspy skin of his upper lip and chin. Not when she could nip at his lips and lose herself as he sucked on hers. She heard her own tiny laugh of pleasure and twined her arms about his neck, pulling him closer, crushing herself to his chest. His hands roamed her back, rested briefly on her hips and squeezed, moved down to cup her derriere. He pulled her hard against him.

Oh, *no,* what had she done? She squirmed out of his embrace, panting. 'We shouldn't have. I'm sorry, so sorry. Thank you *very* much for kissing me. It was wonderful, but I didn't mean to tempt you and then, and then… I'm sorry, but I just can't.'

Cam thought she might burst into tears. What the devil? They'd been kissing and embracing, and things had being proceeding nicely, thank you very much, and he'd pulled her closer…

Ah. She'd noticed his arousal.

'We were only kissing,' he said. 'And enjoying the feel of each other. Nothing more.'

Her worried eyes rested on the bulge in his breeches. 'But—you're erect. It'll hurt if I don't give you the relief you need.' She stared at him. 'Won't it?'

'No, of course not. Did Timothy tell you that?' He didn't need an answer. 'It subsides on its own if one thinks about something else. Or, if you weren't in the mood and it mattered that much to him, he could have taken care of it himself.' She knit her brows. 'Pleasured himself, you know. Like you pleasure yourself in bed.'

'No, I—' Her hands flew to her mouth. She was so transparent; she couldn't admit it, but neither could she deny it.

He couldn't help chuckling. 'Like this.' He squeezed his cock through the fabric of his breeches, pulling on it, half closing his eyes. 'It feels good, as I'm sure you know from playing with yourself.'

'I—'

'Did he ever play with you? Like this?' Before she could stop him, he brushed the back of his hand up the apex of her thighs. She sucked in a sharp breath, and he pulled her close, cupping her mound, kneading gently through her skirts, watching her head fall back and her breathing quicken. She moaned.

He kissed her again. His hand slipped away, and she moaned again, this time with dismay. *Don't stop...* But now he dropped kisses from her ear to her throat, while that wandering hand slowly, tantalizingly raised her skirts.

'Do you want me to play with you?' His voice and hands sent tremors of need shimmering through her.

'Please,' she whispered, and his other hand trailed up her thigh, slowly, unbearably. She whimpered, wanting his touch, wanting it *now*...

His fingers delved into the wetness at her core, slipped and slid over her most sensitive spot, then settled into a rhythm. She pulsed wildly around his caresses. This was *nothing* like she'd done to herself alone in her chamber. She'd controlled it then; now she couldn't think, couldn't speak, could only writhe against his fingers and moan for more. His fingers drove her higher, helplessly higher and faster, on and on until she exploded and convulsed, over and over again.

She slumped against him, heart pummeling against her chest. Throb. Oh, God. Throb. Oh, *God*.

Laughing voices broke the spell. She gasped and wrenched away, staggering.

'Damn it, why are they headed here?' He put out a hand to steady her. 'What a damned nuisance.'

Frantically, she smoothed her gown and patted her hair. 'My God, what am I to do?'

'Act as if that didn't just happen,' he said imperturbably.

'That's easy for you to say,' she snapped.

'Not really. I'm imagining being ducked in the fish-pond, but it's not working quickly enough.' He glanced at the bulge in his breeches. 'Fortunately, I really do have something else to show you.'

'I must have been out of my mind to let you bring me up here.' What would people think when they found her alone with the marquis? 'This will affect not only my rep-utation, but Almeria's, as well.'

He picked up the lamp and strode to a set of three por-traits—a gentlemen to each side and a lady in the centre. 'Stop worrying about Almeria. She will marry well, I as-sure you.'

Because he planned to wed her? That seemed so wrong after what they'd just done. The very thought made Frances ill.

Beneath the portraits was a massive oaken chest with a table next to it. He set the lamp on the table, lifted the lid of the chest and rummaged through it.

Perhaps he merely meant that beautiful heiresses al-ways married well. Or perhaps the sick feeling was be-cause her heart kept thudding and thudding as the voices approached—Lady Warbury's friendly tones, the Druid's cheerful ones and Almeria's laugh.

The marquis brought out a folded strip of linen. He

shook out the herbs placed inside to deter insects, handed it to her and shut the chest. 'Sit.'

She obeyed, he sat next to her, and the door opened. A troop of people armed with bedroom candles entered, followed by the Druid with a lamp. Good grief, *everyone* was here. Alan Folk raised odious brows at the sight of Frances and Cam, while Mrs. Cutlow's expression was positively green.

'Strangely enough,' Lady Warbury was saying, 'the orchard, which is celebrated each year with pagan rites, was first planted by a Puritan. He would certainly have disapproved of such goings-on.' She stopped. 'Oh, there you are, Cam. And Mrs. Burdett. I wondered where you'd gone.'

'We're looking at Margery's embroidery.' Cam didn't sound the least bit discomposed. Which wasn't surprising, supposed Frances, since rakes must often find themselves in compromising situations.

Frances, on the other hand, had never done anything so improper in her life. Horrified that her mortification would show, she kept her eyes on the strip of linen as if she were examining it minutely. On it was embroidered a series of scenes from house and farmyard.

'Oh, yes, the hobgoblin piece,' Lady Warbury said. 'How apropos, since I thought our visitors might like to hear the legend. Isn't the hob a darling?'

In her flustered state, Frances hadn't even noticed him—a dark, knobby little fellow with sparse hair jutting from beneath a brown cap, plucking an egg from under a bored-looking hen. 'Yes, indeed,' she managed. 'Almeria, come sit with me and take a look.'

Obligingly, Cam stood to give Almeria his chair. The bulge in his breeches was gone. He had spoken the truth—his erection had subsided on its own.

She dragged her mind back to more proper subjects. 'See, he's stealing an egg.'

'And there he is amongst the raspberries,' Almeria said. 'What a charming little man.' She pointed. 'And eating cake upon a shelf.'

'And in the boughs of that apple tree,' Frances said. Something chased through her mind, a thought or a memory she couldn't quite catch.

'It's thanks to the hobgoblin that we perform the rites of wassail,' Lady Warbury said.

'Making the orchard flourish,' the Druid added.

Both Alan and Mrs. Cutlow rolled their eyes. Lady Warbury ignored them. She motioned to the Druid to hold the lantern higher, illuminating one of the three portraits above the chest—a grumpy-looking Puritan in a wig and square white collar. 'This is Edward Pale. We lost the estate under Cromwell's rule, and this man bought it. He seems to have been a good master and landlord, but fiercely against any sort of festivities. He died childless, bequeathing the estate to his wife, Margery, who in turn married Camden's great-great-grandfather.'

The Druid moved the lantern to show the other two portraits in the group, a richly dressed courtier and his wife.

'According to the stories, it was because of Duff, our hobgoblin, that she married him,' Lady Warbury said. 'Margery did plenty of other stitchery, but legend says she kept this one a secret, working on it only when no one else could see her. She'd heard the tales that hobs and such were survivors from pagan times, and knew she would suffer if her husband learned she'd seen one.'

'She would have been considered a witch,' the Druid said. 'And they might have tried to catch and kill the hob.'

Mrs. Cutlow yawned, and Alan said, 'Superstitious idiots. There's no such thing.'

'Perhaps, perhaps not,' the Druid retorted. 'There's no proof either way.'

'In any event,' Cam interposed smoothly, 'when my great-great-grandfather came a-courting her—courting his estate, to be accurate—she agreed to marry him only when she was certain Duff approved.'

'What a lot of gammon,' Alan said. 'How could she possibly know? That's a fairy tale if ever I heard one.'

'Fairy tales are fun,' Frances said indignantly. 'Believing in them does no harm.'

'That makes a good first part for the motto,' the marquis said with a grin. Firstly, Believe in Fairy Tales, and Secondly, Do No Harm.'

'What a lovely motto.' Almeria giggled. 'I adore fairy tales.'

Alan snorted, glancing from the marquis to Almeria and back. 'It's a good thing Cam's father isn't alive to hear that. It would have sent him into fits.'

Because Cam was about to propose marriage to a girl who loved fairy tales? Something inside Frances twisted unhappily. He would make her a good husband—would make any woman a good husband… *Please, not Almeria.*

'His motto was, First, Tell Everyone What to Think, Say, and Do, and Second, Beat It into Them,' Edwin said. 'He used to cane Cam for insisting the hob was real.'

'Oh, how horrid!' Almeria cried, all big blue eyes and

fluttering lashes. Frances gritted her teeth and pretended to examine Margery's needlework again. When had she become such a jealous cat?

'Which meant Cam stubbornly insisted all the more,' Alan said, 'even when he was well past the age of believing such nonsense.'

'And I have the scars to prove it,' Cam said ruefully.

'You always were a brave boy,' his mother said.

This time it was Cam who rolled his eyes. 'Stubborn, you mean.'

'And so dedicated to the second half of our motto,' she went on. 'Always kind-hearted, always determined to do no harm.'

Something crossed his face so quickly Frances wondered if she'd seen it at all in the dim light. 'Mother, you're putting me to the blush,' he said, but whatever that emotion had been, it wasn't embarrassment.

'That's a mother's privilege,' Lady Warbury said. 'I was overjoyed when you reinstituted the wassail and giving the hob Christmas treats. These sorts of traditions are worth perpetuating whether one believes in them or not.' She took the strip of linen from Frances. 'Good night, everyone. Cam, please stay and help me for a minute or two.'

Frances went to bed thinking about Cam withstanding his father on principle to the point of being beaten until he bled, and about Margery's courage in embroidering scenes that might have cost her her life. It was long before she slept, but she fell asleep knowing what she had to do.

'No!' Cam said to his mother. 'How can you even suggest it?' Whilst she'd calmly sprinkled herbs and refolded the embroidered linen, she'd also told him he must seduce Frances, of all things!

'But she's a widow, dearest, and a very pretty one. It would be no sacrifice on your part.'

She was right about that. He'd never been so aroused in his life as while watching Frances come. The rise and fall of her bosom, the flutter of her lashes, the flush on her lips and cheeks… He'd brought many women to orgasm, but it had never affected him like this.

His mother talked on. 'She must be lonely, as it's well over a year since Timothy died. As long as you're careful not to get her with child, what better opportunity for a dalliance?'

This was precisely what he'd planned, but when his mother put it like that, he wanted to give her a tongue-lashing such as she'd never had in her life. Instead, he managed to say with commendable calm, 'Frances is a respectable widow, Mama, not a bored wife on the prowl.'

His mother tsked. 'Frances is a woman, Cam, with desires like any other. Poor dear, she can't be more than twenty-three or-four, and she scarcely had a taste of marriage before it was over.' Her eyes gleamed, a sign she was warming to her topic. 'In fact, since you were so close to Timothy, I believe it's your *duty* to bring Frances back into the world of the living.'

'Not with a tawdry house-party tryst.' Suddenly doubting himself and his well-laid scheme, he strode to the window and parted the curtains to gaze at the white night. He shut them again, turning. 'Mother, I don't do that anymore.'

Where had that come from? He had every intention of going right back to his old ways, once he'd taken care of

Frances. Now that he thought of it, though, the prospect didn't hold much appeal.

She gaped at him. 'You don't bed pretty women?' She faltered, looking at nothing but clearly recognizing his recent lack of interest in dalliance. 'Gracious me, I just thought you'd been more discreet lately. Dear boy, has something happened to you?Are youincapable?'

Good God. 'No, Mama, of course not.' He floundered for something to say. 'I expect…I've matured, that's all.'

That had a daunting ring of truth.

'Ah,' she said. 'You've sown all your wild oats.' That gleam in her eye deepened. Next she would take up matchmaking again, certain the time had come for him to marry.

'If you want to be useful, try discouraging Mrs. Cutlow from pursuing me. She makes the corridors hazardous at night.' He left before she could say anything more.

Damn it all, how could he have not seen it before? Frances wasn't the sort of woman one dallied with. She was the kind of woman one married. But she'd refused to wed again, so what choice did he have but to dally with her, if he was to make amends?

Firstly, Bed Frances Burdett, and Secondly, Do No Harm.

It had seemed good enough as a temporary motto when he'd first considered it. Now all he could think about was what might happen to her after she left his home, newly awakened, newly vulnerable to any idiot in the Polite World.

Not that everyone out there was an idiot. He knew plenty of good fellows. He tried to think of someone who might be perfect for her, but there was no one.

Except him.

* * *

Christmas dawned bright and cold, with Jack Frost's etchings on the windowpanes. Frances scraped at her window to peek at the white gardens below. They travelled the half mile to and from the village church in two horse-drawn sledges. In the afternoon, clouds gathered and it began to snow again.

The marquis seemed uncharacteristically subdued, but she caught him watching her from time to time. He didn't try to kiss her again, or touch her, or…or anything. She should be thankful for what he'd done for her so far. He'd made her come alive again. He'd made her want to be new and eager and…everything impossible.

She redrew the design for her embroidery. Now, instead of an orderly flower garden, blackberry canes and wild roses grew in ecstatic profusion.

'What do you think?' she asked, when the marquis finally came to take a look.

'I think you're a beautiful, desirable, courageous woman,' he said in that warm voice. 'No, I *know* you are.' He smiled, and she shivered with wanting him, from her lips and fingertips all the way to her toes.

He wandered away, dividing his attention amongst all his guests. She should be thankful—this was obviously the best way to handle any repercussions from the night before—but instead she felt bereft.

No matter how welcome his compliments, she was inclined to discount *beautiful* and *desirable* as mere flummery—after all, Timothy had said the same before they'd wed…but then, Timothy had lied about his erection. Anger burned in her breast at the thought that she'd believed everything he'd told her. Maybe he'd fed her more lies.

There was only one way to find out. Was she truly courageous? Her needle proved more obedient now, but symbolic abandon and the real thing were far removed from one another.

If Cam intended to propose to Almeria, this was Frances's last and only chance to take him up on his suggestion of a passionate affair. She couldn't do it once he was engaged or married. That went entirely against her beliefs. Even the thought that he *might* marry Almeria made her unsure.

Actually, it made her want to weep, which she set aside as making no sense at all.

Last chance. She trusted the marquis. She couldn't imagine taking this risk with anyone but him. She couldn't even imagine *wanting* to. Only with him could she find out, once and for all, whether she was suited to the activities of the marital bed. Not that she intended to remarry—she didn't—but if she managed to enjoy herself with Lord Warbury, and if she pleased him as well, she wouldn't feel like a failure anymore. She would start life afresh as a new woman.

And if she failed again, he would be kind, he wouldn't gossip about her, and she would return to London resigned but safe.

Finally, alone in her chamber in a silent house, she put on her wrapper and slippers and lit her bedroom candle. Her heart thumping pitifully hard, she opened the door and glanced up and down the empty passage. She crept slowly along, and was almost to the back staircase when a board creaked beneath her feet. She hissed but kept on going.

The staircase door opened. Her heart nearly burst from her chest. Then she blew a shaky sigh of recognition. 'Thank heavens it's you.'

'More hot milk?' asked Cam.

'No, I—I wanted to talk to you.'

A sharp click sounded down the corridor. Someone had opened a door! Quick as light, Cam pulled her onto the landing and shut the staircase door. Her candle flame wavered and went out.

Darkness engulfed them, dense and inviting. Cam drew her close with one arm and took the candlestick with the other. She didn't know what he did with it, but a second later his other hand cradled her head, and his lips descended on hers.

She opened herself to him with a stifled moan of pleasure. She thought she heard the softest of growls in his throat.

A long creak sounded outside—a door opening slowly. They broke the kiss. 'Hush,' he said, so softly she barely heard him. 'No one but family and servants use these stairs, but if need be, I'll hold the door shut.'

'Eek!' A feminine squeal came from the passageway. 'Oh, my God, there are *rats* out here!' That was Mrs. Cutlow's voice. Gasps and sounds of stumbling later, the door creaked again and clicked shut.

Frances muffled a storm of giggles against the marquis's broad chest. Under his breath, Cam said something that sounded like 'thank you,' but so low she couldn't quite hear.

'What would rats be doing up here?' she whispered.

'It must have been her imagination,' Cam said cheerfully. He eased open the door. The corridor was darker than pitch. He hurried her down the passage with sure and steady steps, nudged her ahead of him into a room and shut the door softly behind them.

Glowing coals in the fireplace lit the room enough to show a massive bed against one wall. Arousal, dark and heady, spilled into Frances's veins.

He pulled her close again and pressed his lips to her hair, nuzzling gently, then planted kisses one after another on her brow, her temple, at the corner of her eye. 'Delicious Frances.' One hand caressed her behind, whilst the other fondled her breast, cupping it through the layers of fabric. He licked her ear.

A shudder travelled down her spine and settled in her most sensitive spot. It began to throb. She thought about Cam's fingers and what they'd done to her last night. A wave of desire swept through her so hard that she clung to him, shaking.

'Damn, I want you,' he said, his voice husky, his lips travelling the line of her jaw.

She wanted him, too, but she drew away, battling the insistent throbbing. 'I must talk to you first.'

'Very well.' He let her go and moved swiftly across the room to put a log on the coals. He lit a branch of candles and smiled at her. His smile made her want to forget talking. Made her want to fling herself into his arms, to crawl all over him, to kiss his hot skin and inhale his scent... She'd never felt like this about Timothy.

He reached into the pocket of his banyan, took out her bedroom candle and set it on a table by his bed. His voice beckoned her closer. 'But be warned—my desire for you may affect both my hearing and my brain.' He removed his banyan, tossed it over a chair and prowled toward her.

Desire shimmered through her, playing havoc with her determination. The thought of what he might reply made her throat catch on the words, but she had to say it quickly, before he touched her again, before she lost herself in his arms.

She took a deep breath. 'Are you planning to ask my cousin Almeria to marry you?'

'What?' He gaped at her. 'God, no. Of course not.' Was that what had been bothering her? 'She's young and giggly, and her chatter would drive me mad.'

'Are you absolutely sure?'

'Of course I'm sure. It never even crossed my mind.' He kissed her, long and slowly, but she still wasn't pliant and comfortable in his arms. 'What's wrong, sweetheart?' He pressed kisses to her forehead, her temple, her ear, anxiety prickling him. 'You're safe with me, dear heart, I swear. I'll never harm you, and I don't want anyone but you.'

He'd spent the day pondering marriage. He didn't know why he hadn't seen it before. He couldn't go backwards in life. He didn't even want to. His past of tawdry affairs had lost all its allure.

He'd been so obsessed with his damned motto and making amends that he hadn't realized his real motive was Frances Burdett. It had never once occurred to him that he might be in love with her.

Motto of the night: Woo, Seduce and Win… Whilst Doing No Harm.

* * *

Frances appreciated his kind, comforting words, even though she didn't really believe them. She wished she could confide in him, explaining all that she feared. Instead, she asked another question. 'Is there a way to ensure that I won't become with child?'

'I won't get you with child.' His hands roamed her waist, her hips, her behind. 'Beautiful Frances.'

She shivered at the intent in his voice. 'And you will be satisfied?' Even if she wasn't, he had to be. 'I won't leave you, er, hanging?'

'God, no.' His voice cracked. 'No, you won't.' He undid the top button of her wrapper, and then the next one. The back of his hand brushed her breast. She drew in a sharp breath, and her nipple hardened, tingling. He slipped his hands under the wrapper to cup her breasts through the nightdress. Wantonly, she pressed herself into the heat of his palms.

'Oh, so lovely,' he said, a shudder in his voice. 'Wonderful Frances.' His eyes were closed. Standing there touching her, his face rapt, he seemed almost as vulnerable as she felt. Which was impossible, of course; he'd bedded many women. This was nothing new to him.

'My love, my darling, my sweet.' Did every woman hear those endearments? She didn't want to think about it; she wanted to bask in what felt like love, even as she abandoned herself to what was surely only lust.

She would suffer for it afterwards. She should have seen it earlier, but she'd been blind to everything but her own fears. She had fallen in love with him, and there was no point pretending otherwise. He didn't love her, but wouldn't one night in his arms be better than none at all?

Yes, said that pulse in her nether regions. Her heart disagreed, but her heart couldn't resist him, couldn't control its own heady pounding that sent rich, red, desire-filled blood through her veins, sent anticipation tingling all the way to her fingers and toes. 'Hurry, before I change my mind.'

His rich, sensual chuckle made her groan with need. He slid her wrapper down her arms and tossed it over the chair atop his banyan. She shivered. 'I'll warm you up,' he said, and his words sent more tremors of excitement through her veins. 'Lift your arms.' He stripped her nightdress over her head. For a long second he stared at her, but she shivered again, and he said, 'Sorry, but you're made to be gazed at,' and shucked his nightshirt.

He was beautiful naked—powerful arms and broad chest with a sprinkling of dark hair; her eyes travelled down his flat abdomen to the hard length of his erection. He took it in his hand and tugged it a little. 'It's yours to play with, Frances. All yours, any time you like.'

He scooped her into his arms and carried her to the bed, then burrowed under the covers to join her. 'And you're mine to play with, too.'

Thrills danced through her. At first the sheets were cold, but within seconds, their nest became warm. And dark and close, and pulsing with pleasure.

She couldn't help but twine herself around him, couldn't stop rolling and kissing and rubbing herself against him, reveling in the smooth heat of his skin against hers.

She couldn't get enough of his voice, so deep and warm,

so appreciative, as if he found this as wondrous as she. 'Darling Frances,' he said, running his hands through her hair, teasing her nipples with the strands. 'Sweet, hot Frances.' He explored her breasts with fingers and lips and tongue, and took her into his mouth with a gentle suckling that sent golden shafts of pleasure straight to her core. Meanwhile his hands moved down, feathering across her belly and mound to her thighs, then inched up between her legs, urging them ever so gradually apart.

His fingers slipped inside her, and she pulsed around him as his fingers moved, making her writhe. 'Oh, Cam,' she whispered, and then again, in a stifled groan, 'Cam, I want you *inside* me.'

'In due time.' He crawled down her naked body, kissing all the way, and flicked her sweet spot with his tongue.

'Cam, you mustn't,' she hissed, but he grasped her hips and licked and sucked while she panted and gasped. She dug her hands into his hair and opened helplessly to his lips and tongue. The pleasure grew and pulsed and throbbed and tore through her. She came to pieces all at once, crying out.

He crawled back up her again, kissing and licking all the way, then kissed her hard, tasting of… 'You taste of me,' she said. She'd forgotten such forbidden experiments for a year and more. What a *fool* she'd been, all because of what Timothy had said.

'Delicious Frances.' He pushed himself inside her.

She laughed with helpless joy. 'I'm throbbing all around you.'

'You are, aren't you?' he growled, and began to move within her. She remembered Timothy and how with him she'd felt nothing at all. She'd tried to move with him, tried to like it, but it was just...nothing.

Cam stilled. 'Don't think about him. He was wrong for you, and I'm right.' His eyes burned into her in the darkness. 'Isn't that so?'

'Yes.' Oh, *God,* yes.

'You're hot and passionate and perfect,' he said, his voice husky, his breathing hard. 'Aren't you?'

'Yes!' she cried, and let the past go, let Timothy go forever. Cam thrust into her, each movement a caress, and she answered with loving movements of her own. She watched his pleasure build, entirely forgetting her own. He thrust harder, faster, on and on, and then pulled out of her, spilling his seed onto her thigh. She convulsed again in utter surprise around the space where he'd once been.

He rolled onto his back and pulled her close with one arm, cuddling her against his shoulder. 'What more could a man want in a wife?'

She was good enough. With the right man, she could have been a good wife. She snuggled next to him, satiated and content, glowing with the aftermath of pleasure and new, invigorating knowledge of herself.

Slowly, thoughts crept unbidden into her mind. Memories of little things Cam had said, innocent in themselves, that all added up to something else.

He'd known she found kissing unpleasant, so he'd made a point of teaching her it wasn't.

He'd known she recoiled from passion. Why would he suspect such a thing unless someone had told him so?

He'd known she believed herself useless as a wife...because someone had told him that, too. He'd taken her to bed tonight to prove to her that she wasn't.

She sat up in bed, roiling with unwanted thoughts. 'Why did you keep calling on me after Timothy's death?' She pulled the sheet up over herself, covering her breasts. Not that it did the least bit of good—he had stripped her naked to her soul.

She knew him well enough now to read consternation on his features. When his mother had complimented him on his dedication to the family motto, he'd looked exactly the same. That was his driving passion—to do no harm—but the constant reminders plagued him.

'It doesn't matter,' she said. 'You could easily come up with a convincing lie, something comforting, something to make me feel good. You could say you wanted to offer condolences in person. That you needed to hear me say what I'd already written—that I didn't blame you.'

'You should have. It was largely my fault.' He sat up, so warm and male and kind-hearted that she wanted to burst into tears. Fortunately, she was far too angry to do so. She didn't want kind-hearted, damn it all. She wanted the truth.

She huffed. 'We'll never agree on that. Answer me this, then—if you aren't interested in Almeria, why did you invite us here?'

He sighed. 'Edwin is infatuated with her. It was unscrupulous of me, because she doesn't favour poor Edwin over any of her suitors and likely never will, but I couldn't think of any other way to get to spend some time with you.'

'And to kiss me. And to bed me. Isn't that so?'

'Well, yes,' he said, reaching for her. 'You're beautiful and adorable and completely irresistible. Of course I wanted all that.'

She pushed away and slid down off the bed. What a lot of tripe. 'He told you, didn't he?' She grabbed her night-dress from the floor. 'Timothy told you I didn't like kiss-ing. He told you I was a bore in bed. I thought I already knew the worst of him, but this tops it all.'

'Yes, he told me.' Cam got off the bed, too. 'But I didn't believe him.'

She struggled into the nightdress, cursing. Cam ap-proached, warm competent hands seeking to help her.

'Don't touch me!' Finally she got her arms through the sleeves and yanked the nightdress down to cover her na-kedness. 'I suppose you couldn't resist finding out for yourself. Or perhaps you just wanted to prove what a great lover you are. You could even warm up cold little Frances Burdett.'

'No!' His face twisted. 'No, Frances. It was never like that.'

She clamped her teeth together, aghast at the misery on his face. 'I'm sorry! I didn't mean it. I know that's not like you.' She blinked away a treacherous tear. 'You're dedi-cated to your family motto, just as your mother said. You were making amends, weren't you? You believed that with your great skills in the bedchamber, you could help me feel less horrid about myself.' More tears pricked behind her eyes. 'You'll have to content yourself with the knowledge that to a great extent, you succeeded.'

He'd had his pleasure of her, which was doubtless enough for a man like him; and she'd had her pleasure of him, for which she would be forever grateful, once she got over being hurt and angry and *aching* inside. She must leave, and leave quickly, before he realized she'd fallen in love with him. She couldn't bear that.

He probably didn't even like her much. She was female and reasonably attractive, and he'd done what he'd set out to do…and that was all.

She put on her wrapper and tried to light her bedroom candle, but tears blurred her vision. She squeezed her eyes shut, willing the tears away, but one escaped anyway, trickling down her cheek. She took a deep breath, opened her eyes again and lit the dratted candle.

'I give up,' he said.

He threw up his hands. 'No matter what I do, I can't live up to the motto. Well, to hell with it.' He slumped, naked and exposed and not giving a damn. Not that she was looking at him anyway. 'I don't suppose I can do any more harm than I've already done. I called on you after Timothy died because I wanted to explain to you what really happened that day.'

She had already reached the door in her haste to get away from him. She put her hand on the latch.

'I thought I was doing it because of a burning need for justice and truth,' he said, 'but the justice was for me as much as for you. More so, because telling you about it would have meant also telling you what Timothy told me, which would have made you feel even worse.'

She turned partway. Was that a tear glistening on her cheek? God, what a mull he'd made of it. 'So I stopped pestering and watched you instead, hoping perhaps time would heal your wounds…and then, after your year of mourning was over, you let it be known you would never remarry. I couldn't leave it at that. I thought if I could just show you how perfect and passionate you are, all would be well again.'

Her hand still rested on the latch. 'What do you mean, justice for you? I'd already said I didn't blame you.'

'Because of what people were saying,' he said. 'That Timothy and I were fighting over some doxy. It wasn't true.'

She squeezed her eyes shut and shuddered on a sigh. Why did it still hurt that Timothy had turned to prostitutes so soon after their wedding? 'Why should it matter to me what you were fighting about?'

'Because whatever you believed of Timothy, I couldn't bear that you would believe the same of me.' Last chance. 'Frances, we were fighting about you.'

She dropped her hand from the latch and turned. He stood naked before her, face drawn and shoulders slumped, and she wanted to take him into her arms, hug and hold and comfort him…but she mustn't. She twisted her hands together. She would want to stay there forever.

'I was so angry,' Cam said. 'You were innocent and lovely when you married—I remember thinking what a lucky fellow Timothy was—and a fortnight later you had become pale and listless and so very sad. I asked him if you were ill. He'd hardly noticed, damn him, and he didn't even care. But that got him talking, and then drinking, and gradually it all came out. In two short weeks he'd destroyed you. I told him what I thought of him, and I didn't hold back. I said he didn't know a thing about women. I told him he should be horsewhipped for what he'd done to you, ordered him to mend his ways, and proceeded to give him advice on how to woo you gently and patiently to pleasure.'

'Oh, dear.' Frances hiccupped on something approaching a laugh. 'Timothy had a temper and a lot of pride.'

'We both did,' Cam said. 'Words became blows, and Timothy demanded whether I fancied I drove better than he did, too. He knew I didn't. I suppose he wanted to salvage his pride by beating me in a curricle race. When we met an hour later, ready to start, he'd been drinking even more. I should have insisted on racing some other day when he was sober, but at that point I didn't care. I don't think I've ever been so angry in my life. I even said, "If you want to break your neck, it's fine with me."'

'And then he did.' She set the candle down. 'Oh, poor Cam.' Nobody had told her about that; they'd probably been trying to protect her from the worst. 'If I'd known, I wouldn't have refused to see you.' To hell with the consequences to her own heart. She crossed the room and his arms came around her; he let out a long, shuddering breath.

'You didn't mean him to die.' She caressed his hair and softly kissed his cheek. She loved him so very much.

'No, but it's no wonder people blamed me,' Cam said.

'I don't, and I wouldn't have even if I'd known.' She should pull away again, but she couldn't make herself let go. Not yet. 'It's over, Cam. You did your best to make amends, and you've helped me so very much. Everything's all right now.'

'Not unless I've succeeded in my goal,' he said, 'of convincing you to marry again.'

* * *

She tried to twist away, but he tightened his arms. 'Don't go, Frances. This needs to be discussed.'

'Why?' She pushed at him, but he didn't budge. 'It's none of your business whether I remarry.'

'I beg to differ. What if you choose wrong again? I can't make a habit of accidentally killing your unsatisfactory husbands.'

She huffed. There was nothing amusing about this. 'Since I don't plan to marry again, that won't be a problem.'

'Ah, but you're awakened to passion now. You don't want to live the rest of your life without it.' He kissed her hair. 'Do you?'

'No,' she said into his banyan, softening briefly, then struggling again. 'But if I must, I shall.'

He didn't loosen his hold. His cock was already reacting to her again. With luck this would be a long, lovely night. 'I don't suppose you're willing to try your suitors out in bed to make sure they're both considerate and reasonably competent before marrying them.'

'Definitely not.' None of them would hold a candle to him anyway, and he knew it. She shoved, and he let her go.

'Then there's only one way out of this fix,' he said. 'You'll have to marry me.'

'Marry you?' Her words came out as a squeak.

'You've already tried me out.' His lips curled ever so slightly. 'We can do it again, if you want to make sure.'

Between hope and fury, she barely managed to control her voice. 'This isn't a jesting matter.'

'I'm completely serious,' he said. 'I should have thought of it long ago.'

'Why? There's no reason for you to marry me.'

'Yes, there is. I love you, Frances. I've been in love with you for ages. I was envious of Timothy when he married you. I accidentally killed him because I was so enraged at what he did to you. I've spent a whole year thinking about how to heal the wounds he'd made. If that's not love, what is? It just took me a while to figure it out.'

He loved her? More likely, he was being stubborn—he'd shown ample evidence of that—and fooling himself. 'What about—what about your motto? What about making amends and doing no harm?'

'It was far more than that. If Timothy had married and been unkind to some other woman, I would have chided him, but it wouldn't have come to blows. I wouldn't have raced him while he was so drunk. And God knows I wouldn't have lost interest in other women and thought only about his widow for a whole year.'

He'd lost interest in other women? Maybe that explained all the laments she'd heard. She couldn't help the dawning of a smile.

'I try to make my actions conform to my motto, but it's just a way to ensure I mean well, and it doesn't always work.' He shivered. 'Come back to bed, sweetheart. We can discuss it whilst warm and cozy under the covers. Even I get chilly standing about in the nude.' He smiled at her and pointed up. 'You may not have noticed, but there's a sprig of mistletoe hanging from the ceiling, and several others are hidden above the canopy. We have dozens of kisses to get through before Christmas is over.'

She rolled her eyes but went to him. He stripped her nightdress over her head and they crawled into bed again. They wrapped themselves around each other, hot, smooth skin and long, warm kisses.

'Well, my very own Frances, whom I love with all my heart,' he said, between one kiss and another. 'Will you marry me?'

She let out a breath of utter joy. 'I will.'

'You'll have to fall in love with me, too. Do you think you can?'

'I'll do my best,' she said on a laugh. She wasn't about to tell him she already had. He was conceited enough as it was.

Besides, he probably already knew.

* * * * *

The Pirate's
Reckless Touch

LINDA SKYE

Linda Skye is a travel addict and a self-proclaimed food critic with an insatiable appetite for the written word. She first developed her love for reading and writing by browsing her grandfather's dictionaries and etymology books—a habit she has yet to abandon!

Born to Filipino parents in the United States and raised in Canada, Linda is a modern-day nomad, moving across country and ocean with her military husband. She currently lives in the United Kingdom and spends her free time writing, practising digital photography, updating her food blog and dreaming of adventures at home and abroad. She has travelled throughout North America, Europe, Asia and Africa.

Linda holds a Master's of education and specialises in teaching languages and literature. She has been teaching English as a second language, English literature and literacy courses since 2001. Though she is currently teaching part-time at a local technical college, Linda is a full-time daydreamer with a passion for the strange, mysterious and exotic.

CHAPTER ONE

RAWDEN SCOWLED AT the winter chill, shoving his hands deeper into the pockets of his woollen trousers. Thick, heavy snowflakes drifted down lazily in circular patterns all around him, and a crowd of ratty street children bustled around his legs, laughing and sticking out their tongues to catch the flakes. It was only a few days until Christmas Eve, and even the poorest boroughs of London seemed to have swung into the festive season. A few of the local taverns that lined the narrow alleyway had even hung evergreen wreaths from their doors.

But to Rawden, it just didn't feel like Christmas.

Not when his ship, the *Golden Maiden*, was in such disrepair that he feared going to Davy Jones's locker every time they were at sea. Not when his mutinous, grumbling crew had to be kept in line with constant threats of keelhauling. And not when his personal coffers were practically empty despite months of scouring foreign seas for booty-filled ships.

So it was not the warm glow of the Yuletide season that

had brought him back to the London docks; it was the hope of finding information about fresh plundering grounds.

Rawden's eyes scanned the row of seedy back-alley taverns, stopping to rest on the crudely carved placard of a familiar door. The Mucky Duck. A favourite watering hole for London's less savoury merchants. He strode over quickly and pushed his way past the heavy oak door and into the dank, dimly lit pub. Ignoring the late-night revellers and flirtatious ladies of the night, Rawden made his way over to the bar and lifted a finger. A heavy earthen mug slid his way almost immediately, filled with a dark, frothy brew. He quietly nursed his drink as his sharp eyes discreetly searched out the room for known traders or informants.

But all thoughts of piracy evaporated the moment he spotted her across the room. He didn't know who she was or where she had come from, but she was almost blindingly beautiful. Her golden tresses were loosely pinned up so that a few wayward curls framed her delicate face. Her pale, slender neck was as elegant as a swan's, and her bare arms were the colour of the finest fresh cream. Her light and flimsy frock was cut dangerously low, the sleeves just barely skimming the edges of her slim shoulders.

A drunken sailor might mistake her for a common whore—but Rawden knew better. Though her dress was similar to those of the other pub wenches, the fabric was too white, too clean. And rather than flitting from man to man with a salacious grin, she awkwardly wandered about, subtly cringing when meaty hands reached for her. But most of all, her dovelike face was just too innocent and too sweet to be mistaken for that of a tart. It was painfully obvious that she didn't belong, despite her very best efforts to blend in. An amused smirk quirked the corners of Rawden's lips as he watched her stumble from table to table. He wondered, briefly, what misguided notion had caused the young woman to engage in such a bold and foolish masquerade.

And then a cool blast of December air washed over him as the pub door swung inward and two marine police walked in. Conversation stilled for a moment as the burly men sauntered toward the bar.

Rawden frowned into his mug of ale before tipping it back and draining the bitter drink in one long gulp. Tossing a few coppers onto the bar, he stood abruptly, fully intent on leaving the scene. Finding information with police in the tavern had just become impossible, and he had no desire to get caught up in any shenanigans with the law. He had enough trouble as it was.

As he turned, he saw that the police had stopped in the centre of the tavern, their eyes roving over the raucous crowd of sailors and merchants. Feigning indifference, he casually ambled toward the exit. He felt the officers' eyes on him as he approached, and he carefully kept his eyes averted. A flash of golden hair caught his eye.

Perfect, he thought to himself. *Something to pretend to look at.*

Rawden fixed a leer on his face, gluing his eyes onto the young woman and grinning like a hungry dog. He heard the police snort disgustedly as he passed. But even after the police turned their attention elsewhere, Rawden could not tear his eyes from the innocent girl. It didn't help that she was heading in his direction. Just before he managed to make it to the door, she seemed to trip on some invisible obstacle—which sent her careening into his arms.

A cacophony of catcalls and whistles erupted from the onlookers as Rawden steeled himself against the young woman's soft flesh. She had landed against his chest in a tangle of smooth limbs, and her silky hair was brushing the underside of his stubbly chin. She pulled away more slowly than he expected, bracing her palms on the rough leather of his vest. Then, with her ample bosom still pressed up against his chest, she tilted her head back to meet his gaze. Rawden's arms tightened around her slender frame as he looked down at her sweetly upturned face. She was even more beautiful up close. Thick lashes fluttered over sea-blue eyes, and her pink lips were slightly parted in surprise. Rawden inhaled sharply, and he was overtaken by her pure, bright scent. She smelled clean and fresh, like a crisp summer's day.

Too clean, a voice niggled at the back of his head.

Rawden sighed, remembering himself. He slid his hands to her elbows and steadied her as he stepped back resolutely.

"You should go," Rawden said gruffly as he watched the police from the corner of his eye.

His suggestion was met with silence, and he glanced down at the girl with a dark frown. She had tilted her head to one side and was studying him curiously, blue eyes unblinking.

"Why?" she asked quietly.

Rawden's fingers tightened at her elbow and he leaned in, his lips brushing her ear.

"Because I know you don't belong here," he breathed, his warm breath moistening her neck.

He leaned back, certain that the daring gesture had shocked her to her senses—only to watch incredulously as the girl took a bold step forward and placed an open hand on his forearm. Leaning against him, she rose to her toes and mimicked his actions, pressing her open mouth to his temple.

"And what makes you think that?" she whispered, allowing the very tip of her tongue to graze the ridge of his ear.

She smiled and slid down the length of his body, letting him feel her every curve glide down the steel planes of his torso. Rawden felt raw heat surge through his limbs, pooling where her hips meet his. Logic lost to lust as he revelled in the warm glow of her body pressed to him. His eyes dropped to trace the curve of her bare shoulder and the swell of her breasts. His rough hands fisted in the fabric of her airy shift and he walked her back into the door—through which he had been trying to escape just moments before. He pressed her firmly up against the rough wooden surface and smoothed his hands down her sides to grip her hips. She responded by wrapping her arms around his middle, her fingers tracing a distracting pattern on his lower back.

"Girl," he growled low in his throat, "this is a dangerous game."

"So?" she answered coyly, nipping at his chin. "Are you going to play?"

"Perhaps," he said as he twisted his fingers in her hair and gently pulled her head back. "You certainly need to learn a lesson or two."

"Oh?" she questioned playfully, allowing him to plant a row of rough kisses up the length of her exposed neck. "What lessons would those be?"

"Foolish lass," Rawden grunted as he reached down to give her pert bottom a light pinch. "For one, that innocent, high-born girls should not pretend to be strumpets in sailors' taverns."

"I'm innocent, am I?"

Rawden stilled immediately, closing his eyes. For a brief moment, he allowed himself to imagine her creamy legs wrapped around him, her pliant flesh yielding to his desire and her cries of passion at his ear. He could have her now if he wanted—let her think she'd won at her game of masquerade and sate his lust with her sweet body without caring about her reputation. And then…he would leave her ruined and sullied.

His breathing heavy, Rawden reluctantly pushed away from her. Planting his palms on either side of her head, he lowered his face to hers. *Yes,* he thought as he took in her flushed cheeks and bright eyes, *you're still innocent.* Though her seductive confidence may have been the result of some previous carnal experience, her expression was not the jaded, calculating look of a wharf prostitute. Neither was her face marred by the bitter wrinkle lines of a woman forced to pleasure others at her own expense. He inhaled deeply. Her skin was too soft and smelled of expensive oils. Rawden sighed.

"You don't belong here," he repeated gruffly. "Go home before someone ruins you."

"Someone?" she asked, arching an aristocratic brow.

"Not me," he warned through gritted teeth, pulling her

away from the door. "But if you stay here, someone else will certainly force you to do something you'll regret." He stood back, his eyes hard. "So go home, little girl."

With that, he brusquely brushed past her, pulling open the tavern door with enough force to send it slamming into the wall. He stalked out into the cold, frustration clawing through his veins. He tried to banish the phantom feeling of her body under his as he strode hurriedly away. It was so darned *cold*, and he quickened his steps. He shoved his hands back into his pockets—and then stopped cold.

Slowly, he reached deeper into his trouser pockets, fingers fumbling and searching. Jaw dropping, he turned out the fabric to be absolutely sure.

Nothing, he thought in disbelieving wonder.

That *innocent* young girl had just stolen all his money.

CHAPTER TWO

JULIANA WRIGHT PULLED her thick cloak more tightly around her shoulders and hurried through the twisting alleys. She was on a mission. She'd finally found the right man for the job—a rare type of honourable villain—and then he'd vanished into the night without so much as whispering his name. She frowned crossly. For a moment in that seedy tavern, she had really thought that she'd had him in the palm of her hand. Thankfully, it hadn't taken too long for Juliana to pry his name off of a few inebriated sailors; apparently he was legendary for his former exploits abroad.

Captain Rawden Wood.

He had once been one of the wealthiest pirates in the Western seas, ravishing treasure-laden ships along the Mediterranean and African coastlines. His ship, the *Golden Maiden,* had been a shining example of marine engineering—a sleek and swift pirate vessel equipped with the latest cannons and the most cutthroat mercenaries. 'Twas a shame for him that the illicit gold had all but dried up in Europe. It caused his ship to fall from the pinnacle of its past. It had his crew biting at the bit with restless greed. It made Captain Rawden Wood desperate for money.

And that made him perfect for her job, Juliana thought to herself with a sly smile. *Just perfect.*

Now, she just needed to find him *again*.

Her steps were light and sure as she skipped toward her destination. But when she rounded a corner, she almost stumbled to a stop.

A trio of shabbily dressed thugs was casually leaning against the walls, as if they had been expecting her. One of them was picking his teeth with the tip of a nasty-looking dagger. He turned to size her up, and a cruel grin lit his face. He took a menacing step toward her.

"Well, well, well," he said in a voice as gritty as sand. "What do we have here?"

Juliana spun around, ready to run back the way she came. But another pair of goons emerged from the gloom, their grubby hands reaching for her. She ducked out of their reach and turned to face their leader, realising grimly that she'd been cornered. Her eyes darted from him to his cronies and back again. Their clothes were crusted with salt, their hair matted with dirt and their fingertips blackened with grime. She recognised the sort immediately. *Swabbies.* They were the grunts of a ship, spending most days mopping up the deck. Their leader—a heartless, soulless pirate, no doubt—was still grinning maniacally as he invaded her personal space, thrusting his face close to hers. His greasy, foul smell assaulted her nostrils, so she did the only thing she could think of.

She turned up her nose at him.

He laughed. "Is that any way to treat an old friend? Surely you remember me—good old first matey Clegg?"

"What do you want, you dirty sea dog?" she demanded, tinting her tone with arrogance.

"You know what I want, my little lassie."

"I am *not* your little lassie," Juliana hissed.

She suddenly felt very crowded as the small group of scallywags tightened their circle around her, cutting off her view of the end of the alley. Her hand slipped instinctively to her thigh and she hitched up the hem of her dress.

"Plan on giving us a show?" the pirate asked suggestively, waggling his bushy brows at her exposed leg.

"Not likely," she snorted as her fingers found the hilt of her concealed dagger.

"Come on now," Clegg chuckled. "Just hand it over."

"Not on your life," she bit out.

"My life?" Clegg asked with a false smile. "I don't think it's *my* life you should be worried about, lassie."

Juliana did not answer. She kept her eyes trained on his every move, her hand tightening on her weapon.

"Just give us what's ours, and we'll be on our way," the pirate said, his voice unnaturally coaxing.

"It's not yours. And it never will be," Juliana declared.

The pirate's face turned ugly in rage. Before she could blink, he grabbed her by the upper arm and began to shake her violently.

"Stupid wench," he shouted, spittle flying. "Give me what's rightfully mine!"

"Oh? That's an odd coincidence." A deep booming voice echoed off the alley walls. "That's what I want too."

Her assailant's hand slipped from her arm as the thugs turned to see who had spoken.

Well, well, well, Juliana thought sardonically, *if it isn't Captain Rawden Wood. What impeccable timing.*

But this was not the way she had wanted to approach him, and she considered slinking off into the dark—except that the swabbies' bodies formed a solid wall against her back. She tensed, waiting for whatever would happen next.

"Just be on your way, bucko," Clegg sneered. "We have some unfinished business with this here lassie."

"So do I." Rawden paused and then added sarcastically, "*Bucko.*"

"You looking to get hurt, matey?" Clegg threatened.

Rawden paced calmly into the alley, his hands still lightly resting in his pockets. As he neared, Juliana saw just how intimidating he could be. He was tall and dark-haired with piercing green eyes. His gait was sure and measured, as deadly as that of a pacing lion. He stopped when he loomed over Clegg, who had to look up to meet his eyes.

"I hope you're not mistaking me for a dashing young dandy out to save a damsel in distress," he said, his voice pitched low. "Because that would be a fatal error."

"No disrespect, matey—but why bother us?" Clegg said, unable to keep himself from stammering slightly. "She's just one little wench."

"That's my business, not yours."

"I've got men here—"

Rawden interrupted him with a deep sigh.

"Look here, you rapscallion," Rawden said, tapping the gold pin adorning the lapel of his coat. "Do you know this crest?"

Clegg squinted at the gold pin; a winged woman resting on a thin circlet of gold. It was a well-known symbol. He paled and stepped backward.

"Captain Rawden Wood," Clegg rasped.

"Aye, then," Rawden replied, his voice hard and dangerous. "So you do know of me."

Clegg didn't bother to answer. Instead, he waved a hand at his swabbies and backed his way out of the alley as quickly as he could, disappearing with the sound of scurrying feet. Silence reigned in the nearly empty back street as Rawden watched their shadows disappear around the corner. Juliana regarded him warily, her fingers still tight around her dagger.

"You can let go of that knife, missy," Rawden grunted, his eyes sliding to hers. "I've no plans to hurt you just yet."

Juliana didn't so much as twitch. Rawden sighed.

"You have my money, girl." Rawden held out a hand expectantly. "That's what I'm here for."

She raised a thin brow, her eyes slowly trailing down his body. His eyes were the most uncanny shade of emerald green, and they gleamed in the half light, making him look even more devilish than before. He had a hard-set, square jaw that was covered in light stubble, and his thick dark hair tumbled in messy curls around his temples. Though he wasn't stocky by any means, he was tall and had sturdy, broad shoulders and a lean, muscular build. He was fairly well dressed for a down-and-out pirate, and his clothes were reasonably clean and neat. *Yes, he would do.* Juliana straightened, fixing him with a resolute stare.

"I will return your money," she told him in a clear, unwavering voice. "If you will hear my request first."

It was Rawden's turn to arch a brow.

"Why should I?" he asked, curious.

"What have you got to lose?" Juliana countered.

"Time."

"I will make it worth your while."

"Do you think you are in any position to be bargaining with me?"

"Do you want your money back or not?"

"You realise that I can just *take* it from you, do you not?" he asked incredulously.

"You said you would not hurt me."

"*Yet*," he clarified pointedly. "I said I had no plans to hurt you *yet*."

Juliana narrowed her eyes and planted her hands on her hips.

"You are an impoverished pirate at risk of losing your ship to decay. And any day, your gold-hungry gang of bandits will turn on you," Juliana declared haughtily. "I think that you *need* to hear my offer."

Rawden's lips thinned as his patience waned.

"Not so innocent after all," he muttered. "Well then, little lass, what is your offer?"

"I am looking for something," Juliana began.

"What is it?"

"Not your concern," she snapped before continuing. "I am looking for something of mine but I am also being pursued."

"I can see that," Rawden acknowledged. "And by some less than savoury characters, I assume."

"So," Juliana said with a quick nod of her head, "I need protection."

"For how long?"

"Until I find what I am looking for."

"Which is where?"

"I can't tell you yet," she said evasively. "But I require a ship to get there."

"I see," Rawden said curtly. "You're looking for something—but you won't tell me what. You are going somewhere along the coast—but you won't tell me where. And you need me to be your personal bodyguard for an indefinite length of time?" He barked a laugh. "I think not, lassie. I'll have my money and be on my way, thank you very much."

Juliana remained impassive as she drew a small pouch of coins from her cloak. She tossed it in his direction, and he caught it deftly with one hand. Rawden chuckled as he dropped the pouch back into his pocket.

"Good luck finding someone," he said as he turned away. "But I'm sure you couldn't pay enough for anyone to—"

"A gold sovereign," she cut in sharply.

He glanced at her over his shoulder.

"One gold sovereign is not nearly enough to—"

"One gold sovereign every day," she announced, blank-faced. "Every day from today until the day I safely have what I am looking for."

Rawden slowly turned on his heel, his eyes studying her serious expression.

"A gold sovereign every day," he repeated carefully. His voice dropped to a deadly timbre. "That is quite the dangerous promise, young lady. How do I know you can deliver? After all, you did swindle me for just a few shillings."

Her answer came in the form of a shining gold disc flying through the air, which he caught with a quick swipe of his hand. When he opened his fist, a single gold sovereign blinked up at him; he didn't need to bite at it to know it was real.

"That's for today," she was saying as she flicked a second gold coin his way. "And this is an advance for tomorrow." She paused before adding, "And I robbed you because it was the only way I knew to make you come find me."

"And where is the rest of my payment?" Rawden asked slyly, still staring at the two shining pieces of gold in his palm.

"Hidden," she answered sassily. "In spots along the way to what I'm after."

"Clever girl," Rawden mused aloud. He looked up, his eyes appraising. "One minute an innocent little aristocrat, the next a petty thief. And now," he said, "a cunning little merchant."

She wasn't quite sure if he was praising or berating her tactics—but one thing was for sure. There was *something* in his intense green eyes that sent her heartbeat racing. There was an electric pull between them that she just couldn't ignore. And if she played her cards right, their magnetic attraction might just work to her advantage—if she could keep her own jumbling emotions in check. Juliana tilted her head slightly, causing one perfect golden curl to fall over her porcelain cheek.

"Oh, I can be much more than just that," she answered in a lilting voice.

"Is that right?" Rawden prompted, a feral grin spreading his lips.

With all the grace of a svelte cat, Juliana sashayed toward him. When she was so close that their misting clouds of breath mingled, she touched his cool cheek with a fingertip. Moistening her red lips with the tip of her tongue, she slid her fingers down the line of his jaw. He caught her wrist in an iron grip.

"Planning to rob me again?"

She smiled and pulled her wrist from his grasp.

"Not if you accept my offer."

"It is quite a generous offer," he said thoughtfully, his hands wandering instinctively to her waist.

"You have no idea," Juliana purred seductively as she smoothed her hands up his arms and wound her arms around his neck. "Just imagine—a gold coin for every day you spend with me."

"*Protecting* you, you mean," Rawden corrected her, his voice a husky rasp.

Juliana felt him wind his arms more tightly around her as she stepped in even closer. She took a deep breath, inhaling his musky scent. He smelled of salt and oakwood, and his evening whiskers tickled her fair skin. She laid her cheek against his shoulder and pressed her lips to his neck.

"Yes," she murmured against the skin of his neck. "Protecting me."

Rawden's hands fisted in the fabric of her thin shift as he pulled her even closer and buried his nose in her soft hair.

"And what is to stop me from taking your gold *and* whatever it is that you're looking for?" he rasped.

"You couldn't if you tried," Juliana said with a short laugh punctuated by a soft moan as his hands slid to her bottom.

"Is that right? Won't you need protection once you've found your treasure?"

"No one else will know I've found it."

She twisted her hips against his and sighed when he thrust back.

"So how will I know when you have found this *thing* you are so keen on?"

"When I find what I want," Juliana said in a seductive whisper, "I can assure you that you will be the first to know." She laughed huskily. "Besides, I'm not so foolish as to keep paying a pirate for the pleasure of his company."

She gently nudged the underside of his jaw with the bridge of her nose. Then she lifted her lips to graze his earlobe with her teeth. He groaned softly, lost in the sensations. He abruptly pulled her away to hold her at arm's length.

"Fine," he said, meeting her playful eyes with a stern stare. "But I have one condition."

"Name it," she answered with a smirk.

"You are to obey me," he stipulated firmly.

"Obey?" She arched an imperious brow.

He nodded and took her chin between his thumb and forefinger.

"I will not be bound to a wench who will not allow me to protect her in my own way."

"Fair enough," Juliana replied with a slight shrug.

"It's settled then," Rawden said as he released her and stepped back.

With a curt nod, he turned and stalked away toward the docks. She followed, one step behind him. Her sharp gaze trailed over his masculine form. She knew it was a dangerous game she was playing, stoking the flames of desire between them while trying not to get burnt.

But she had cast her lot—and she was determined to win.

CHAPTER THREE

"I DIDN'T EXPECT you to get us into trouble this soon," Rawden muttered darkly.

"Apologies," Juliana said tightly, her slight form hidden behind his. "I most certainly did not plan for this to happen."

They stood at the edge of the docks, their backs to the channel. Nearly a dozen men brandishing pistols had them surrounded. Rawden's eyes flicked from one man to the other, his mind racing. They were clearly pirates, probably sent after them by Clegg. He might have been able to escape had he not been hindered by two very important facts: first, he had the girl to worry about. And more importantly, he had no weapon.

He sighed deeply and slowly raised his hands, ignoring Juliana's hiss of protest.

"Fine," he conceded with a flippant grin. "You win."

The pirates eyed him warily, their fingers tightening on their triggers.

"What?" Rawden said innocently. "You don't trust me?"

"Throw your weapons into the channel!" one pirate shouted.

"I don't have any on me," Rawden said with a slight shrug. "You can check if you want."

None of their attackers seemed to be inclined to get near the notorious captain. Instead, they began muttering softly amongst themselves.

"Look," Rawden said impatiently, "why don't you just take us to your fearless leader. It's what you were supposed to do anyway, right? If you don't trust me, just keep pointing us in the right direction with those shiny pistols of yours. I can assure you that I won't try to outrun your bullets."

"We just want the girl," one of them called out.

Rawden felt Juliana stiffen beside him. She dug her fingers into his sleeve, and he gently placed his hand over hers in what he hoped was a reassuring gesture. Really, did she think he would renege on their contract so soon? It hadn't even been a quarter of an hour since he'd given her his word. Besides, he had only gotten two sovereigns out of her so far.

"Unfortunately, we're on a two-for-one deal at the moment," he called back unyieldingly. "And I'm sure you'd rather I tag along willingly rather than pick you off one at a time from behind."

The pirates grumbled but reluctantly acquiesced, waving them toward the looming shadow of a ship moored a short way down. Rawden tucked Juliana's arm in his and strode along, his gait relaxed but his hand firmly gripping hers. Though she was stone-faced, he could feel the faint tremor in her fingers. He cast her a meaningful look, hoping she would fulfill her end of the bargain to follow his lead.

Not very long after, Juliana and Rawden found themselves standing on the deck of a massive ship—and, yet again, completely surrounded. The first mate, Clegg, pushed his way to the front.

"Remember me, dearies?" he drawled, spinning a blade with his fingers. "You were quite rude that last time, so I won't be so lenient now."

"Hold your tongue, Clegg."

The harsh voice rung out over the deck, and the whole crew quieted. As Rawden and Juliana watched, the captain of the ship slowly descended the wooden steps from the forecastle toward them. His eyes were sharp as he thoughtfully thumbed his greying beard.

"Greetings, Captain Wood," he said to Rawden amicably with a toothy grin. "Welcome to my vessel, the *Grey Gull*."

"What a pleasant surprise, Captain Elijah Hawkins," Rawden said, bowing with a flourish. "You're certainly looking well."

"More than I can say for you," Elijah replied lightly. "This is an awkward situation, isn't it?"

"Yes, isn't it?" Rawden echoed softly, his eyes never leaving Elijah's wizened face.

But Elijah's eyes were already sliding to Juliana, who stood half-hidden behind Rawden.

"Well now," Elijah said with false affection. "Aren't you all grown up now, Miss Juliana Wright."

Rawden felt Juliana tense and slide even further behind him. She was not even trying to hide her trembling now. Though he certainly understood her fear, such a blatant display of fright surprised him. She had not seemed the type to cower under pressure.

"Now don't be rude, young miss," Elijah chided, his voice dangerously soft. "We were good friends once, you and I. In fact, wasn't it your father who—"

Juliana stepped out from behind Rawden suddenly.

"Don't you dare speak of my father," Juliana demanded in a flinty voice, her eyes dancing in anger.

Rawden's eyebrows rose slowly. The fine tremors shaking her body hadn't been the result of fear at all. She'd not been afraid; she had been angry—no, not angry, absolutely *furious*.

"There she is," Elijah said, rocking back on his heels. "I thought you'd become a proper little damsel in distress for a moment. But that never was your style, was it?"

Juliana's lips tightened into a thin line, and she simply glared at him silently.

"I guarantee you won't be giving me the silent treatment for very long," Elijah said with a cruel smile. "But it will be easier on all of us if you would just give me the map."

Rawden studied Juliana's stony expression from the corner of his eye. *Map,* he thought, *what map?*

"I won't."

Elijah sighed heavily.

"I thought you might say that, my dear."

He shook his head, imitating regret. He turned to his crew and raised one hand high. While his back was turned, Rawden leaned down to whisper in Juliana's ear.

"I hope you can swim," he breathed quietly.

Juliana was about to ask what he meant when Elijah's booming voice rang out again.

"Shoot Captain Wood and feed him to the fish," Elijah commanded. "Then strip the girl and tie her to the mast. Have some fun too, while you're at it!"

The crew roared with delight as their captain egged them on with more promises of violence. But when Elijah turned back to his captives, he found them near the railing of the ship.

"Stop them!" he called belatedly.

But it was too late. With a wink and salute, Rawden jumped overboard with Juliana under one arm. The crew rushed to the edge of the deck and fired blindly into the dark water.

"Stop, stop you fools!" Elijah raged. "We need the girl alive!"

But only the faintest sounds of the commotion aboard reached Rawden's ears. Frigid water sloshed around him as he struggled to free Juliana from her heavy wool cloak. For once, he was happy that he wasn't carrying a firearm— at least he wouldn't lose anything to rust! Then, ignoring her sputtering and coughing, he dragged her kicking body through the water.

"I can swim," she panted. "Let go!"

He released her immediately, and she pushed away to tread water. He paused to stare at her pale silhouette as they rose and fell with the swell of the waves.

"Let's go," he said finally.

"Where?"

He didn't answer but turned and began to cut through the water in a strong, elegant front stroke. He glanced back over his shoulder to see Juliana catch up to him with equally skilled strokes. They swam for what seemed an eternity in the chilly water, forcing their muscles to strain against the cold. Rawden muttered curses on his salty lips as he cut through the icy waves. It just had to be winter-time, with the warm lights of Christmas blinking at their back and nothing but bone-chillingly cold water pulling at their heavy limbs. Just perfect. He could have been en-joying a sweet Christmas pudding in his cabin by now if he hadn't met this confoundedly alluring woman.

Finally, when the *Grey Gull* was a mere shadow be-hind them, a smaller shape emerged from the dark in front of them. It was a small rowboat, manned by two men— one at the bow and one at the stern. As soon as Juliana touched the rough wood with her fingers, she felt herself being hauled aboard. She collapsed at the bottom of the boat in a wet tangle of soaked limbs and cloth. Cough-ing and shivering, she rubbed her hands up and down her arms, trying to revive her numb limbs. She felt Rawden sit on the bench in front of her and heard him bark orders to his men, who began to row immediately. Juliana slowly crawled into sitting on the bench opposite her pirate pro-tector. When she lifted her eyes to his, he was glaring at her with a clenched jaw.

"Care to explain that to me, little miss?"

"Explain what?" she asked shortly.

"This business of a map."

"What business is that of yours?"

He leaned forward, and shook the excess water from his hair with long fingers.

"Don't fool yourself into thinking that I'll blindly endan-ger my life or the lives of my crew for you, Miss Wright," Rawden said in clipped tones. "I don't care what history you seem to have with Captain Elijah Hawkins, but he is a dangerous opponent. And I'll bet my boat that he'll come after you again. So you'd better tell me right now—what kind of map do you have that makes you so important to him?"

Juliana looked away into the darkness, her fingers tightening around her arms until her knuckles were white. Her gaze grew distant as her lashes lowered.

"There was once a legendary map," she began softly, "that was hidden in the Royal Navy's archives." Her tone took on an almost singsong quality. "It was an ancient map—so old that the paper would crumble into dust if you touched it carelessly. It was so precious that no one knew of it except the highest ranking officers, and they were sworn to secrecy. The map may have even belonged to the great King Arthur. It may have even been penned by Merlin himself."

Juliana closed her eyes and took a deep breath. When she spoke again, her voice was hard and cold as stone.

"My father found this map. And Captain Elijah Hawkins killed him for it."

"But your father kept its secret safe." Rawden's voice was flat. "And now only you know where the map is."

"Only I."

For a few long moments, there were no sounds but the lapping of the water against the sides of the dinghy and the grunts of the rowing men. And then Rawden heard something else—the chattering of teeth. With a sigh, he shrugged out of his long coat and reached forward to drape it over the girl's huddled form.

"And," he asked quietly, "what does this map lead to?"

"Treasure."

Rawden gripped the lapels of the coat he'd put on her and pulled her closer. She met his sharp eyes and stared back defiantly.

"What kind of treasure?"

She pulled away from his grip, her chin tilted back.

"Roman gold," she informed him. "More Roman gold than has ever been found before. And all hidden in secret sea caves."

"Where?"

She glared.

"Tell me," Rawden demanded. "Our agreement will still stand."

"In Cornwall," she said in a hushed voice. "Sea caves in Cornwall."

Rawden leaned his elbows on his knees and steepled his fingers in front of his face. He regarded her calm expression through hooded eyes. His job had just gotten much more complicated. On top of protecting a headstrong lass with more secrets than she cared to share, he would have a bloodthirsty pirate on his tail looking for an unmatched treasure map. He considered her serious face with calculating eyes. She was watching him with guarded hopefulness. His lips spread into a slow smile. He had much to lose— but so much more to gain: his pay in gold and perhaps a cut of the Cornish treasure. Yes, he thought, he would see this adventure to its profitable end.

"Well," he said, leaning back with a mild chuckle, "at least now I know the direction we are sailing in."

CHAPTER FOUR

WHEN JULIANA SET her bare feet aboard the infamous *Golden Maiden*, she knew she was getting a small glimpse of the Golden Age of piracy. Smooth wood gleamed and billowing sails hung from imposing masts. It was a beautifully designed ship.

And then she felt the stares. All the men—from the burliest swabbie to the scrawniest deck hand—had stopped whatever it was they had been doing to stare, slack-jawed. Juliana's chest tightened. She recognised the look in their eyes.

Hungry. Wanting. Waiting.

Even if they may have once been the most disciplined and steadfast pirate crew in existence, they now resembled a pack of rabid dogs more than anything else. A hand descended heavily on her small shoulder, and she looked up in time to see Rawden level his crew with an uncompromising glare.

"Listen up," he boomed thunderously. "This here girl is my guest—so no one touches her but me."

A collective cloud of loud grumbling rose from the mean-looking crew.

"She's also your meal ticket, you scallywags," Rawden announced. "She's leading us to a stash of gold. So no one—and I mean, *no one*—" he punctuated dangerously "—is to lay a finger on her. Except me."

The groaning turned to cheers as Rawden took her by the upper arm and began to drag her away from their leering eyes.

"Give it all away, will you?" Juliana hissed angrily.

Rawden hustled her towards the forecastle, and her feet slapped against the deck as she skipped to keep up.

"You should know it's important to give them a reason *not* to hurt you," Rawden muttered under his breath. "Now where to first, missy?"

"Portsmouth," she said without hesitating.

"Wilkins!" Rawden shouted above the din. "Full sails to Portsmouth harbour."

"Aye, aye Captain!"

And then Rawden pushed her into his quarters, closing the door behind him.

Juliana padded slowly into the centre of the luxuriously appointed cabin, tossing away his sopping long coat. The room was filled with dark wooden furniture and rich carpets. The cabin was lit by a slow-burning fireplace at the far end. In the centre was an imposing, ancient oak table, and in one corner was a wide, magnificent bed.

"And I suppose that this is where I'll be sleeping?" she asked sweetly.

"This is where *we* will be sleeping, my darling," Rawden

corrected. "Unless you'd rather take up a cot down below with the crew."

"No, thank you," Juliana said caustically, flipping her dripping hair over one shoulder. "Though your decor is sorely lacking. No Christmas candles, no holly—not even a pine bough to celebrate the season!"

"Well then," Rawden returned curtly. "You'll have to make do with my company."

"Why don't you take up with your crew," she snapped, hands on hips. "And leave a lady to her private space."

"A *lady*—" he slurred the word "—wouldn't have taken up with a pirate in the first place."

Juliana's eyes narrowed.

"So what would you say that I am, then?"

"Important cargo, perhaps?" Rawden quipped, tapping his chin lightly with a finger. "And for your information, cargo does not move around my ship."

"What is that supposed to mean?"

"It means that you are not to leave this cabin—not for anything and not for even an instant—unless I am escorting you," Rawden commanded sternly.

"You cannot be serious," Juliana countered, her voice rising.

"I assure you that I am." Rawden shook a finger at her. "You will not venture from these quarters."

"Important cargo?" Juliana protested indignantly. "More like a prisoner! I will not be so treated, dear sir!"

Rawden took a good, long look at her. Her dress was still soaking wet, and the sheer material clung to her curves scandalously. Desire spiked in his gut as he traced the shadowy lines beneath the thin fabric, trailing from her shapely calves up to her flushing shoulders. When his hooded eyes reached her face, he discovered her sweetly blushing despite her angry glare.

"You are quite the sight for hungry eyes," he said huskily, his feet moving before he realised it. "Do you even realise what my men would do to you if they caught you alone?"

"I can protect myself, thank you very much," she huffed.

"What? With this?" Rawden asked, his fingers nimbly clamping over her thigh, blocking her access to her only blade. "You're much too naive, my dear."

"I do not like being *handled*, Captain Wood," she breathed in a furious hiss. "Remove your hand at once."

"No," Rawden answered, fingers clenching around her shapely thigh. "You need to understand. You are not as invincible as you think."

His other hand shot out to grab a fistful of her long hair. Though his grip was not at all painful, it was firm. He drew her closer slowly, his eyes smouldering and resolute.

"Even if my men are loyal to me, their...baser instincts would override logic." He leaned in to inhale the scent of her. "And not one of them would be able to resist plucking such a ripe fruit. The minute one of them caught you alone, you would find your clothes ripped away and your body ruined. Is your freedom to roam the deck worth such a price?"

Juliana studied his earnest expression, her lips turned down into a frown.

"Are you trying to tell me that keeping me a prisoner in your cabin is for my own good and not for your own?"

Rawden shrugged, adopting his cavalier facade once more.

"Believe what you will, little missy," he chuckled. "But like it or not—you will not be leaving this room without my say-so."

Juliana did not like the current turn of events. She felt another string slip from her control as the pirate captain took command of yet another aspect of their tenuous relationship. She forced a flippant smirk to her lips.

"Fine. As long as you understand the repercussions of annoying a lady," she quipped.

"Which are?"

"You'll soon find out. Have you never lived with an irritated before?" she said breezily.

He let his gaze trail up and down her svelte form.

"I'm sure the magnificent view will temper any minor inconveniences," he said with a sultry grin. "You do cut quite the scene, my darling."

She did not flinch when his arms closed around her; rather, she twined her wrists behind his neck. Rawden smoothed his palms up her sides, relishing the feel of the wet fabric sliding over her slick skin.

"As do you," she replied, fingering the edge of his open collar.

"I am quite sure that you cannot see through my clothing," he answered devilishly, his lips at her neck.

"Perhaps," Juliana countered with a laugh. "But from this angle, I am quite sure that my modesty is intact."

In response, Rawden spun her in his arms, anchoring her to him with a forearm around her waist. His other hand skimmed the swell of her breasts. He leaned forward to peer greedily over her shoulder and got an eyeful of her heaving bosom and her erect nipples under sheer fabric.

"And now?"

"Now, you are being quite cheeky."

"I'll show you cheeky," he grunted.

With his free hand, he began to massage her chilled flesh, his fingers deftly searching out the curves and crevices of her body. Juliana's breathing hitched in her throat as she threw her head back against his shoulder, her nails digging passionately into his bicep. Rawden smiled at the wanton flush creeping up her chest. As he smoothed his rough palm under the hem of her wet dress and up her silken thigh, he began to tug at her short sleeve. The damp material slid down easily, baring the curve of her creamy shoulder. He nipped lightly at the exposed flesh, his breath making her shiver.

"Now," he whispered against her skin as his hands began to search her body with more fervour, "I wonder where you've hidden that map."

In a sudden flash of white cloth and golden hair, Juliana was halfway across the room, standing by the fireplace. Though her chest still heaved with desire, her eyes were cold and wary. She was tense, and her hand was again at her thigh. Rawden watched as she gripped her dagger's hilt with white-knuckled ferocity.

She's too quick, he thought, *and more dangerous than she seems*.

"You press too far," she warned, her gaze unblinking.

"And you assume too much," he returned evenly. "Why would I settle for just one sovereign a day when I could have a whole cave of Roman gold?"

"You will not reach the Roman gold without my directions."

"And yet," he said, taking a step forward, "here you are, in my quarters with only your short dagger as a defence."

"You promised to protect me," she reminded him.

"And I will," he affirmed with a smirk. "But I did not promise to let you keep your map."

"Do you mean this map?"

Juliana dropped the hem of her skirt to lift a damp, folded-up square of aged paper between two fingers. Then, without a moment's hesitation, she flicked the paper into the low-burning fire. It crumbled into ash and disappeared with a quick plume of grey smoke.

"There now," she said, voice steady. "Now I am well and truly the only one that knows the way to my treasure."

Rawden narrowed his eyes and studied her for a brief moment.

Quick-witted. Defiant. Fearless. Miss Juliana Wright had once again proved herself a force to be reckoned with. A breathtakingly beautiful force.

He walked to her with slow, deliberate steps. Though she stiffened at his approach, she did not flinch when he reached out to brush a stray strand of hair from her cheek with the back of his hand. His touch was tender, but his eyes were hard and calculating.

"Clever girl," he said softly, dangerously.

He moved in closer, sliding his palm up her neck to cup her cheek. Lowering his face to hers, he dragged one fingertip across her bare shoulder. Briefly, he caught a glimpse of black-and-green inking on her shoulder blade— a tattoo, perhaps? But he did not have time to dwell on the curiosity; at the moment, there were important negotiations to be made.

"I believe we need to revisit the terms of our agreement," Rawden told her, his hands gliding down her arms.

"And why is that?" she asked, tilting her head to give his lips access to her collarbone.

"Because there is something new on the table, Miss Wright," he announced.

"Something new?"

He spun around suddenly with her in his arms. Lifting her effortlessly, he set her atop the wooden table so that she was perched on its edge with his hips wedged between her thighs. With one hand, he carelessly swept a pile of papers to the floor; with the other, he gently pushed her shoulder to the rough tabletop. He planted one open hand beside her surprised face and stared down, leaning over her.

"Yes, there is the matter of the gold—and my share of it."

"I already promised you one gold sovereign for every—"

"Every day *until* we find your treasure." He paused to pin her with a serious stare. "Will you make me your enemy after that? Your gold coins will be nothing but crumbs when we lay eyes on the treasure."

"Clever man." Juliana threw his words back at him with brief smile. "So you would claim a share of what is mine?"

"Yes. And why not? I will have helped you find it."

"Very well," she acquiesced. "You may take ten percent for your troubles."

Rawden chuckled and then lowered his face to press a kiss to her jaw. The bargaining had begun.

"Half of the treasure," he countered. "And no less."

Juliana gave as good as she got, tightening her thighs around his waist and twining her fingers in his hair as she twisted *just so*.

"Too much," she sighed into his hair. "You can have twenty percent."

Rawden groaned and thrust the evidence of his arousal against her core. He splayed his fingers over her ribs and bent lower to drag his teeth against her earlobe. The air became heady and thick with the heat between their bodies.

"You drive a hard bargain, my dear," he grunted, at the edge of losing all control. "I'll take a quarter of the treasure—and in exchange, I'll protect you for a fortnight after you've found your treasure."

Juliana stilled, pushing him back to face him squarely. Her blue eyes searched his expression, weighing every nuance in his face. After a moment, she grinned and pulled him close—and the deliciously carnal spark they had been nursing burst into full flame.

"I accept your terms, Captain Wood," she said, her pink tongue darting out to lick her bottom lip. "How shall we seal this agreement?"

"Let me think," he answered, leaning down and bracing himself against the table. "A kiss?"

She arched a coy brow before tugging his face close to hers, and he was briefly surprised by the sheer intensity of her kiss. The minute her lips touched his, it was as if they had both been swept up in a raging typhoon of lush sensations. She suckled greedily at his lips, and he returned her open-mouthed kisses with equal fervour, his tongue sweeping past her sweet lips. His hands found their way to her smooth thighs as hers found the opening of his shirt. With a swift jerk, she pulled his shirt open and slid her hands over his chest. As the pads of her fingers swept over the ridges of his abdomen, he pulled his shirt off and threw it to the floor. Her hands kneaded his taut muscles, and he tangled his fingers in her long hair, pulling her into an even deeper kiss. She rocked against him and moaned, hands clawing at his back. Growling with desire, Rawden pushed her back down onto the table and stretched her arms up above her head, threading his fingers between hers. He continued to ravage her with hot, insistent kisses, and she bucked beneath him in response. Rawden smoothed his rough hands down her long arms, around the column of her neck and over her slender shoulders. Then, with his palms flush against her heated skin, he pulled down the thin fabric of her gown, hitching the elasticated collar under the generous swell of her breasts. Juliana's teeth raked his bottom lip, and she arched up off the table as Rawden's calloused fingers grazed the smooth contours, catching lightly on her hardening caramel peaks. He wound his arms around her waist and drew her upward as his lips left hers to trail nibbling kisses down her throat and past her collarbone. He trailed a slick line down her sternum with his tongue and grinned when she gasped and clutched blindly at his hair. He cupped one generous mound with a hand and then latched on to the other with his mouth, his tongue swirling seductive patterns on her sensitive flesh. Juliana could not help but cry out in pleasure, her toes curling and her thighs tightening around his grinding hips.

It was perfect. It was absolutely perfect. And their agreement was about to be sealed with much more than just a *kiss*.

Rawden was just getting ready to reach down to unbutton his trousers when a loud knock sounded on his door.

"Not now!" he barked shortly, his lips barely leaving Juliana's exposed skin.

"We need you at the wheel, Captain," his first mate called insistently, rapping on the door again.

Rawden growled, gathering the girl into his arms and pressing his nose into her skin to inhale her sweet scent. Then he straightened and pulled her off the table, gently setting her down on her feet. She slumped against his chest, and he could feel her heart racing.

So close, he thought to himself, *they had been so close.*

Juliana sighed disappointedly—and then stepped away. She moved closer to the fire, unobtrusively fixing her garments as she did so. Rawden let loose a string of expletives under his breath before turning to scowl at the closed door.

"Wait for me at the wheel," he commanded, his voice rough with unspent passion.

He glanced at Juliana, eyes still slightly wild.

"You should dry out that dress," he suggested. "We have no other women's clothes aboard. We will reach Portsmouth by tomorrow's eve."

Juliana nodded and watched as he stormed away, his footfalls heavy with frustration. Just before he pulled the door open, he spun around to wag a finger at her.

"This *conversation* isn't over, my dear," he said with a wicked grin that promised more to come.

But by the time Rawden stumbled blindly back into his quarters, the fire had died down to burning embers and the dark furnishings were cast in shadow. The ship still shifted in the angry waves, but after a moment of adjusting his eyes to the semi-darkness, Rawden strode into the cabin easily, shutting the door firmly behind him. Heavy silence hung like a blanket, and he spied a small figure curled up in his sheets. He sighed.

Apparently their steamy conversation was over after all.

Rawden slowly stripped to his underclothes, tossing his damp, salty garments over the back of a chair. His attention turned to the bed. He briefly wondered if she'd taken his advice to dry her damp clothing, or if she'd stubbornly been shivering away all night long. She looked warm enough at the moment.

His eyes surveyed the scene. Juliana had evidently decided that his entire bed was now her personal domain; for though she was small, she had planted herself firmly in the middle of the mattress.

Well, that was a misconception that just begged to be corrected.

Setting his jaw, Rawden stalked over to the bed and sat on the edge. Lifting the corner of the blankets, he slid under the warm sheets and lay down. As soon as his bare skin touched hers, he felt her stiffen. He smirked and slid even closer.

"A gentleman would take the floor."

Her voice was clear and sharp, untainted by sleep.

"I am not a gentleman."

Juliana let out a low growl and scooted to the far edge of the bed, wrapping the sheets around her like a protective cocoon.

"Now, now," Rawden crooned, edging closer. "You were so…amiable before. And we are to be bedmates for a while, after all."

His hands slid over her curves under the covers, his rough skin sending prickles of pleasure through her body. Juliana tensed as he hooked an arm around her waist and pulled her back into his warm chest, his hands smoothing over the flimsy shirt she had thrown on as a substitute for proper nightclothes. He began to rub slow, sensual circles over her slim limbs with his calloused palms, and Juliana felt her muscles yield to the exquisite pressure. His warm breath tickled her ear as his hands trailed lower, and Juliana bit back a sigh, her fingers twisting in the sheets. Almost lost in a fog of warm and budding desire, Juliana felt the insistent tug of caution at the edges of her mind.

No, she thought hazily, *this isn't right.*

How did the pirate see her? As a meal ticket. A luscious treat to be had in his cabin. A wanton woman who *needed* him—needed his ship, needed his help, needed his protection—and needed his affection?

Her mind at odds with her body, Juliana tried to reason through her conundrum. She couldn't let him control that one last bit of leverage she had over him or she would be completely at his mercy. She had to seduce *him* and not the other way around.

Rawden's fingers dipped lower. And when they skated down the length of her inner thigh, Juliana felt a jolt of pleasure that shocked her into action. She pulled away suddenly, rolling away so that she faced him in the dark.

"Stop it," she panted, curling her fingers around the coverlet and pulling it close to her chin.

Rawden raised an eyebrow and met her eyes, which were luminous in the half light.

"Don't be coy," he urged, reaching a hand out to her.

"No!" she cried out. Using her very last trump card, she whispered pitiably, "You'll ruin me."

Rawden froze and stared, slowly retracting his hand. Cursing, he rolled away and pulled the covers over his bare chest. Juliana watched his hulking form in the dark and gradually edged even further away. She could practically feel his unspent desire building into tense frustration.

There, she thought triumphantly, *now* you *want* me. Once again, she had gained the upper hand.

CHAPTER FIVE

MOST BRITONS WANTED a bit of snow around the Yuletide season—if only to watch the large, heavy snowflakes drift down from the sky. But sailors hated the blanket of ice and snow that turned the decks into deadly ice rinks and churned the waves angrily.

Sailing had been miserable all day, and the gale-force winds had only died down once they were nearing Portsmouth harbour. Rawden had been wrestling with the wheel for hours on end, barking orders to his exhausted crew and cursing the tumultuous waves.

Even so, his thoughts had managed to stray to the vixen residing in his room. He doubted she'd been much perturbed by the inclement sailing conditions. Recalling her ease in swimming and her steady footing on the ship, he reckoned she'd spent quite a bit of time at sea. He'd even glimpsed lines of green and black on her shoulder—a tattoo? What decent young lass had a tattoo? He began to suspect that her father had been more than just a man holding a legendary map; could her father have been a pirate?

That would explain how she knew Captain Elijah Hawkins, and how she could face his kind so fiercely and fearlessly.

And yet...

Her voice was so velvety and sweet—not roughened by the salty sea air. Her manner of speech was elegant and smooth—not crass from a life lived in taverns and brothels. And her skin smelt of roses and peaches—and was just as soft to the touch and sweet on the tongue. Just thinking about having his hands and lips on her body was enough to send Rawden into a dizzying state of desire, his very skin tingling with need.

He was hungry—and not just for food.

So, when he finally managed to leave the upper deck, he made a brief stop at the galley before striding impatiently back to his quarters, a tray of food on his arm. He pushed his way into his cabin, kicking the door closed behind him. Then he stopped abruptly, his eyes transfixed on the vision waiting for him.

Juliana was standing with her back to a floor-length mirror. In one hand, she held up a priceless, ornately fashioned hand mirror. Her head was tilted back as she studied the reflection, her long curls cascading over one shoulder. She was wearing nothing but one of his white shirts, the buttons undone. It hung loosely from her elbows, and Rawden caught a glimpse of her back in the tall mirror before she stepped away. He registered more ink lines in blue and green, but quickly dismissed the observation in favour of watching her glide toward him. She pulled the shirt up to cover her shoulders and only bothered to close the bottom few buttons, leaving a long line of creamy skin down to her navel open to his greedy eyes. She swayed

over to the large wooden table and carefully set down the
mirror, leaning to rest her hip against the table's edge. His
shirt's bottom hem just barely covered her bottom, gently
grazing the top of her thighs. She cocked her head to one
side, watching him expectantly.

."Hungry?" Rawden asked, his throat suddenly dry.

He set his tray—which had nearly been forgotten—on
the table. Then he pulled out a chair. Juliana smiled. Her
eyes never leaving his, she stepped close and ran a finger
from his temple to his chin.

"How considerate of you," she murmured, pressing a
kiss to his stubbled chin.

Rawden swallowed. Just moments ago, he had imagined
himself as the dominant one, intent on ravishing her after
two quick bites of food. But now…now it seemed that she
had caught him in a web of feminine charm he had never
experienced before—and she knew it.

Juliana's eyes gleamed as she watched Rawden go rigid
with want. She had him just where she needed him to be
for her plan to work—completely enamoured with her. But
as she gently pushed his damp overcoat from his shoulders,
she wondered if she had already fallen for him as well.

No matter, she thought as she admired his broad shoulders. It was far too late to back out now.

Juliana took him by the collar of his shirt and gently
pushed him into sitting in the chair he had just pulled out
for her. He began to protest, and she smiled at his apparent show of chivalry, her heart warming to her cocky pirate captain. Confidence in her choice grew.

"I'm cold," Juliana purred, pressing a chaste kiss to his
lips. "Don't make me sit alone."

With that she eased herself into sitting across his knees, revelling in the feel of his hard, corded muscles under her thighs. Rawden immediately placed his hand at the small of her back for support.

"So," she asked conversationally. "What have you brought us to eat? I'm absolutely starving."

"You're lucky," Rawden said, his eyes drifting to her exposed legs. "We were just in port so the food hasn't had a chance to go rotten yet."

Juliana surveyed the tray. There were two bows of steaming meat stew, a few hardtack biscuits, a couple of pieces of fruit and two small mugs of hot rum. It smelled delicious. Her stomach rumbled, and Rawden chuckled.

"I haven't had a meal in half a day," Juliana huffed. "And I can't eat the gold stashed in this cabin."

"True," Rawden said, dragging the tray closer. "So eat up. We are almost in Portsmouth."

Juliana began to delicately lift spoonfuls of the hearty stew to her lips, carefully savouring each bite. Rawden reached around her to dip into his own bowl, amusedly watching her dainty way of eating. When both bowls were scraped clean, Rawden grabbed one of the apples. With his arms still around her, he began to cut the apple into slices. Then, with a teasing smile, he offered her one of the slices, holding it in front of her. Juliana took the crisp slice in her mouth, suggestively sliding her lips over it before taking it with her teeth. While she chewed, she selected another slice and offered to him. She giggled as he took the whole piece in one bite, his teeth lightly grazing her fingertip.

Rawden tightened his arm around her waist and leaned in, nosing his way forward until their lips touched. But unlike before, this kiss was languid, slow and deliberate. With the taste of fresh apples still on their tongues, they indulged in each other, feeling every nuance of lips, tongue and teeth. The orange glow of the fire warmed their skin, and they engaged in a slow exploration of each other's bodies. Hands sliding up limbs, fingers tangling in hair and sighs escaping moist lips. They hadn't even realised how much time had passed or how closely they were twined around one another—until there was another loud rapping at the door.

Rawden dropped his forehead onto Juliana's shoulder.

"Not again," he groaned.

The knocking came again.

"What?" Rawden shouted, exasperated.

"We are docking in Portsmouth harbour, Captain."

"Fine, fine," he answered with a drawn-out sigh. "We've arrived at your first stop. Shall we go, my lady?"

Juliana offered him an apologetic shrug and stood reluctantly.

"I suppose we should," she said with a rueful smile.

She walked over to the fireplace and carefully pulled her dress from the mantle, where it had been hanging to dry. To Rawden's surprise, she spun around to face him before dropping his shirt to the floor, giving him a quick glimpse of her naked body before she pulled on her high-waisted evening dress.

"It's cold," she said, grinning at the way he had dropped his jaw. "May I trouble you for a cloak?"

He wordlessly grabbed a heavy, hooded cloak from a trunk while she rummaged through his things for some semblance of small footwear. Finding a worn pair of slim leather boots—which looked as if they were from his child-hood—she pulled them on and laced them up. When she stood, he draped the cloak over her shoulders. Juliana pulled the wide hood over her head and took his prof-fered arm. Together, they stepped out onto the deck and headed for the gangway.

"Will I need to take my men?" Rawden asked.

"I'm sure you can handle me on your own," Juliana quipped lightly as she nimbly skipped down the ramp.

Rawden raised a brow but followed her lead as she marched straight into the roughest borough of Portsmouth. With Christmas only a few days away, even this dimly lit neighbourhood was awash with festive trimmings. Holly boughs and brightly coloured lanterns adored the doorways and window sills of many a public house. And there were even a few drunken revellers singing traditional Christ-mas carols in the streets.

Juliana walked purposefully through the sludgy streets, her eyes fixed on some unknown goal. Then without bat-ting an eye, she pulled them into the seediest tavern of them all.

It took Rawden a minute to adjust his eyes to the dimly lit pub. It was crowded and dark, crammed full of burly men hunched over rickety tables. No one seemed to notice their entrance, however—it seemed the tavern's patrons were already far too drunk to even lift their heads. Juli-ana quickly scanned the room. Her hand tightened on his arm before she slipped away toward a dark corner booth.

"Wait for me here," she instructed him quietly as she glided effortlessly through the boozy throng.

Huffing, Rawden eased himself into leaning against

the doorpost, his arms crossed over his chest and his eyes trained on Juliana. His overlarge cloak seemed the perfect camouflage for his stunning protégée. Her golden tresses were completely hidden, and the bulky material obscured her feminine form. He watched as Juliana slid into a shadowy corner booth at the other end of the room. A man leaned forward to greet her, his expression relieved. He was handsome in an older, dignified way, with silver hair at his temples and wrinkles at the corners of his eyes. As they began to talk, the man fervently clasped both her hands between his.

Rawden stood straighter. He'd guessed that she had planned to meet someone in the tavern—probably some business associate—but she was meeting a man who was acting much too *friendly* for his taste.

For her part, Juliana gently extricated her hands from the man's grasp and put a reassuring hand on his shoulder. Rawden could not hear their conversation, nor see Juliana's face because of her hood, but he could very clearly see worry etched into her companion's handsome face. Juliana's slender hand reached out to pat his, her head bobbing underneath the voluminous hood. The man gripped her fingers tightly, his expression ardent as he leaned in. Rawden frowned. This was no ordinary business meeting.

He pushed away from the door frame, intent on stalking over to the booth to find out exactly what was going on. Was he a friend? A lover? An accomplice?

But before he could take two steps, Juliana had risen from her seat. Though the man looked longingly up at her, she only patted his shoulder before turning away. She

wove her way back through the crowd, pausing to touch
Rawden's elbow and then turning to the door.

"Let's go," she whispered urgently.

Rawden remained rooted to the spot.

"You two seemed cozy," he commented blandly.

A line appeared between her brows.

"So?"

"He looked a bit old for you, don't you think?"

Juliana looked up at him, her blue eyes flashing. Rawden
stared back down at her, stone-faced.

"Yes, he *is* a bit old for me," she retorted sharply.

"So then, you're stringing him along?"

Juliana stepped back, momentarily stung by his words
and the bitterness in his green eyes. A spark of bitter anger
took root in her heart.

"Aren't you doing the same to me? In any case, what
business is it of yours?" she blurted before she could check
herself. "I'm paying you to be my bodyguard, not my conscience."

Rawden's face went blank, his eyes shuttering all emotion.

"Indeed," he said tonelessly. "So you are nothing more
than a common strumpet after all."

Rendered speechless, she glared at him, slack-jawed
and indignant. She allowed him to take her by the arm
and brusquely pull her from the tavern and into the cold
night air.

"Minx," he muttered as he towed her back toward the
boat. "Clever little liar."

The chill in his voice was colder than the biting wind
that whipped through the December air. All the Christ-

mas merriment around them did nothing to lighten either
of their dark expressions or moods. Juliana fumed silently,
occasionally skipping to keep up with his long strides. Confusion thickened her thoughts; she didn't know why she
was so angry—so much so that hot tears stung the corner
of her eyes. She shouldn't be angry at all, she told herself.
She shouldn't even care. Captain Rawden Wood was nothing but a means to an end, a tool to be used.

But still…

His wrongful, caustic accusations had her stewing in offended ire. She wasn't sure why she was so affected; only
that she was—and thus the situation needed to be rectified.

So, just before they reached the gangway to his ship,
Juliana wrenched her arm away and spun around to face
him, the edges of her cloak flapping in the wind. Throwing
back her hood, she jabbed at his sternum with one finger.

"Just what is your problem, Captain?" she demanded
furiously.

"My problem?" He barked a short, humourless laugh.
"Only that I've been taken for a complete fool."

"What are you on about?" she exclaimed incredulously.

"That old geezer," he said frostily. "You had him
wrapped right around your little finger."

Juliana nearly stomped a foot in irritation.

"Joffrey? He's old enough to be my father!"

"Precisely," Rawden spat. "And yet you still stooped
low enough to seduce him."

"Seduce Joffrey?" Juliana shook her head in frustration.
"I don't know what you're talking about!"

Rawden snorted and leaned in to say, "You nearly had me

fooled too, you know. Your sweet little act almost reeled me in completely. But all this time, and I wasn't the only one!"

Juliana reeled backward, her eyes wide.

"Now wait just a minute," she said, her voice dropping to an icy whisper. "You actually think I take Joffrey to my bed?"

Rawden threw his hands in the air.

"Why else would you hold his hand and cozy up to him in a tavern?" he sneered. "I just wonder what deal you made with him!"

Juliana stared, blinking hard. Then she suddenly doubled over, choking in laughter. *He was jealous.* The thought was at once a source of relief and amusement. *Just jealous.* And then a realisation hit her—she was happy that he hadn't truly been disgusted by her, and that somewhere deep inside of him, he wanted her for his own. A second, more important realisation dawned on her then: she wanted him for her own as well.

Rawden looked on, feigning indifference. After a long moment, Juliana straightened, blinking away tears. Then, with a burst of speed, she rose to her tiptoes and grabbed Rawden by the lapels of his jacket, pulling him down so that they were nose to nose.

"Listen closely, you fool," she said sternly. "Joffrey— that old geezer as you put it—was my father's first mate. He has been watching out for me since the day I could walk—so *no*," she emphasised, "I was not seducing him. I was just telling him about our arrangement and collecting a few important items from him."

"Like what?" Rawden challenged stubbornly.

"More of your payment, for one. But that's not what's

important," Juliana said with a sly smirk. "But there is something you need to understand."

"Oh?"

"Yes, that's right. You need to understand that I do need you to take me to the gold. And I do need you to protect me. But I'm not playing you for a fool—because there's something else I need from you."

"And what's that?" Rawden asked skeptically.

"I also need this."

Without warning, Juliana pushed her lips against his, capturing him in a searing, passionate kiss. She hooked her arms around his neck and let him drag her to his body with eager arms. After showing him just how much he wasn't a simple cog in her plans, Juliana pulled away to offer him a triumphant smirk.

"Do you understand now?" she asked affectionately.

"Oh I think I do," came a strange voice from a distance.

Rawden carefully set Juliana on her feet and wrapped a protective arm around her shoulders. He was absolutely exasperated. Completely and utterly frustrated. Not only had they been interrupted *again*, but now—for the second time in as many days—they were completely surrounded by a crowd of enemies.

CHAPTER SIX

"Don't you know when not to interrupt a couple?" Rawden lazily drawled, adopting a relaxed stance as he faced their adversaries.

"So," Captain Elijah Hawkins leered. "You're a couple now? You've really grown up, Miss Wright."

"You still can't have the map," Juliana told him, sassily placing a hand on her hip.

"If I can't have that map," Elijah threatened, "then I'll take your ship, Captain Wood."

He snapped his fingers and his gangly crew lit up dozens of bottles, all filled with oil. The home-made bombs glittered menacingly in the dark, illuminating the cruel smiles of the rival pirates. Rawden's jaw clenched. There was no way that his crew could put out the fires fast enough—but they would definitely try, leaving himself and Juliana vulnerable to any sort of attack that Elijah could devise. Even Rawden couldn't best two dozen armed men. He glanced down at Juliana, his mind scrambling for an out.

"Ready to really make the *Golden Maiden* glow, boys?"

Elijah hooted, lifting a hand to give the signal. "It will be a most beautiful Christmas ornament!"

"Wait!" Juliana called out suddenly.

Elijah grinned and lowered his hand slightly.

"Had a change of heart, lassie?"

Juliana stepped out from under Rawden's arm and drew a weathered scroll from her cloak. She held it up so all could see it.

"Will you leave us in peace if I give you this map?" she asked, her voice grave.

"Of course," Elijah answered with a gracious shrug. "That is all I ever wanted from you."

Juliana's lips thinned.

"I will give you this map, and you will leave without causing us or the ship any harm," Juliana stipulated calmly. "Swear by the sea."

Elijah dropped into a gallant bow.

"I swear by the seven seas," he said with a flourish.

Juliana nodded and then tossed the scroll high in the air. Elijah caught and unrolled it, his eyes greedily poring over the parchment. Then he chuckled deeply and re-rolled the ancient map.

"Finally," Elijah said in a self-satisfied voice. "How does it feel to know that if your father had only done what you did just now, he would still be alive today?"

"Stow it, Hawkins," Rawden snapped, voice tight with anger.

Rawden's fists clenched at his sides. They had been defeated. All had been in vain. There would be no treasure now, not even the promise of gold sovereigns.

"And a merry Christmas to you all!" Hawkins said with a mocking bow.

Elijah laughed viciously while Juliana just glared, tight-lipped. One of his crew took up a mutilated version of a Christmas carol, and the others joined in cruelly. Beckoning to his men, Elijah turned and melted into the mists. Juliana stared after them until the last traces of his infuriating humming died out. Then, with a heaving sigh, she turned and began to march up the gangway. She headed straight for Rawden's cabin and entered the lush quarters without saying a word. Rawden followed a step behind, his eyes leaving her only when he turned to push the heavy oak door closed, shutting the world away. He watched as she let his cloak drop to the floor with a thud. Yet, she still did not look back at him.

Rawden felt regret creep up his throat as his eyes traced the swirling lines of her shimmering gold hair. He had broken the terms of their agreement. He would not be able to take her to the sea caves in Cornwall. He had not been able to protect her or her map from her enemies. In fact, he thought crossly, it had been she who had protected him in the end. She'd saved his ship from imminent destruction by giving up the one thing she had left of her murdered father. Self-loathing joined regret as a bitter taste on his tongue.

But a small detail began to niggle at the back of his mind. Rawden frowned. If she had just given away her father's map…then what map had she burned in front of his very eyes on that first night?

"I thought you burned your father's map," he blurted suddenly into the awkward silence.

"Yes, I burned a map," she replied evenly. "Just not my father's. It was yours—I stole it from your table when you weren't looking."

Rawden smiled ruefully. Always the trickster, he thought fondly.

She had said she'd needed his ship and his protection—but those were only two of the three things she'd demanded—a point she'd made abundantly clear with her lips before their disastrous trip into Portsmouth.

So, was this a complete loss?

He had lost the treasure and his pay, but he might still have...her.

"I see," Rawden said slowly. "It's a shame you had no maps to pinch tonight." He paused, then added quietly. "I am sorry you had to surrender your father's map to Elijah Hawkins."

Juliana let out the breath that she'd been holding. She looked at him over her shoulder, her eyes searching. He might think she was useless to him now.

"You are?"

"I am," he replied, meeting her eyes sincerely, "You protected that map for far too long to just hand it over to protect my ship." He stopped for a moment, and then continued. "I am grateful for that sacrifice," he said in a voice gravelly with pent-up emotion. "And I want you to know..." He stopped again. "I want you to understand that it's not the treasure that I'm worried about right now."

"It's not?"

"No," he said, looking away as he awkwardly scratched behind one ear. "It's you," he admitted finally in a soft voice. "I want the map and the treasure—but I want you more."

Juliana stared at him, trying not to gawk in amazement. Her heart felt full to bursting, and all doubts melted away.

"You can still have all three," Juliana said with a happy laugh.

"What?" Rawden asked, stunned. "How?"

"I didn't give Hawkins the map," Juliana announced mischievously.

"I saw you—"

"That wasn't my father's map," she interrupted, a devilish glint in her eye, "I'm sorry to say that the map I gave to Elijah was just another of your old maps. I took one before we left."

"You stole another of my maps?"

"Yes," she said with a nonchalant shrug. "And I'm glad I did. Hawkins will figure out sooner or later that it's a fake—but it'll be too late in either case."

"Just how many of my maps are you going to burn or give away before this is over?" Rawden exclaimed with mock exasperation.

"No more, I hope!"

"But see here," Rawden demanded, shaking a finger at her. "I demand you show me the real map, right now and once and for all. I need to see the real thing with my own eyes."

"Say please."

"*Please*."

"Very well," Juliana said, lifting her chin. "Since you asked nicely."

With that, she turned away once more. She pulled her

LINDA SKYE 321

arms from her sleeves and let her gauzy dress slip down her body and pool at her feet. In one graceful movement, she swept her thick golden locks away from her back and pulled them over her shoulder.

Rawden understood immediately.

An elegantly beautiful tattoo was spread over her svelte back, from the base of her spine to her shoulder blades. It was the most intricate and complex design he had ever seen in his life, inked with delicate swirls of blue, green and black.

The map had been tattooed to her back.

"Do you understand now?" Juliana asked.

Yes, Rawden said to himself, *yes.*

This was the true reason she could never give away her father's map—not to anyone. This was why she had been peering into a hand mirror earlier that day—not to admire herself but to study the reflection of the map on her back in the mirror behind her.

"My father knew that all sorts of men would come after the map," Juliana supplied quietly as Rawden paced slowly towards her. "So he had the map copied onto my body—and then he destroyed the original. Now there are once again only two people in the whole world who know the location of Merlin's map."

Rawden stopped when he was right behind her. He placed his hand at the base of her spine and lightly traced the curving lines of her tattoo with his fingertips. She shivered, a curl of excitement spreading up from her lower belly.

"This is my father's legacy."

"You were wise to hide it," he rumbled approvingly.

Rawden placed his other hand on the curve of her hip and lowered his lips to the shell of her ear.

"Let me touch you," he murmured.

His breath sent frissons of pleasure skittering down her neck to pool in the tips of her breasts. She turned her head so that his lips brushed her temple. She met his heated gaze, and the wide, wanting look in her eyes was answer enough. He gently pressed a row of kisses on her shoulder as he splayed the fingers of one hand over her lower belly. Then, with slow, deliberate, feather-like touches, he traced every line of black ink on her back with the very tip of one finger. As he did, the hand he had planted on her stomach dipped lower, and lower…until she gasped with pleasure and curved her body over his muscled arm. She grasped at his sleeve and moaned aloud as his swirling fingers continued their devastating patterns. He was merciless in his lewd ministrations, not even stopping when her nails dug into his bicep and her panting grew desperate. He caught her lower lip between his teeth and teased her with his tongue.

"Rawden," she whimpered, twisting in his arms. "Oh, Rawden."

With a grunt, he swept her effortlessly into his arms and carried her to his bed. He sat down with her cradled against his chest. She straddled his thighs and rocked her hips against his, mewling plaintively as he showered her with open-mouthed kisses. As his calloused hands swept over the smooth planes of her body, he realised one very important fact: that she was completely naked and that he…was not. Grunting as she tangled her fingers in his dark locks, Rawden shrugged off his shirt. He stood for a moment, and Juliana wrapped her long legs to his torso, anchoring herself to his body as he jerked open his trousers and quickly kicked them off.

When he sat back down, the feeling of his naked skin on hers nearly made him lose all control. He could feel the moistness between her thighs, and she could feel his stiffness rubbing against her. They ground against one another until they could take no more. So when Rawden finally lifted her hips, Juliana eagerly positioned him at the entrance to her core. Hands on his shoulders, she slowly eased herself down onto him. She cried out passionately at the sensations coursing through her entire body; his hands hot on her hips, his velvety voice cracking with pleasure—and his wide girth entering, parting, stretching her very core. They were fully joined, as close as humanly possible.

They both leaned back, planting their hands behind them—he on the mattress and she bracing herself with open palms on his knees. She began to move up and down, gradually increasing her speed until she had to throw her head back in joyous passion. Rawden watched as her heavy breasts bounced, and unable to resist, he leaned forward and grabbed them with greedy hands. His lips closed around one of the tight caramel peaks, and his tongue swirled delicious patterns that made Juliana cry out in ecstasy. She arched into his touch, riding him desperately. Juliana felt as if something electric was trying to crawl its way out of her pores, and her movements became wild jerks.

"Not yet," Rawden growled huskily. "Not just yet, my dear."

He gathered her in his arms and stood, turning to lay

her down across his bed. Still joined, he lay over her and braced himself against the mattress on his elbows. He kissed the tip of her nose and slowly, slowly withdrew. She felt every ridge of his shaft as he pulled away. She almost protested, but when he was just about to pull free, he then pushed back in—again, ever so slowly. He repeated this slow torture over and over again until Juliana dug her fingers into his shoulders and sobbed for more.

Rawden chuckled darkly. Then, just as he was about to pull out, he drove into her in one quick motion. Juliana gasped in delight. He pulled away slowly, and then slammed back into her, hilt deep. This new, sweet torture drove Juliana half-mad, and she writhed beneath him.

Finally, he paused. Leaning back, he took her chin between his fingers.

"Look at me," he commanded hoarsely.

Juliana blinked up at him with hazy eyes. Rawden waited, his eyes dark with desire. But still he waited.

"Yes," Juliana breathed with a soft smile. "Yes, I'm yours."

His response was immediate. Hooking her knees over his elbows, he began to plunge in and out of her with such force that she was driven back against the headboard and had to brace herself with her hands above her head. Their bodies, slick with sweat, crashed together. It was wild, it was furious…it was love at its basest and most passionate. Juliana could not fight the flow of pleasure that crashed through her body, so she just hung on blindly. And just when she thought their lovemaking could be no more intense, Rawden grabbed her hips and turned her so that she was on her hands and knees in front of him. He dug his fingers into her hips and began anew, his thrusts hard and fast.

Juliana had never felt anything so deep or so wonderful in all her life. Her hands fisted in his sheets, her sobs of bliss echoing though the cabin. Rawden leaned forward, and Juliana felt his tongue on her skin. Her breath caught in her throat as she realised he was trailing his tongue over the lines of her tattoo, lines she had studied and hidden for so long. Tears welled in the corners of her eyes as she relished the feeling of him laving the precious design on her back with his open-mouthed kisses. Then he rose, hooked an arm around her shoulders and pulled her up. He grabbed onto her for leverage as his pace became more frantic. His frenzied thrusts hit deep, and she felt a carnal exhilaration spread through her veins, she lost all control over her voice. Stars burst behind her eyes as she heedlessly screamed his name. She felt him shudder inside her, and she clenched around him as he released deep within her core.

Panting harshly, they sagged against each other, limp and sated. As one, they collapsed to one side. He curled around her, pulling her back into his chest. Nuzzling her tattooed shoulder, Rawden sighed into her moist skin. She trembled under his touch.

"I think I should study this map more often," Rawden said, pressing his lips to her neck.

"Any time you want, my dear captain," Juliana giggled, squirming deeper into his embrace. "Any time you want."

CHAPTER SEVEN

THEY SPENT THE next few days holed up in the cabin. Rawden would spend hours poring over the map on her back, leaving only when it was necessary to guide the ship or supervise his crew. Juliana would sometimes venture out onto the deck to breathe in the fresh salty air and catch a glimpse of the distant shoreline. On occasion, Rawden would let her hold to the ship's wheel, his hands on hers, as they cut through the waves. There was laughter and song and lovemaking even when the fresh rations dried up. One day, when Juliana thought she would rather go hungry than eat hardtack biscuits and broth again, Rawden breezed into the cabin bearing a tray of something that smelled—impossibly—of Christmas. Hopping up from her perch by the fire, Juliana crowded in to see just what treasures her captain had brought. With a proud, boyish smile, Rawden gestured to his surprise: two bowls of hot Christmas pudding and two mugs of sweet-smelling malt wine. As Juliana savoured a spoonful of gooey, sticky pudding and sipped her mug of wine scented with orange and cinnamon, she thanked the seven seas for sending her such a marvellous pirate. And excitement continued to grow as they drew nearer to the majestic coastline of Cornwall.

Finally, on Christmas Day, Juliana heard the barked command.

"Drop anchor!"

They had arrived. Rawden pulled her from the cabin and led her onto the deck. With a sweep of his arm, he showed her the towering cliffs of Cornwall. Juliana felt light and warm, despite the cold Atlantic wind whipping through her hair.

Grey, jagged rocks jutted imperiously from the sea. Grey-green grass covered the tops of the cliffs, draped over the sloping hills like a thick, mossy carpet. A blanket of snow and ice shimmered here and there—the only indication of the winter weather apart from the icy mist of the waves.

And there, nestled atop one of the flat peaks were the ruins of an ancient castle—Tintagel Castle, the rumoured home of the legendary King Arthur. Juliana's eyes dropped lower. For it was not the imposing castle that interested her; it was the secret that lay hidden beneath. The winding sea caves below: Merlin's caves. She looked eagerly up at Rawden, who chuckled.

"Aye then mateys!" Rawden called to his crew. "Get a longboat ready! We sail to treasure today!"

A great guffaw rose from the crew as they scrambled to prepare for the landing. And within the hour, Juliana and Rawden were perched at the centre of the lead longboat, headed for shore. They tied up the boats close to the rocky shore, and Rawden lifted Juliana into his arms before she could protest, gallantly wading through the cold water to set her booted feet on dry stones.

"Lead the way, my lady," Rawden said with a flourish, taking her hand as she nimbly skipped from one rock to the next.

Soon, they were marching up a pebbled beach, and the dark, cavernous mouth of Merlin's cave loomed above them. The tide was out, so the entrance was clear of water, leaving only a smooth sandy passageway in its place. Juliana took the torch that Rawden had just lit, holding out in front of her to illuminate the dark passageway. She smiled.

"Follow me," she said confidently. "I know the way."

They trod slowly into the yawning cave, their feet leaving deep marks in the soft sand. Juliana led the group through the snaking passageways without fear. She had been preparing for this day for more than a decade, and she already knew which turn to take at every fork in the passage. The rocks were slimy and slick, so Rawden steadied her with a hand cupping her elbow. As they progressed deeper and deeper into the forbidding cave, the tunnel grew tighter and the air staler. It was a frightening maze.

Just when the crew began to grumble about unending marches and unlikely treasure, they rounded a tight bend and spilled into an unbelievably vast chamber. It was so wide and large that their footfalls echoed off the rock walls. Anyone who thought to look at the walls would see intricate carvings and tall pillars. The uneven ground beneath their feet turned to carefully tiled marble slabs. And then, Juliana dropped her torch into a round basin.

Fire shot out from half a dozen railings, almost instantly lighting a series of lamp stands around the colossal chamber. The shine of gold flashed from every corner; coins were piled in pyramids taller than most men, golden jars and vases were haphazardly heaped together, weapons glittering with precious stones were scattered everywhere. It was more treasure than Rawden had ever seen in his lifetime, much less in one place.

With hoots of glee, the crew surged past them, digging into the coins and shouting to one another. After a few minutes of revelry, they turned to their captain, wondering how they ever dared doubt him. Rawden grinned from ear to ear.

"What are you waiting for?" he shouted. "Pack it all up!"

The men began scooping gold into the chests they'd brought along. Rawden surveyed the treasure. It would take more than a few trips to empty the chamber. Nay, more than a few ship loads! He shook his head in amazement and turned to look at Juliana, who had stooped to pick up a single gold coin. She turned it over in her fingers, marvelling at the Latin inscription and engraving of an unknown Caesar.

"Roman gold," she whispered to herself, closing her fist around the coin. "It was here all this time."

She looked up at Rawden, her face glimmering with the reflection of a century's worth of gold.

"Merry Christmas, Rawden," she said with a laugh and outstretched arms. "This is my gift to you."

"You found it," he said, pulling her into his arms and resting his chin on the top of her head. "Your father would be proud. A true daughter of a pirate."

Juliana pulled away slightly to peer up at him, an impish smirk playing on her lips.

"Who said I was the daughter of a pirate?"

Rawden frowned lightly, his mind whirring.

"You have a treasure map. You know ships. And you can be a right little swindler." He inclined his head to one side. "What else would you be?"

Her sly little smile grew wider.

"I have another Christmas gift for you, Captain Wood," she said, flouncing out of his arms.

"Oh?"

"Yes," she said with a toss of her head. "And I'll have you know that I am not the daughter of a pirate. My name is Juliana Wright, and I am the only daughter of the late Rear Admiral Wright of the Royal Navy."

Rawden felt his bones grow stiff with dread. The Royal Navy? Just what was going on now? But Juliana wasn't done speaking, so he forced himself to focus on the melodic sound of her voice.

"As his daughter, the Royal Navy has tasked me to complete his mission in his stead. I have been given the honourable duty of selecting a privateer to be in the service of the Crown. I have chosen to offer this privilege to you."

"What?" Rawden nearly choked.

"This is a letter of marque," Juliana said, and pulled a sturdy scroll from her cape. "It entitles you to pillage and plunder foreign ships for your own profit and with no risk of prosecution by the Royal Navy or any other law enforcement serving England. Should you accept, you will no longer be a fugitive pirate, but a respectable privateer. And," she said, opening her arms, "you may consider this Roman gold as your signing bonus. Do you accept, Captain Rawden Wood?"

"Do I accept?" Rawden took two long steps and pulled her off her feet, muffling her giggles with a kiss. "Of course I accept!"

"Well, there is one more condition," she cautioned, tapping him on the nose.

Rawden groaned. This woman and her conditions!

"The Royal Navy requires you to have a watcher, someone to send reports back to headquarters. So you'll have to take me along with you, wherever you sail."

"Wherever?" Rawden asked, raising a crafty brow.

"Yes," Juliana whispered conspiratorially. "Even if you plan to sail to a tropical island somewhere in the South Pacific, you must take me with you. Perhaps you can bribe me into silence by ravishing me on a secluded white sand beach somewhere," she added thoughtfully.

Rawden laughed and spun her around once before sealing her lips with his in wild abandon. Breathless, he pulled away to meet her brightly cheerful eyes.

"You had this planned from the very beginning, didn't you," he playfully accused.

"I did," she admitted, kissing his cheek.

"Well, then," Rawden said, gathering her close, "it *is* a merry Christmas, after all."

"Yes, it is," Juliana murmured, pressing her lips to his. "Merry Christmas, my pirate protector."

* * * * *

Three Regency Christmases to remember...

A charming, seasonal collection from top
Mills & Boon® Historical authors—
Louise Allen, Lucy Ashford and
Joanna Fulford

4th October

www.millsandboon.co.uk

Come home this Christmas to Fiona Harper

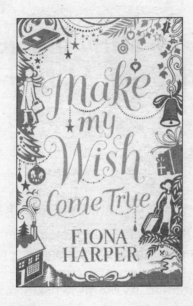

From the author of *Kiss Me Under the Mistletoe* comes a
Christmas tale of family and fun. Two sisters are ready
to swap their Christmases—the busy super-mum, Juliet,
getting the chance to escape it all on an exotic Christmas
getaway, whilst her glamorous work-obsessed sister,
Gemma, is plunged headfirst into the family Christmas
she always thought she'd hate.

Wrap up warm this winter with Sarah Morgan…

Sleigh Bells in the Snow

Kayla Green loves business and hates Christmas.

So when Jackson O'Neil invites her to Snow Crystal Resort to discuss their business proposal… the last thing she's expecting is to stay for Christmas dinner. As the snowflakes continue to fall, will the woman who doesn't believe in the magic of Christmas finally fall under its spell…?

4th October

www.millsandboon.co.uk/sarahmorgan